PARADISE GARDEN

by
ELENA FISCHER

Translated by
ALEXANDRA ROESCH

The beginning was the last day before the summer holidays.
The beginning was a song on the radio.
The beginning was big plans.

Fourteen-year-old Billie rarely crosses the boundaries of her high-rise housing estate. By the end of the month their money just about stretches to pasta with ketchup, but her mother, Marika, lights up Billie's world with her imagination and big heart.

One day they receive an unwelcome visit from her Hungarian grandmother, and Billie loses much more than the colourful everyday life she shared with her mother. No longer able to ask Marika questions, Billie sets off alone in their old Nissan – determined to meet the father she never knew and find out why she keeps dreaming about the sea, even though she's never been there.

Longlisted for the German Book Prize 2023, *Paradise Garden* is a spellbinding journey and a deeply affecting story of class, resilience and belonging.

Julia Sellmann / © Diogenes Verlag

ELENA FISCHER studied comparative literature and film in Mainz, Germany, where she lives with her family. In 2019 and 2020, she participated in the Darmstadt Text Workshop, led by Kurt Drawert. In 2021 she was a finalist at the 29th Open Mike with an extract from her debut novel *Paradise Garden* and won the Mainz provincial government's prize for young authors.

In 2023 she was nominated for the German Book Prize and for the Harbour Front Literary Festival's Debut Prize.

ALEXANDRA ROESCH studied languages and business and worked in banking before becoming a literary translator.

She has an MA in translation from the University of Bristol. Previously translated authors include Hans Fallada, Stefanie vor Schulte and Seraina Kobler.

© Farideh Diehl

PRAISE FOR
Paradise Garden

'A gripping coming of age tale full of soul and heart. I absolutely adored this amazing book.'

KATE HAMER

'Elena Fischer writes so lovingly about sadness that it is comforting.'

ALINA BRONSKY

'I read *Paradise Garden* in the summer while I was travelling with friends and every time they found me reading, I held up the book and said, "Oh my God, this is so good, you must read it!"'

BENEDICT WELLS, *SRF 2 KULTUR*, BASEL

'A really good debut.'

MARIETTA BERNASCONI, *WDR 2*, COLOGNE

'*Paradise Garden* is an accomplished debut about the courage to get to know one's own origins and to accept them as they are.'

URSULA NOWAK, *DEUTSCHLANDFUNK*, COLOGNE

'You will want to read more from this author.'

RUHR NACHRICHTEN, DORTMUND

'The blurb sounded promising. What followed were hours in which I couldn't put the book down.'

DEBORA SCHNITZLER, *DIE ZEIT*, HAMBURG

'There is a surprising lightness to the quiet sadness that runs through the book, which is repeatedly underscored by witty dialogue and whimsical twists.'

CHRISTINE WESTERMANN, *STERN*, HAMBURG

'We will be hearing a lot more from Elena Fischer.'

HELMUT ATTENDER,
OBERÖSTERREICHISCHE NACHRICHTEN, LINZ

'This novel is a small miracle – and a big surprise.'

CLAUDIO ARMBUSTER, *ZDF*, MAINZ

'It is impressive, to say the least, how masterfully and down-to-earth she tells of life in a high-rise suburb.'

OLAF PRZYBILLA, *SÜDDEUTSCHE ZEITUNG*, MUNICH

PARADISE GARDEN

ELENA FISCHER

Translated by
ALEXANDRA ROESCH

THE
INDIGO
PRESS

THE INDIGO PRESS
50 Albemarle Street
London W1S 4BD
www.theindigopress.com

The Indigo Press Publishing Limited Reg. No. 10995574
Registered Office: Wellesley House, Duke of Wellington Avenue
Royal Arsenal, London SE18 6SS

COPYRIGHT © ELENA FISCHER 2023
ENGLISH TRANSLATION © ALEXANDRA ROESCH 2025

First published in Great Britain in 2025 by The Indigo Press

First published in Germany in 2023 by Diogenes Verlag
Copyright © 2023 by Diogenes Verlag AG, Zurich. All rights reserved

Elena Fischer and Alexandra Roesch assert the moral right to be
identified as the author and translator respectively of this work in
accordance with the Copyright, Designs and Patents Act 1988

A CIP catalogue record for this book is available from the British Library

ISBN: 978-1-911648-95-6
eBook ISBN: 978-1-911648-96-3

This is a work of fiction. Names, characters, places and incidents are
products of the author's imagination or are used fictionally and are
not to be construed as real. Any resemblance to actual events, locales,
organisations, or persons, living or dead, is entirely coincidental.

All rights reserved. No part of this publication may be reproduced, stored in a
retrieval system or transmitted, in any form or by any means, electronic, mechanical,
photocopying, recording or otherwise, without the prior permission of the publishers.

The translation of this book was supported by a grant from the Goethe-Institut

Cover design © Sarah Schulte
The Sunglasses Woman illustration © CSA images
Flamingo (iStock) © Nadtochiy
Art direction by House of Thought
Author photograph by Julia Sellmann /© Diogenes Verlag
Translator photograph © Farideh Diehl
Printed and bound in Great Britain by TJ Books, Padstow
Typeset in Goudy Old Style by Tetragon, London

EU GPSR Authorised Representative
Logos Europe, 9 rue Nicolas Poussin, 17000, La Rochelle, France
e-mail: contact@logoseurope.eu

1 3 5 7 9 8 6 4 2

PARADISE GARDEN

1

My mum died that summer.

A song on the radio was just noise, no longer an invitation to sing along even though neither of us knew the lyrics. A downpour was just weather, no longer an opportunity to dash outside and dance barefoot in a puddle.

That might sound poetic, but only on paper. Fourteen is a shitty age to lose your mum. The grief comes and goes like the tide, but it's always there.

Mum was buried on the hottest day of the year. The birds faltered in the white sky and the lizards sheltered in the shade of the headstones. Rose bushes blossomed by the side of the path, and the wind carried their sweet scent all the way to the grave. The heat prolonged time and slowed all movement.

I wiped my sweaty hands on my dress and stared into the hole at my feet. The coffin was down there, with sunflowers on top and Mum inside. Her dark curls framing her face, her red lips smiling mockingly, her feet in her white cowboy boots, that's how I imagined her.

I also imagined Mum suddenly appearing next to me and rescuing me. She'd smooth her skirt and run her hand through her hair. Then she'd say something like 'Stop making such sad faces, I can't stand it!' She'd kiss me on my parting, take my hand and whisk me away like she'd done so many times before.

But of course Mum didn't come back.

Instead, I started my first period.

The priest cast earth onto the coffin. 'Earth to earth, ashes to ashes, dust to dust, in sure and certain hope of the Resurrection to eternal life,' he said in a strange sing-song as warm, living blood seeped out of my body. For a second, I thought I was dying too, and I longed to lie down beside my mum. It felt like my body was betraying me by choosing this moment to start my period. I didn't move a muscle. I closed my eyes and hoped it would make me invisible. I hoped no one would notice I'd just become a woman.

I wished I could make the blood flow back into my body, but I couldn't stop gravity. My blood trickled sluggishly down my leg; everything was propelled downwards, towards the earth. I clenched my thighs together and my yellow summer dress was ruined.

If my grandma had been there, she'd have pressed her lips together, two thin lines that turned downwards at the corners. She'd have sobbed endlessly. My grandma seemed to have a hidden reservoir in her body that she sourced her rivers of tears from. Perhaps her face was so wrinkled because the tears poured out uncontrollably, leaving nothing but dryness behind.

On the day my mum died, I fell apart. All that remained was a jumble of letters that had once been my name.

Mum called me Billie. B-i-l-l-i-e.

When she said my name, her lips would briefly brush together. I didn't hear my real name until I was seven. On the first day of school, the teacher called out our names. I was left over, along with a name I didn't recognize.

'Billie is short for Erzsébet,' Mum said. Her pronunciation was perfect. I did understand Hungarian, but all I heard now was 'arse bed'.

'Why didn't you just christen me Billie?'

'Your grandma was against it,' Mum sighed. I didn't know my grandma, but I knew she disagreed with everything my mum liked.

'Why was she against it?' I wanted to know.

'The name Billie doesn't appear in the Bible,' Mum said.

'Is Marika in the Bible?'

My mum shook her head. Then she said: 'Not directly, but Marika means "gift from God". At least, that's *one* of the meanings.'

'There are others as well?'

Mum grinned so widely that I glimpsed her gold molar.

'"Rebellious". But your grandma didn't think of that.'

2

But now, let's rewind to the beginning.

The beginning was the last day before the summer holidays.

The beginning was a song played on the radio.

The beginning was big plans.

Maybe the beginning was everything, all together.

In any case, I got back from school just in time to join in the quiz question. Mum and I were mad about this one competition.

'Turn it down,' I said when I came into the lounge. I'd heard the radio presenter from the walkway, and all our neighbours probably had too.

'Shh,' Mum said, placing a finger on her lips. She held the phone in her other hand. I knew she'd already keyed in the numbers. We had done it a thousand times.

Mum was sitting on our sofa. Her left leg bobbed up and down and sweat glistened on her forehead. It was scorching that afternoon. She'd opened all the windows in the flat, but the air in the lounge was still stifling.

I'd barely sat down next to Mum when it started. 'Three, two, one,' the presenter said, and then came the first notes of the song.

'"Wicked Game"!' Mum called out.

'No way,' I said. I'd recognized the song straight away. 'It's "All My Tears"!'

'Are you sure?' Mum asked.

'Quick, call them!' I said.

Identifying the song was one thing, getting through was another. The most annoying part was getting through but having the wrong answer. Mum pressed the green button and held the phone to her ear.

Winning money was a big deal for us. Where we lived, most people had erased the word 'win' from their vocabulary a long time ago. No one willingly chose to live here, on the edge of the city. Our block, the tallest of five arranged in a semicircle, formed its own vibrant little community. Each building was painted a different colour; ours was a faded yellow. If you gave the address, at an interview for example, people immediately knew. *Thank you for your interest, next please.* My mum could tell you a thing or two about that.

I held my breath and counted four rings. It rang four times, and then we were live on air.

My mum and I were so ecstatic that we kept interrupting each other. Mum kept switching from German to Hungarian and back again, as she always did when she was excited. But the radio presenter still understood us. At the end, he told us to stay on the line. We could barely believe our luck.

'I hope being on hold doesn't eat into our winnings,' Mum said. She put the phone on loudspeaker and rubbed her right ear. It was glowing.

We were only on hold for five minutes. Then a woman congratulated us and asked my mum for her account details. Mum read the numbers off her bank card. It was like she was reciting a prayer she already knew was going to be answered.

When Mum had hung up, she said: 'This summer we're going to go on holiday!'

'On a proper holiday?' I asked. I pictured palm trees swaying in the breeze, sandy beaches, and of course the sea.

'A proper holiday,' Mum said. Then she got up to get ready for work.

I stretched out on the sofa, feeling drowsy from the heat. I closed my eyes and listened to the sound of water running in the shower. At some point, Mum came back into the lounge in her 'I-can-be-anything' outfit. Her sequinned top shimmered in the sunlight, and her jeans were skintight. With it she wore her white cowboy boots with the cherries. She gave me a kiss goodbye and took the bus into town to her evening job.

My mum had two jobs.

In the mornings, she worked in a big glass box consisting of lots of little glass boxes. She cleaned for the staff, who wore expensive suits and ties. She also brought them their paper clips, envelopes and text markers – and sometimes even an ice pack. Accidents, like bumping into doors or walls, weren't uncommon. In the evenings, Mum worked as a waitress in a bar. 'The bar job keeps us happy,' she said when she counted her tips at the end of her shift, 'but the cleaning job keeps us alive.'

Mum saw the weirdest things in the company where she worked. That was because no one noticed her. When she went down the corridors in her jeans and pinny, refilled the paper in the printer or cleaned the toilets, she was invisible. They'd got used to her over the years, like a filing cabinet or a lamp. Only when she came home, changed her clothes, undid her hair and put on some red lipstick did she become the person she actually wanted to be.

Once a shift, my mum went through all the offices to empty the wastepaper bins. 'You can tell a person's true character from the way they treat things they no longer want,' she said.

The man at the end of the corridor stuffed everything into his wastepaper bin: leftovers, half-full takeaway coffee cups, CDs, shoes. Once my mum even found a bloody tissue. She couldn't just empty the bin, she had to reach in with her hands and help things out. She took half a life out of that man's bin.

I was still awake when Mum got back from the bar that evening. 'Budge up a bit,' she said, slipping into bed next to me. She turned to face me.

'Can we use the money to go to the sea?' I asked.

'Sure, which one?' my mum asked and smiled.

'Atlantic, or Caribbean?'

When I thought about the sea then, it was never boring. Either it was wild, or turquoise, like on the posters in the windows at the travel agent. Regardless, I longed for it. Sometimes this longing was like a mosquito bite somewhere on my body that I couldn't scratch.

'I want to go to Florida,' Mum said. 'I'll eat pancakes every morning on the beach.'

'Course you will,' I said, and my stomach started growling.

My mum had been crazy about Florida ever since she'd watched that film. In it, a little girl and her mum live in a camper van. Nothing happens in the film. 'Why do people make films where nothing happens?' I once wanted to know. When I wrote stories, lots of things happened in them. 'As long as nothing happens, everything is possible,' Mum had said, and in a way, she was right.

Mum got up. 'I'll make us some pancakes now,' she said. Then she disappeared into the kitchen.

My mum's pancakes were the best I'd ever eaten. She always made them when we had something to celebrate. And believe me, we found plenty of reasons to celebrate. Birthdays, for example. Not just ours, but the birthdays of all the children who lived in our block. And there were loads of them.

After a while, Mum brought a fully laden plate to my bed and asked: 'Haven't you got them coming out of your nose?' She asked that every time.

'It's coming out of my ears,' I said, dipping my finger into the maple syrup and licking it. My mum still had an issue with idiomatic expressions. She was often 'on cloud seven' or 'in some jam' and she'd say: 'That guy is as thick as a brick wall!'

Mum sat down on the edge of my bed. 'Everything fades over time.'

'Like a song, for example,' I said. Sometimes I listened to a song so many times that after a while I no longer knew why I'd liked it in the first place.

'Yes, for example. Or a person,' she said. 'But not you. You never fade.' She wrapped her arms around me and my plate almost landed on the floor.

Later, after Mum had been asleep in the lounge for quite a while, I got out of bed again. I opened my window wide and leaned out into the warm summer air.

We lived almost at the top. It was the seventeenth floor. You'd have been able to see the sea from here if there had been one. But there was only an autobahn. The autobahn snaked through the nature reserve, cutting the greenery in two. The roaring of the cars was always there; we hardly noticed it any more. In the past, the roaring had often lulled me to sleep. 'Hey, can you hear the sea?' my mum would whisper.

During the holidays, there was more traffic. Sometimes my mum would pour juice into tall glasses with ice cubes and decorate them with pink straws and paper umbrellas. She'd hand me the cocktails and take two deckchairs and place them out on the walkway between our front door and the balcony with the peeling paint. Then we'd play holidays. We'd sit side by side, my mum in a white bikini, me in my swimming costume, and we'd let the sun shine on our tummies. We were glad we'd already got there while other people were stuck in their cars.

I stood by the window and listened.

It was only now I realized the truth. The truth, of course, was that we'd have swapped places with them in a heartbeat. We'd have loved nothing more than to be stuck in a car on our way to Italy, France or Spain.

3

I was sitting on the walkway, flicking through the travel brochures. They were thick and had glossy covers.

The man in the travel agency had asked where I wanted to go, but I wasn't really sure. All I knew was that I longed to surprise Mum with a good idea. 'To the coast!' I said.

'Europe?' the man queried, and I nodded.

'Portugal, Spain, France, Italy, Greece?'

'Exactly,' I said. 'And can I also have a brochure for Hungary?'

'Hungary isn't by the sea,' he pointed out, packing a pile of brochures into a bag.

Of course I knew Hungary wasn't by the sea, and I knew Mum would never consider it for a trip, but I liked looking at pictures of it.

I was already at the door when I remembered something: 'Do you have a brochure for Florida?'

Now I shifted my gaze between the pale blue sky above me and the road that ran straight through turquoise water. I saw palm trees on sandy beaches and pastel-pink hotels with sprawling pools and verandas with wicker rockers and gardens boasting blossoms as large as footballs.

And then I saw the prices.

They were so high we couldn't afford the flights out there. We couldn't afford a single flight, even if they'd let us share a seat.

I closed the Florida brochure and then my eyes. The sun was high in the sky, tinting the darkness behind my eyelids red. I had the entire walkway to myself, but I knew it wouldn't last. My mum and I weren't the only ones who moved their lives outdoors as soon as it got warm. We shared the walkway with our neighbours, who like us didn't have balconies.

Take Luna, for example. Luna was older than me, but younger than my mum. We didn't know exactly how old she was – sometimes she said twenty-three, sometimes thirty-two. The truth was somewhere in between. Luna's age depended on how she was feeling. She worked nearby, at the Sunset Tanning Salon. If she liked someone, she'd let them tan for free. She always had one or two tokens in the pockets of her jeans that you could put in the slot instead of coins. We liked Luna and Luna liked us. However, her generosity wasn't much use to us. I was too young for the tanning salon; you had to be sixteen to use it. I kept trying to convince Luna, but she just shook her head so much that her pink hair whirled around. Mum didn't need a tanning salon. While most people around us watched their skin fade back to the colour of raw sausage meat, she was still tanned. 'That's my Romani blood,' she said and sighed. She couldn't believe she was missing out on the chance to get something for free.

I opened the next brochure. Italy. Italy wasn't Florida, of course, but there were nice beaches and good pizza – nothing to turn up your nose at. I compared hotels and campsites. I flicked back and forth and back again. It didn't take long for me to realize our winnings fell short. Perhaps it was enough for a new mattress or a couple of trips to the big leisure park, or even a season ticket for the swimming pool. It was probably even enough for a trip to Italy in our Nissan, but what then?

'Are you going away this summer?' a voice asked suddenly beside me. It was Ahmed, his sports bag slung over his shoulder, boxing gloves dangling from it. Ahmed's skin glistened with sweat, though in this heat it was hard to tell if someone was heading to or returning from training. Ahmed was even darker than my mum. Officially he was Israeli, but he was actually Palestinian. I didn't understand how that could be, but I didn't really care either.

For a moment I thought about telling him about our win, but then I thought better of it. I didn't want to make him sad. Ahmed had come to Germany to study chemistry, but for some reason he wasn't getting anywhere. When my mum asked him how he was doing, he used to laugh and say 'Good, good!' But recently he'd started saying nothing. I knew he'd lost his job handing out leaflets.

'We wanted to go to the sea,' I said instead. 'But we'll probably stay put.' I set the Italy brochure down on the floor next to me. 'It's way too expensive.'

'Why don't you go to the North Sea? It's not far, and I heard it's very beautiful.'

Ahmed unlocked his door. He lived right next to us. If we needed help with anything, we knocked on his door. He was super strong and had large hands that he could open any jam jar with. I liked Ahmed. He smelled of soap and shisha, and had the longest eyelashes I'd ever seen. He also had good ideas.

I stood up. I felt like going straight back to the travel agents to get a Germany brochure, but they were closed in the afternoons.

Instead I went inside and brought out my school atlas, a pen and paper and a calculator. I opened the atlas and looked for a general map. There was more than one autobahn heading north from here. The autobahn didn't go all the way to the sea, though. No one wanted to sit on the beach with cars shooting past behind them. But there were enough country roads. I plotted the shortest route and wrote down the name of the town. Then I started calculating. We had enough money to pay for the petrol. Perhaps we could even spend a night in a hotel.

Finally I drew a sun, a beach and the sea on the piece of paper and wrote *North Sea* above it.

'What are you up to?' Mum asked from behind me.

She'd got back from work ten minutes ago. I didn't need to turn around to know that her jeans and T-shirt were strewn across the floor in the hallway. When she got back from the office, she just dropped her clothes. Then she put lunch in the microwave.

Mum leaned over the back of my deckchair with a steaming plate of lasagne. 'I thought it was the school holidays,' she said, looking at the atlas.

'I'm planning our holiday.'

I took the plate and put it down on the floor next to me. Mum pulled the other deckchair over next to me. 'Let me see,' she said.

Three seconds later, she handed the paper back.

'No. Absolutely not. What gave you that idea?' She crossed her arms in front of her chest.

'Why not?' I asked.

'What are we supposed to do at the North Sea?' she asked. 'Freeze on the beach? We don't like wind, have you forgotten?'

'It's a thousand degrees out. We won't be cold.'

'Let's go to France,' Mum said, leaning back in her chair.

'France is too expensive,' I said. 'We could just about afford the drive. Where are we supposed to sleep?'

'We'll figure something out,' Mum said and took a sip of my Coke.

'Oh yeah, like what?'

'It's warm. We could sleep outside.'

'And if it rains?'

'Then we'll sleep in the car.'

When Mum saw my face, she said: 'Did you know there are people who spend their whole lives in cars? I bet they give their cars a new paint job each year.'

I liked our Nissan; that wasn't the problem. The Nissan was the only luxury we allowed ourselves. We mostly took the bus. Sometimes we even bought a ticket. Only sometimes, at the beginning of a new month, we drove into town in the Nissan.

The problem was that our car had no MOT. Not for a year now. One headlight was broken and the passenger door didn't close properly. My mum was inventive with the door, though: she had fastened it to the frame with a thick piece of rope. But whenever we went around corners I still had to hang on to it like someone I loved who was dangling over a cliff. 'Think of the overzealous policemen who reprimand you for something like that instead of chasing proper criminals,' she once said.

But I wasn't giving up that easily. 'It's beautiful at the North Sea,' I said.

'How do you know?' Mum asked.

'Ahmed told me. How do you know it isn't?'

'Some things I just know.'

I had no idea what Mum had against the North Sea. I stood up, took the pile of travel brochures and dropped them on the floor.

'Hey, what's that for?' Mum asked.

'If you already know everything, then why did I bother getting them?'

Mum stared at the brochures. A flamingo was depicted on the cover of the one on the top of the pile. 'Is that Florida?'

I nodded.

Mum pushed her sunglasses on top of her head. 'Did you fetch that especially for me?'

'Yes,' I said, then Mum gave me a hug. I hugged her back. If it's just the two of you, it's easier to make up quickly.

'Hey, what's going on with you two?'

Luna had come out. Her flip-flops made a slapping noise on the tiles. She wore them the entire summer. She'd discovered them online; a pair cost no more than a scoop of ice cream. But because the shipping cost four times as much, Luna had ordered a big pile of them. Now she owned flip-flops in all the colours of the universe. The flip-flops were made of plastic and came from China. My mum said Luna would get skin cancer on her feet from them, it was just a matter of time.

We moved apart.

'We're going on holiday,' Mum said. Luna picked up one of the brochures and sat down between us on the floor. And then my mum told her we had won. In the end Mum said: 'Billie wants to go to the North Sea, but I want to go to France.'

'France!' Luna said in my direction. 'Think of the croissants. And isn't the weather better too?'

Why was everyone so hung up on the weather? I was on the point of saying something, but Luna was talking again.

'Plus the French have such a cool lifestyle. What do you call it?'

'*Savoir vivre?*' I asked.

'No, it's something else.'

'*Laissez-faire?*'

'That's the one,' she said.

Mum looked at me and grinned. I knew I didn't stand a chance any more. I'd just been overruled by someone who basically had no vote. I sighed. When my mum set her mind on something, you couldn't budge her. And Luna was right about the croissants.

Luna dug out a bottle of nail polish from the pocket of her shorts. She dropped the bottle in Mum's lap and laughed as if someone had told a joke.

She often laughed without a real reason. Maybe it had something to do with the fact that Luna was both the happiest and the saddest person I knew.

Luna had more dreams during the day than I did during the night. Her biggest dream was to marry a man who'd pay off all her debts. 'She's got a long wait coming,' my mum once said.

Mum unscrewed the bottle and took Luna's hand. Mum and Luna often painted each other's nails. Luna painted Mum's right hand because Mum was right-handed, and my mum painted Luna's left hand because she was left-handed.

The nail varnish looked like melted vanilla ice cream.

'When am I going to finally get a postcard from Hollywood?' Mum asked.

While Luna waited for Mr Right, she was trying to become an actress. She was constantly learning lines: down by the washing machines, in the queue at the discount store, when she disinfected the sunbeds. She was waiting to be discovered.

'Soon,' Luna said. 'And then I'll buy you a big house we can live in together.'

Luna constantly had ideas like that. I thought we already lived in a big house together, wall to wall even, and said nothing.

'And you? What are you dreaming of?' Luna asked my mum.

Mum was quiet for a while. Then she said: 'Air conditioning.'

Luna laughed. 'Okay. And now for real?'

'Of France. From now on, I am dreaming of France.' Mum leaned back and closed her eyes.

'And what's your dream?' Luna asked me.

I didn't need to think long. 'I want to be a writer,' I said.

'Watch what you say,' Mum said to Luna. 'She spends the entire day writing things down in her notebook.'

Later I filled a bowl with popcorn and put it on the coffee table in the lounge, together with Coke and glasses. Luna brought crisps. 'Sweet and salty,' she said, putting crisps and popcorn in her mouth at the same time. 'If you had to choose… what would you take?'

'Sweet,' said Mum.

'Salty,' I said.

We put the telly on and waited for Luna's moment. I had the scent of her freshly washed hair in my nose. It smelled of coconut.

'There! At the back!' Mum suddenly shouted.

Luna was sitting in the train carriage holding her ticket out to the inspector. We replayed it about seventy-eight times. We loved getting a taste of what Luna called her 'glam life'.

4

A few days later, Mum had a day off. That was one good thing. The other was that it was the start of a new month. A new month was like a new life. At the start of each new month, Mum tried to make up for the end of the previous month. At the start of each new month, Mum said: 'Let's do something.'

I listened to the faint squeaking coming from the living room. Mum would wake up in a moment. She tossed and turned on the big air mattress. In the evenings, she pumped the air in; in the mornings, she let the air out and folded her bed into a small package she slid behind the sofa.

Then I heard her walking around barefoot in the kitchen. She filled the kettle; she opened the oven, pulled out a baking tray, pushed it back in and closed the oven again.

I lay in bed, dreaming about our holiday. Over the last few days, I'd compared pictures of the North Sea with pictures of France, over and over. I'd picked up a North Sea brochure as well, of course. When I came home with it under my arm, Mum had raised her eyebrows but said nothing.

Then something weird happened. The longer I looked at the pictures of France, the paler the ones of the North Sea became. The longer I stared at endless palm tree-lined promenades, colourful old towns, huge yachts in harbours and crêpes with chocolate, the more I longed to go to France. In the end, I wasn't sure if it was even a real holiday if you stayed in Germany.

And when Mum came into my room with warm croissants and a coffee with milk, I was already convinced.

'Everything tastes a hundred times better in France,' she said.

'Okay, let's go to France!' I said with my mouth full.

Mum did a little jig and bowed. '*Merci, Madame!*' I think those were the only French words she knew, apart from 'croissant' and 'crêpes'. And then Mum said: 'Let's do something. Let's go into town. You can choose a new dress.'

We parked the Nissan in the underground car park by the river. It was a ten-minute walk from there into the town centre, but it was worth it. The underground car park was the cheapest of them all, and you got to walk along the river.

The river divided our town into two halves. On our side, there was an area where you were allowed to barbecue. When it was warm, extended families gathered there. They were so large, you couldn't determine who was the father and who the uncle, or who was the sister or cousin. But it didn't matter, because everyone belonged to someone. The women sat on colourful blankets, the men played boules or Frisbee. Later, they put huge skewers on the barbecue. The children danced around, and sometimes they argued. But then they just found someone else to play with.

Sometimes Lea and I lay on the grass by the river after school. Lea was my best friend. We lay together on the riverbank and did our homework. Or at least I did my homework, while Lea commented on the clothes of the people passing by. Lea was obsessed with clothes. For her, clothes were like having enough money to fly to the seaside – first class, mind you – or ordering a three-course meal without being hungry; or going shopping when your old stuff wasn't worn out.

When Mum and I arrived at the town centre, I headed towards our second-hand shop, but she held me back. 'No, you're getting something new today.'

'But —' I said, but Mum put her finger on my lips.

And so I spent the whole afternoon in a changing room in the town's largest department store. Mum brought me one dress after another. I tried them all, and I felt strange in each of them. I didn't feel like flowery purple or colourful stripes.

'We'll just keep looking,' Mum said.

But we didn't need to.

My dress wasn't hanging with the others. I knew immediately that I'd found the perfect one. It was as if it had my name on it. It was lemon yellow and fitted like it had been made for me. The shoulder straps were two fingers wide and double-layered. The length could be adjusted either side with a button. And the best thing was: the buttons looked like sunflowers.

'And what do you think?' I asked when I came out of the changing room.

'The buttons!' Mum said. 'Beautiful! Are they made of porcelain?'

My mum loved sunflowers. Thousands and thousands of them grew near our flat. Sometimes when she needed cheering up, she said: 'Hey, Billie, let's go to the sunflowers!' We would stay until the yellow leaves glowed in the setting sun. 'They are clever,' Mum said. 'They always turn towards the light.' She'd never have cut a sunflower and put it in a vase. 'Violence has many faces,' Mum said, 'and cutting flowers is one of them.'

The saleswoman wrapped the dress in pink tissue paper and put it in a white box. She put the box into a white bag. At that moment, I knew I'd never throw the packaging away.

Mum and I left the department store hand in hand. We walked through the sunshine and Mum asked: 'Do you fancy an ice cream?'

We went to Café Venezia, and I was allowed to order the Paradise Garden, the largest sundae the cafe had to offer. 'You're not eating, you're painting,' Mum laughed when I mixed strawberry, passion fruit and coconut and called the new flavour flamingo.

After I'd sucked up the thick mixture through a straw, Mum asked for the bill. She gave a big tip. Then she said: 'Today we're going to jump off the ten-metre platform. It's a good day for it.'

I recognized her look. That was the way she looked when she surprised herself. For my mum, spontaneity was the same as routine was to other people: security.

At night I'd dreamed about jumping. But every time, just before plunging into the water, I flew away. When I woke up, my heart would be pounding against my chest.

Just before we reached the pool, it started to rain, and thunder rumbled in the distance. The ticket lady didn't want to let us in. 'The ticket office closes an hour before the end of swimming time,' she said through the barred window, placing her fat fingers with red fingernails and cheap rings down on the board in front of her. A packet of cigarettes lay there too, opened, with one cigarette sticking out. She'd probably take a smoke break soon.

'We could sneak in,' I whispered in Mum's ear, but she shook her head and made that noise with her tongue she always made when she thought I was talking rubbish. Then she turned to the ticket lady.

'This young lady,' Mum said, nodding towards me, 'has something she needs to do. And it is' – she looked at her watch pointedly – 'sixty-two minutes before closing time.' She crossed her arms in front of her chest. Although she was petite, the gesture was effective.

Apart from a few swimmers, there was hardly anyone left. We put our bags down on the grass and stripped down to our underwear. Fortunately, Mum was wearing normal pants and not a pair of her 'I'm going on a date and need to look hot' knickers.

She went first. Looking straight ahead, Mum walked to the end of the platform, where she stood quite still. Then she stretched her arms up, as if she wanted to touch the sky with her fingertips, and put her hands together. Her body tensed like a bow and finally she dived, almost silently, into the water. Her dive was perfect.

'Now you.' She smiled as she pulled herself up on the edge of the pool and squeezed the water out of her hair. 'It's not about making it look good. It's about daring to do it.'

Mum always had the right words.

I climbed the metal ladder. Mum grew smaller, the blue surface more threatening. I imagined the tower as a cliff and the pool as the sea. I imagined I was a mermaid and the sea was my home.

And then I jumped. When I clambered out of the water with shaky legs, Mum pulled a small package out of her bag. 'For the bravest girl I know,' she said. I ran my hands over the wrapping paper. It crackled. Inside it was a red swimming costume. It had a shark's fin on the front, and underneath it said *Beware of the shark!* It was the coolest swimming costume I'd ever seen.

'Where did you get it?' I asked.

Mum laughed. 'From the department store. You took so long, I could have bought ten other things.'

I hugged her. 'And how did you know I was going to jump?'

She shrugged. 'I'm your mum.'

All this was the best non-birthday present I'd ever had.

At home, we waited for the storm to come, but nothing happened. We had the door to the flat and all the windows open. We hoped a fresh breeze would come in, but it stayed really hot. And then the heavens opened and the water evaporated from the ground and from the leaves on the trees.

Mum and I sat on the sofa and ate watermelon.

The sofa was our favourite place. Mum had got it from the dump years ago. Ahmed had helped her, and he'd come up with the idea of using carpet shampoo. That was how he cleaned his prayer rugs, which dried in the sun in front of our flat. Mum used it to clean the blue velvet cover, which was stained in several places.

Something about our sofa was magical, I was convinced of it. It made Mum talk. I knew almost nothing about her past. I didn't even know who my dad was. But sometimes I did find something out.

I found out, for example, that Mum had grown up in the countryside near Budapest. Her dad had built their house with his own hands.

There were three children's rooms, but only one of them was used. The other two rooms were planned for my mum's siblings.

'They were never born. They all died before.'

'Why?' I asked.

'I don't know.'

There was a garden and stables next to the house. Mum played with cats, chickens and goats as a child. There was a photograph of her in our living room that showed her sitting on a huge pig, laughing into the camera. There was a lot to do back then, but no dad. Cancer had taken him from her, month by month, a little more. When she was ten, she'd sat down on her dad's bed and taken his hand.

'His skin was almost transparent,' Mum said. She'd had to promise him to always manage on her own. He died that same day.

'What was the worst thing about not having a dad any more?' I asked.

'Being alone with my mother,' she said curtly. 'Her hand was always faster than her mouth.'

That was probably the reason why we had never visited her in Hungary, I thought.

I took a big bite of watermelon. The juice ran down my chin and dripped onto the notepaper lying on my thighs.

'Sun cream, sunhats and sunglasses,' Mum dictated, happy about the fact that everything she said began with 'sun'. Mum was in a very good mood. I don't know if it was because of the bubbly she'd poured into her fruit juice or because of France.

We wanted to leave as soon as possible. Mum had to check a few things at work first.

Half an hour later, the list was finished. And then I suddenly remembered something.

'We don't have any suitcases. Do we?'

Mum looked at me for a moment as if she had to process what I'd just said. Then she burst out laughing. The laughter burst out of her like lava from a volcano, and I was sure everyone on our floor could hear her. When she'd calmed down again, she shrugged and said: 'We'll just chuck it all in the car.'

That night I crawled onto the air mattress, over to Mum. I'd woken up at some point because I'd had a bad dream. First, I'd ridden a seahorse through colourful underwater worlds, had rested in giant clamshells and clambered up algae towards the surface of the water, where the sun was glimmering. Then, suddenly, it got dark around me. The darker it got, the less air I got. When I woke up, my heart was pounding.

'I dreamed about the sea again,' I said.

'What?' Mum asked, still half asleep.

'Did we ever live by the sea?' I asked.

'Perhaps in another life,' Mum said, and then she was asleep again.

5

Over the next few days, Mum and I gathered stuff from all over the flat that we wanted to take with us. In the kitchen, we laid everything out on the table; in the lounge, on a chair; in the bathroom, on the shelf under the mirror; and in my room, on the floor. Everything except our clothes. It was clear we wouldn't be able to pack them until shortly before we left. We simply didn't have enough clothes to leave them lying on the floor for days on end without being worn. We didn't yet know exactly when we were going to head off, but we knew it was going to be soon and we wanted to be ready.

My mum still had almost her entire annual holiday to take. It wasn't common to take more than two weeks off at a time in the place where she worked. But luckily Mum got on well with her bosses.

When she got home from work one evening, she said with a grin: 'Turn the telly off and put the washing machine on!'

'When does your holiday start?' I asked.

'Tomorrow!'

Mum said 'to-o-mo-o-o-ro-o-w' and danced to the rhythm of her own words. Then she disappeared into the kitchen. I heard her take a madeleine from its packet. Since we'd known we were going to France, she'd only eaten things like that.

'And how long?' I called into the other room.

'Four weeks!'

'Four weeks?!' I couldn't believe I'd be spending two-thirds of my summer holidays, or a whole month, or thirty days, in France.

I had to tell Lea straight away. Whenever something new happened, she was the first person I told. I'd known her phone number off by heart since she joined our class last school year. At first I thought her parents had moved, and that's why she'd changed schools, but then she plopped down in the only free chair, right next to me. She smelled of smoke, perfume and chewing gum. She said: 'I got expelled.' 'Where from?' I asked. 'From school.' 'Oh. Why?' Lea brushed it off. 'Got caught doing something.' I didn't ask any more questions. I wasn't sure I wanted to know what had happened. Lea's mix of thoughtlessness and energy confused me.

'Let's meet in town,' she said when I called her and told her we were going on holiday. 'I have something for you.'

All the way into town, I wondered what Lea wanted to give me, but I had no clue.

We met at the fountain. Lea hugged me and put down her backpack. Something purple was poking out of the top of it, plastic or rubber, I couldn't quite tell.

'What's that?' I asked.

'It's for you,' Lea said and grinned. Then she took the object out of her backpack and handed it to me.

'Swim fins?' Then I realized. It wasn't just a swim fin. 'A mermaid tail?' I almost screamed. Then I hugged Lea so tightly she nearly lost her balance.

'It's called a mono fin,' Lea said and sat down on the edge of the fountain. 'Do you like it?'

I'd already taken off my shoes and put my feet inside the fin. Then I turned around and dipped my fish feet into the fountain water. Lea also took off her shoes and rolled up the legs of her jeans.

'Where did you find it so quickly?' I asked and moved the fin back and forth in the water.

'My mum gave it to me once,' said Lea. 'I remembered when you said you were going to the sea.'

'I can give it back afterwards,' I said.

'Don't be silly,' said Lea.

I was so happy that I wanted to do something nice for Lea too. I thought for a few seconds, and then I had an idea. I fumbled around in my pocket for a coin. 'Make a wish,' I said, holding the coin between my index finger and my thumb in the air.

Lea gave me a sceptical look. 'Do you believe in that stuff?'

'I don't not believe in it,' I said. 'Come on, make a wish. But it has to be something you can't buy.'

Lea thought for a moment. 'Can I say it out loud?'

'Definitely. You have to.'

In truth, I had no idea. I knew you absolutely shouldn't say shooting star wishes out loud. But this was different, and I was curious what Lea had come up with. I showed her how to stand, and then she threw the coin behind her into the fountain. She closed her eyes and said: 'I wish for Billie and me to be friends forever.'

I thought it was a waste. We'd be friends forever anyway. But it was Lea's wish and I didn't interfere. Besides, it was too late now. You couldn't just swap wishes like a pair of jeans.

'Shall we get an ice cream from the kiosk?' Lea asked.

'Do I have to take the fin off?'

Lea laughed. 'I think so.'

'All right,' I said. I knew Lea fancied the ice cream seller. 'But then I have to go home.' I hesitated. Then I said: 'To pack my suitcase.'

We didn't have a towel with us, but that was okay. Lea was wearing sandals anyway, and I went barefoot; it wasn't far. I put my socks into my trainers, and tied my trainers to the straps of the fin.

The kiosk was tiny and so was the selection. Lea still needed ages to decide on an ice cream, though. This was because she wasn't focusing on the freezer cabinet but on David. He was sitting on a folding chair among the magazines, sweets, cigarettes and alcohol, reading a book. The cover was quite worn and the pages were tattered. I tried to make out the title, but his fingers were covering it up. When we arrived, he glanced up briefly, nodded to us and continued reading.

When Lea finally pulled off her wrapper, I'd almost finished my ice lolly. 'Too bad they don't cover the whole lolly with that crackling stuff,' I said. I liked the tiny explosions in my mouth.

'Meanies,' Lea said, biting into her ice cream sandwich.

We hung around outside the kiosk for a while longer, flicking through some of the magazines.

At some point David said: 'Are you actually going to buy one of those?'

Lea gave him the finger. 'Not any more.'

And that was the end of the kiosk and David.

Back home, I nestled the fin at the foot of my bed, allowing it to peek out from under the covers.

Then I sorted my dirty washing. I picked up each item of clothing individually.

To a red, faded T-shirt, I said: 'You're perfect for the journey.'

To my denim shorts, I said: 'We're playing volleyball together on the beach.'

And to my new dress, I said: 'I'll wear you when I walk along the beach.'

'Now?' my mum asked when I came past with a full basket of washing. She was sitting on the sofa zapping through the channels.

'Sure,' I said. 'Then we can leave the day after tomorrow. At the latest!'

Doing the laundry was my job. We didn't have a machine of our own, but there were several in the cellar, along with two dryers. The machines wound me up all the time. They were either busy or out of order. Sometimes I'd insert a coin into the slot, only to find that nothing happened. Then I'd slam my hand against the metal box. Hanging on it was a lock with a piece of paper in a plastic sleeve: *BREAKING OPEN POINTLESS. EMPTIED DAILY!* I'd never seen anyone actually open the box. In my mind, I'd bid farewell to a scoop of ice cream and feed the box with two coins. Usually, the water would gurgle through the tube, and the drum would start moving.

This time I was in luck. Because most people were asleep at night, all the machines except one were free. I washed and dried clothes into the early hours, but I didn't mind.

You don't mind if you believe the summer of your life is going to start the next day or the day after.

6

The summer of my life ended before it really began. It ended with a phone call.

We'd just loaded the car with our things. It had taken longer than we'd planned. We'd suddenly remembered all sorts of things we needed to take with us. The small salt shaker, in case we fancied eggs on the way. My mum's swimming cap, in case there was no hand shower in the place we'd be staying. Two new notebooks for me because I wanted to write on our trip. And of course books. I packed so many books into a bag that Mum just shook her head. She claimed the bag would be to blame if we ended up having to refuel more than planned. 'Finish that one first,' she said and pointed to *On the Road* by Jack Kerouac. I'd found the book at a bus stop. *For someone dreaming of moving on* was written on the first page in blue biro. Now it rested at the top of my bag.

Then we were finally ready, but half the day had gone by and we hadn't even left the parking space. We decided to leave the next morning. We wanted to set off as soon as the sun came up.

Mum and I settled down on the sofa and ate crisps. We had tried lots of different sorts until she finally found some that were super spicy. Spicy in a way that made your lips tingle and your mouth water.

I leafed through a magazine Luna had left at our place. 'Read me my horoscope,' Mum said, licking the chilli powder from her fingertips and turning the telly down.

My mum is an Aquarius. Under Aquarius it said: *Why hold back? You only live once. Go ahead and take some risks. Enjoy the change and try something new.*

Mum was always starting new hobbies, especially when they involved men. I knew it wasn't a good idea to read her this horoscope. I skimmed through the others and settled on Taurus: *Use your common sense when planning something important, otherwise you could slip up badly!* I read the words out, attempting to sound as serious as a news presenter.

Just as Mum opened her mouth to object, the phone rang. She closed her mouth again, got up and went over to the dock, but the phone wasn't there. She checked behind the sofa cushions and picked up a stack of brochures from the floor.

'Billie, give me a hand, will you!'

I couldn't be bothered to get up. I thought it would stop ringing any moment anyway. But it kept on going. I found the phone in the bathroom. Before I could answer it, Mum took it from my hand. 'Yes?' she said. Then she sat down on the toilet seat and didn't say anything for a long while. Her face was completely expressionless, but I could see something was wrong by the way her right arm hugged her body. I made faces, tried to find out through sign language and gestures, but Mum brushed me off, avoiding eye contact. I nudged her arm, but she waved her hand impatiently and shooed me out of the bathroom.

I gave up and decided to return Luna's magazine before my mum noticed I'd read her the wrong horoscope.

Luna opened the door straight away. Her tanned legs were in light blue frayed denim shorts. Her top was sleeveless and the colour of the Caribbean Sea. Sometimes I thought all the photos of it had to be fake. It was impossible for something to be so beautiful.

'Hey sweetie!'

Luna often called me 'sweetie', but I didn't mind. In fact I liked it. There was something comforting about it. It was a bit like having a sister.

We sat cross-legged on the floor. Luna didn't have any furniture except a bed, a chair draped with clothes, and a dressing table with a stool in front of it. Her flat was even smaller than ours; when you came in, you were right in the middle of her bedroom, which also contained a tiny kitchen.

'You didn't come to bring the magazines back, did you?' she asked now. Luna had a sixth sense for these things.

I shook my head. Mum had never hidden in the bathroom before to take a phone call. I guessed it wasn't good news.

'She'll tell you what's going on,' Luna said. 'Think about something else.'

Luna could just block things out. She said she had to so she wouldn't go mad – for example, when she was waiting at home to hear if she'd got a part. My mum said it was the reason Luna was still alive. And the cakes helped her too. If she couldn't sleep, then she made cakes. They were so beautiful she could have charged people just to look at them. Luna's cakes were pastel coloured and always a bit too sweet.

As if she'd read my mind, Luna got up and fetched last night's cake from the fridge. She cut two slices. 'It's filled with raspberry cream,' she said.

'It's yummy,' I said with my mouth full.

'Shall we listen to some music?' Luna asked.

Luna was a massive Janis Joplin fan. 'She is unhappy in an attractive way,' my mum had once said, and I hadn't known if she meant Luna or Janis. 'Both,' had been her response to my question.

We lay on Luna's bed. The ceiling fan was turning sluggishly. I tried not to blink. I counted to eleven before succumbing to the urge.

'What's she singing about?' I asked.

'About love. And about longing. About how you don't want what you get, and don't get what you want.'

'That sounds exhausting,' I said.

'Life is exhausting,' Luna said, lighting a cigarette and then offering me one. I took it and she gave me a light. I didn't really smoke. I only smoked when someone offered me one. I didn't have the money to get addicted. She inhaled deeply. 'Maybe your mum was on the phone with a man?'

'I don't think so,' I said.

I thought of Adam. My mum had been crazy about him last summer, but that was long over. Since then she hadn't mentioned anyone else. But that didn't have to mean anything. Mum didn't talk about my dad either. This didn't change the fact that there was a man somewhere out there who was my father.

In any case, the thing with Adam had started in church, of all places. Suddenly my mum had insisted on going to church. At first I thought she'd found the perfume in my room. Maybe she wanted to drag me to confession.

I had stolen the perfume with Lea. But that's another story.

'Since when do you want to go to church?' I'd asked my mum.

'Since today. And you're coming too.'

'But God is at home everywhere.'

'Don't steal my sayings,' Mum said and smiled.

I thought about the strong smell of incense, the uncomfortable wooden pews and the boring stories. 'Can I bring a book?' I asked.

'If you must,' Mum said, and disappeared into the bathroom.

When she came out, she smelled lovely, and her curls shone. She slipped into her high-heeled sandals and a top I'd never seen on her before.

'Is that new?'

'Super special offer,' Mum said and ran her fingers through her hair. Her bangles jingled.

I immediately suspected Mum hadn't got dressed up for God.

And of course I was right. The reason was the organist.

When we arrived, the service had already started, and the church was pretty full. Mum walked right to the front and squeezed herself into the second row. That way she had a perfect view of the man sitting at the back in the gallery at the organ. She just had to turn around. And she did so repeatedly. 'Isn't he playing like a young god?' Mum whispered in my ear, her breath a couple of degrees warmer than usual.

The organist leaned back and forth dramatically, tilting from side to side. I thought it was quite exaggerated. 'Not bad,' I said and immersed myself back into my book. I'd just got to an exciting bit, but I couldn't focus with Mum's ongoing commentary.

'He's as blonde as an angel,' Mum said, and the words tumbled from her mouth like ripe apples from a tree. 'Do you think that's his natural hair colour?'

'No idea,' I said, but Mum wasn't listening any more. She was sitting up very straight and kept running her fingers through her curls. I knew she was imagining herself draped across the keys. I nudged her, forming a heart with my hands and rolling my eyes until only the whites were visible. I resolved never to fall in love.

Since Mum didn't know his name, she called the organist Adam. She thought the name suited him. 'If I believed God had created man, then this would probably be his masterpiece,' she said.

It turned out later that Adam's real name was Samuel. My mum was pleased she hadn't been entirely wrong. After all, Samuel was also a biblical name. And the more she thought about it, the more she liked it. Suddenly she got enthusiastic about all sorts of things: a puddle, a smile, a fizzy sweet. And then one evening she didn't come home after her waitressing shift. After I'd waited for over an hour, the phone rang. 'See you tomorrow, sweetie. Order yourself a pizza, okay? There's money under the right-hand cushion on the sofa.'

She spent a few more nights with the organist, and then this stopped. When I asked her the reason, she just said: 'Samuel has more women than his organ has keys.' Mum's voice had finally gone back to normal. All the time she'd been seeing him, her voice had gone up half an octave, regardless of who she was speaking to.

My mum had had a few dates with men in the last few years, but I rarely saw any of them more than once. None of them were good enough for us. When she came back late at night and watched a romantic film, I knew it was over again. The truth was that Mum never stayed with a man for long.

In physics class, I'd learned how magnets work. It was as if Mum was a super strong magnet. She attracted men like the North Pole attracts the South Pole. Then she switched her opinion from plus to minus and repelled them all.

'Billie?' Luna asked now.

'Luna?'

'I want to get a new tattoo,' Luna said. 'Look.' And then she showed me various drawings of the sun. 'Which one do you like best?'

'This one,' I said and pointed to a sun with a friendly face and rays that looked a bit like flames.

'That one goes best with the moon, right?'

I nodded. There was a moon tattooed on Luna's shoulder. You could even see the craters and mountains. Her name was written in cursive above it. As if Luna needed to assure herself that she existed.

'Why are you called Luna?'

Luna combed her hair with her fingers. 'When I was born, my hair was as white as the moon. That's why my mum chose Luna.'

I didn't know if Luna had just made that up.

Mum once told me that Luna's mother had died a few years ago.

'They found her with a syringe in her arm. Did you see the handbag on Luna's shelf and all the stuff around it?'

I nodded. An ID card, two childhood photos of Luna, a toothbrush and toothpaste, a pair of knickers, an empty notebook and banknotes in a small porcelain dish. Luna never touched it. Dust lay on the banknotes like butter on bread.

'Luna's mother's life fitted into a single handbag,' Mum had said. We were both a bit sad about the shrine in Luna's flat.

'Do you think Luna's crazy because her mum took so many drugs?'

'Maybe. But remember you don't say "crazy". It's called mentally ill.'

Sometimes I didn't understand my mum. She said 'damn' and 'shit' all day long, but calling others crazy wasn't allowed.

I jumped off Luna's bed. 'I have to go home now.'

Luna turned the music down. 'Okay. See you soon, sweetie. Good luck!'

As I closed the door behind me, I spotted Uta. She pushed open the door to the walkway with her shoulder. Then she dragged herself and her two shopping bags down the corridor. I ran over to help, but she'd already reached the door of her flat. Her door was the second one along as you entered the corridor. 'Lift is broken again,' she said, but it was more a pant and a wheeze.

'Shit,' I said. I remembered what Mum had once said about the lift: 'If you live on the seventeenth floor, then the gym is included.'

'Can you tell your mum I need to talk to her?' Uta asked.

'Sure.'

Lately, Uta had been talking to my mum all the time. I had no idea what about. Whenever I asked Mum, she either said nothing or changed the subject. Mum was good at saying nothing.

She was especially quiet when I wanted to know something about her past.

As Uta leaned forward to unlock her door, the gold chain swung forward from between her breasts. Attached to the chain was a locket containing a photograph of Lady Di. Everyone here knew Lady Di dangled between Uta's huge breasts.

Uta often talked passionately about the British royal family. She summed up Lady Di's death as 'scandalous and consistent'. Scandalous because Lady Di had been driven to her death, consistent because she'd died for the love of her life.

I was pretty sure Heinz wasn't the love of her life. Heinz spent the entire day in front of the television. In summer in his underpants, in winter in his purple-and-green tracksuit. He only got up for two reasons: either to fetch himself another beer from the fridge, or to take care of his birds. The entire flat was full of birdcages. Luna had once said he loved his birds more than he loved his wife.

Sometimes Heinz invited us to have a sausage when he barbecued in the walkway, despite it being prohibited, but who was going to report him? The caretaker didn't care about anything. Not about the lifts and not about us. And we didn't care about him. My mum had learned to take care of things herself. She knew how to put up a shower rail and sand down a tabletop.

7

I found my mum in the bathroom. She was sitting in exactly the same place as before, staring into space, not moving. The telephone lay on her lap.

'What's happened? Who were you speaking to?' I asked.

Mum slowly turned her head as if she'd just woken up. 'Are we going to eat something? I'm starving.'

Now it was my turn to stare. Was that all she had to say?

Mum's hand wandered to her mouth. Then she chewed on the nail of her pointy finger. She hadn't done that in a long time.

'Who were you on the phone to?' I asked again.

'Your grandma,' Mum finally said and sighed.

I couldn't remember my mum ever having spoken to her on the phone. 'What did she want?'

'She's sick.'

It didn't sound like she just had a cold or a cough.

'Has she got cancer?'

Mum shook her head. I didn't know my grandma, but I was still relieved. I'd learned that nothing was worse than cancer. I knew how my mum had lost her dad.

'The doctors don't know where her pain is coming from,' Mum said and got up. 'Why do they study for years on end if they still can't work out the cause?'

I didn't have an answer to that.

Mum started clearing the table in the kitchen. I always did my homework there, Mum painted her nails, mended our clothes or learned English vocab there while our dinner defrosted in the microwave. Then we'd eat in the living room on the sofa, plates balanced on our knees. But now Mum cleared everything into the living room, and then she laid the table. She laid the table like she was expecting guests. She even folded the napkins and put them next to the plates. 'What are you looking at?' she asked when she saw my face. 'I'm fed up with the chaos.'

We were already sitting at the table when Mum realized we'd run out of butter.

'Can you go grab a packet?' She pressed a coin into my hand. It wasn't enough to buy a packet of butter, but I didn't say anything.

On the way to the discount store, I realized there was no way we could finish off an entire packet of butter in one evening. We'd have to chuck it out when we got back from the holiday. But then I saw the bike and didn't think about it any more. The bike was simply leaning against the wall. It was red and had a cream-coloured saddle. It was exactly the bike I'd always wished for. I looked around briefly, then I got on. My hair flapped in the wind, and when I cycled down the hill, I spread my arms out. It felt a bit like flying.

Shoplifting at the discount store was easy. I dropped the packet of butter in my backpack. Then I barged my way past the queue at the checkout. Easy-peasy. But there was a difference between a packet of butter and a bicycle. I did an extra lap, and then I put the bike back. I comforted myself with the thought that summer would nearly be over by the time we got back from France anyway.

From the hallway I could hear Mum wasn't alone. At first I thought she was on the phone again. But the phone was on the sideboard in the hallway.

Before I saw Uta, I saw her black eye. It shone at me from the doorway. Uta was sitting on our sofa, sniffling. My mum was talking to her softly, one hand holding Uta's, the other holding a packet of mozzarella. It took a moment for me to understand that Uta had been using it to cool her eye. The eye was almost completely swollen shut. Uta didn't look at me, not with her good eye either.

'She fell down the stairs,' Mum said and sent me to my room. I didn't believe her. I wasn't stupid. I recognized a black eye when I saw one. And I knew Heinz had done it.

Whenever I ran into Heinz with my mum, he ignored me. But one time he'd stroked my arm in passing. I was speechless with shock. Afterwards I immediately jumped in the shower and lathered my arm with soap three times, from shoulder to wrist, but I still felt his fingers on my skin for days afterwards. When I told Mum about it, she said: 'Kick him in the balls if he touches you again, you hear me?' Then she tied a pillow between her legs and ordered me to attack her. I hesitated. I didn't want to hurt her. I'd been stronger than her since the age of twelve. My mum imitated a man's voice, dark and crude, and said: 'Come on, love, don't be like that.' She looked aggressive, like the pit bulls that lived in our block. I had to giggle and the exercise was over.

I lay on my bed and listened to music. Then Mum came in. 'Shift over,' she said and sat down next to me.

'She didn't fall down the stairs, did she?' I asked.

Mum wiped her hands across her face and shook her head. 'No, but she didn't want you to know.'

'Know what?' I wanted her to say it.

'That Heinz brings her flowers.'

I sighed. Mum liked to package ugly things into nice words.

'Is it my fault?' I asked.

'No! Why would you say that?'

'I forgot to tell you that Uta wanted to speak to you.'

'Even if you'd told me, it wouldn't have changed anything,' Mum said.

We stared at the ceiling for a while; my stars were up there. They were made of plastic and glowed in the dark. Our city was too bright to see many real stars.

'Do you think she'll leave him?' I asked.

'No,' Mum said. 'She loves him.'

'How can you love someone who hits you?'

'Some things are complicated, Billie.'

I didn't know what was complicated about it.

'Come on, let's have dinner now,' Mum said and got up.

'Did you lay the table for Uta?' I asked.

Mum shook her head. 'I didn't know she was coming over.' She held out her hands to me. 'I laid the table for us.'

The cheese and ham looked all sweaty by now, and the bread was slightly stale. The butter had gone all soft in the heat. I'd forgotten to put it in the fridge. Our knives slithered across the bread and the butter disappeared into every single pore, like I'd stolen cheap margarine.

That evening my mum didn't speak about my grandma any more, and I didn't ask. My grandma was a stranger to me, and

I knew very little about her. My grandma was as far away from me as far as the Earth is from the Moon.

It was only the next morning that I realized this wouldn't stay that way.

8

The first thing my mum said the next morning wasn't: 'Go and take a shower, we're leaving shortly!'

She didn't even say: 'Good morning.'

The first thing she said was: 'When you're sick, you need your family around you.'

When I came into the living room, it was getting light. I'd set my alarm clock extra early. I couldn't wait to get going. Perhaps we could even take a dip in the sea tonight.

Mum was sitting cross-legged on her inflatable mattress. She was still wearing her clothes from the night before, and it didn't look like she'd taken off her make-up. It also didn't look like she'd slept. She ran her hands across her pale face, and then she said: 'Sit down.'

I didn't feel like a long chat. 'Can't we talk in the car?'

'I need to tell you something. Please sit down.'

I felt dizzy. I wasn't sure if it was because I hadn't had breakfast yet, or if it was because my mum looked so serious.

Mum didn't look at me. 'Your grandma is coming to stay.'

'What? When?' I asked.

'The day after tomorrow.'

'The day after tomorrow? That won't work,' I said. 'We'll be lying on the beach the day after tomorrow.'

'We need to postpone our holiday.'

My mum couldn't be serious. I jumped up. 'What?'

'I know it's stupid, but —' Mum started.

'It's not stupid, it's a catastrophe!' I said.

Mum said I should stop shouting.

'What about your holiday time?'

'I still have to take it.'

'But then we can't go on holiday any more this year!'

'We'll go next year,' Mum said. 'I promise!'

'Can't she come after our holiday?'

Mum shook her head. 'She isn't well enough.'

'So why don't we go to Hungary?'

I rapidly switched the images of the Atlantic to those of Lake Balaton, and the French seafront to the glittering skyline of Budapest. Perhaps my mother could first take care of my grandma, and then we could have our holiday in Hungary. Hungary wasn't France, but it was better than nothing.

But Mum said: 'She needs the best possible medical treatment.'

'Aren't there any good doctors in Hungary?'

My mum clicked her tongue and made a dismissive gesture. 'The hospitals are badly equipped, and everything is way too expensive.'

'But we don't have any room. Where's she going to sleep?'

'In your room.'

'And where am I supposed to sleep?' I couldn't believe Mum had first cancelled our holiday and had now thrown me out of my room without batting an eye.

'In the living room.'

'But that's where you are!'

Our living room had three doors. It was between my room and the kitchen and opened into the hallway. I would never have any peace.

'Since when does that bother you?' Mum wanted to know.

'It doesn't bother me, but she shouldn't live with us.'

'Where else is she supposed to live? If you've won the lottery and bought a villa, then feel free to tell me.'

'Why can't she just stay in hospital?'

'A hospital isn't a hotel.'

'But it's already too full here,' I said.

'Billie, I have decided.' Mum got up. She looked tired.

'You don't even like your mum,' I said.

'But she's my mum.'

'But she was mean to you.'

'People can change.'

I imagined an old woman who I didn't even know lying in my bed. My room would probably smell weird for years.

'Then I'll move into the car.'

Mum looked at me like I'd lost my mind. Then she laughed out loud.

'You wanted to sleep in it in France. And you said yourself that there are people who live in their cars,' I whinged.

'Yes. But not you.'

'Why not?' The more I thought about it, the more I liked the idea. I'd be able to look at the stars through the rear windscreen at night.

'Do you want child protection services coming and putting you in a home?' Mum took me by the shoulders and rested her forehead against mine. Then she wiped my tears away with the end of her sleeve. 'We'll still go on holiday together, I promise. She won't be here forever.'

'Not forever' sounded like shortly before eternity, and the sun wouldn't radiate forever either, but would expand for 3.5 billion years and then cause all the Earth's oceans to evaporate. I knew people only said 'not forever' for two reasons: either when they didn't know how long something was going to take, or when they wanted to cheer someone up. Sometimes both at the same time.

'But I don't want to unpack everything again,' I said. 'And I'd like a hot chocolate now.'

My mum brought me the hot chocolate in bed and then went to lie down again. I listened for sounds from the living room. Mum tossed and turned; there was an occasional sigh in between her breaths.

At some point – I was reading at the time – Mum got up. Then she started cleaning and didn't stop. During the week, she barely had any time for it, and at weekends she was tired. But now she suddenly started dusting the tops of the kitchen cupboards.

'How tall is your mum?' I asked, but Mum ignored my comment.

When Mum was done with the kitchen, she moved on to the bathroom, and then the living room. In between, she called her bosses. She wanted to cancel her holiday leave and go to work as usual. There was no flexibility with her office job. That meant that for the next four weeks, Mum would be off work until around five. Then she called Larry. He was the manager of Ocean's Bar, where my mum waitressed. Her coming to work as usual wasn't a problem for Larry. 'Can I also take on a couple of extra shifts?' she asked.

'Extra shifts?' I asked when she'd hung up.

'Your grandma needs to shower, eat and watch TV,' Mum said. 'I need to earn some extra money.'

I pictured my grandma grabbing the remote and changing the channel I'd selected.

'Do you want to go outside for a bit?' Mum asked.

'It's raining,' I said without looking at her. Then I switched on the TV.

One day later, our flat was cleaner than ever before; Luna whistled her acknowledgement through the gap in her front teeth. Then she plopped down on our sofa and pulled a large stack of papers from a folder. Luna spread the papers out in front of her on the small table, and because there wasn't enough space, she continued on the floor. Soon half the living room was covered in white paper. She'd written all over the sheets of paper. Luna wiped a strand of hair from her sweaty forehead and said: 'I've written a novel.'

We had been standing in the doorway the entire time, simply watching Luna.

'When?' my mum wanted to know.

And Luna said: 'Last night.'

Mum and I looked at each other. No one wrote a novel in one night. I was pretty sure of that. My mum teetered across the living room like a flamingo, trying not to step on any pages. Then she sat down next to Luna. The pages of the novel crackled under her bum, but Luna didn't notice. She kept changing her position and ran her hands over her face and through her hair. My mum put an arm around her and spoke to her gently. Then she gave me a signal.

I ran outside and went next door to Luna's flat. It was a problem if Luna didn't sleep at night. We had learned to see the signs. We often heard noises from her flat in the middle of the night. Luna would pace around, move furniture, cook, bake, make phone calls. When she was done, she'd start all over again. Luna was like a toy clock that was constantly rewound. If Luna had several nights like these, then it wasn't long before she disappeared, sometimes for days, once for almost two weeks. When she reappeared, she would hide in her flat like a wounded animal. We'd press our ears against the living room wall, but all we could hear was the muffled, rhythmic sound of the television and our own breath. If Luna even opened the door, she'd be in her pyjamas. Her eyes said 'no' to the world, and her words were stuck somewhere inside her, in a place we couldn't reach. 'Luna is like the sea,' Mum told me. 'When the water recedes after the tide, all that's left is grey mud.'

I switched on the light and went straight into Luna's bathroom. There was a washbag on the shelf. I tipped it out into the sink. Packets of pills and pillboxes rolled into the white porcelain. I picked up each one and dropped one after the other back into the washbag until I found the box with the pills I was looking for. It was almost full.

'She forgets that she's ill, just like we forget in summer what winter feels like,' Mum had once said.

At first Luna refused. Mum spoke to her until she finally opened her mouth. In the meantime, I picked up all the papers.

I spent the rest of the afternoon lying on my bed and writing in my notebook. Writing was the only thing that helped with my bad mood. I'd tried to call Lea. I wanted to tell her about our cancelled holiday and ask if she wanted to go to the shopping centre with me, but no one had answered the phone. So I carried on writing.

I wrote: *These are the most boring summer holidays of my life*, and I immediately felt better. Normally I didn't keep a diary but wrote proper stories.

My notebook was full of stories, and they all had a happy ending. Some stories had actually happened that way, almost at least. If I didn't like the end, I simply rewrote it. I just carried on writing until everything got better.

9

My mum's heart was too big. She always gave the homeless man outside the discount store the euro from our shopping cart although he hadn't even asked for it.

She listened to each one of Uta's stories, although she knew they were always the same.

And she opened the door to my grandma, although some doors are supposed to stay closed. As my grandma stepped into our flat, I held my breath and didn't breathe out again.

Mum had gone to fetch my grandma from the train station in our Nissan. My grandma had come on the night train from Budapest.

Through the bathroom keyhole I watched Mum heave my grandma's suitcase into the hallway.

My grandma followed. Her skin was a bit darker than my mum's and much darker than mine. Like we grew lighter with each generation.

My grandma was tiny, much smaller than my mum. But her suitcase was all the larger by comparison. It was as big as a small cupboard. For a moment, I hoped she'd say: 'Look, I brought my own bed.' Then she'd open the suitcase, lie down and demonstrate how comfy it was to sleep in a suitcase.

My grandma was sweaty. A long grey strand of hair poked out of her headscarf. She pushed it back and looked around. We didn't have a coat rack, just three hooks on the door. The hooks were all full.

'Is that your scarf, Marika?'

I'd given Mum the scarf for her birthday. My grandma ran the scarf through her fingers and said: 'Red would look better on you.'

I flushed the toilet. Then I went out into the hallway. My grandma looked me up and down. Before I could say anything, she said in Hungarian: 'You must be Erzsébet.'

I nodded.

Mum came up behind me and rested her hands on my shoulders. 'Yes, this is Billie.'

My grandma looked directly at me. 'Hello, Erzsébet. It is an honour to be called Erzsébet, don't forget that.'

Mum's hands felt heavy on my shoulders. Finally I replied, also in Hungarian: 'Hello, Nagymama, how was your trip?'

My grandma clasped her hand to her heart. 'Burdensome!' Then she said to my mother: 'You taught her Hungarian!'

'Of course,' Mum said.

Mum had never made much of an effort to teach me Hungarian, but she'd taught me not to lie. I immediately realized that other rules counted now.

'A child without a mother tongue is like a house without a foundation,' my grandma said.

I thought that I already had a mother tongue. It was German. But my father tongue was Hungarian. I'd been eight when I'd told my mum I wanted to learn Hungarian. I imagined how proud my dad would be if he turned up outside our door and I greeted him in Hungarian. 'Your dad will never stand outside our door,' Mum said, but I wouldn't be put off. When I'd learned the first few bits of vocabulary, she said: 'What do you want with a language that no one speaks?' My mum hated it when people realized straight away that she wasn't German. 'To speak to other Hungarians,' I replied. 'All the Hungarians I know speak German,' Mum said. We only knew one Hungarian person; he was our dentist, and I didn't care about him. 'But if I go to Hungary one day to find my father, then I can speak to him,' I said. 'How do you know he lives in Hungary?' Mum asked in an annoyed voice. 'So he doesn't live in Hungary?' Mum went silent, like she always did when I tried to find out something about my father.

My grandma didn't wait for us to show her the flat. She inspected one room after the other, like she'd come to buy it. I waited for her to start haggling over the price because she didn't like what she saw.

Mum had put in a lot of effort. She wanted the place where we lived to look nice. She didn't want anyone who visited us to immediately see that all we ate at the end of the month was spaghetti with ketchup.

The effort Mum had made lingered in the air in every room like the shisha smell in the corridors of our building. Her effort had settled on our furniture. None of it was new, everything was from the flea market or from the dump. The varnish was flaking off; there were scratches or cracks everywhere. Nothing really went together. Wood stood next to plastic, plastic stood next to metal, metal next to glass.

My mother's effort was reflected in the worn velvet cover of our sofa, in the stools she'd made from pallets, in the pictures on the wall. The pictures we'd hung up in our living room and in the hallway were cut out from old calendars. At the end of the year, the employees of the company where my mum cleaned threw away their calendars. Mum took the nicest ones home. Then we cut out the images and stuck them on the wall with Sellotape. 'Places are like people,' Mum once said. 'At some point you get used to their flaws.'

Under my grandma's gaze, each flaw grew into a blemish we could never repair. 'This isn't necessary,' she sighed, when she'd completed her tour and Mum put the kettle on in the kitchen.

'What isn't necessary?' I asked.

'To live like this,' my grandma said and waved her hand like she could simply wipe away everything she'd seen.

'Tea?' Mum asked. Before anyone could reply, she poured the hot water into our cups so enthusiastically that it poured over the rims. 'Oh,' she said. She wiped, rubbed and dabbed at the wet spots with a tea towel.

My grandma shovelled sugar into her tea without saying a word. I dipped my wet finger into the sugar bowl and sucked it. My grandma gave me a dirty look. I then put the fingers of my other hand into my mouth, one after the other.

'Billie, stop that!' said Mum.

I couldn't resist. My grandma was to blame that we weren't going on holiday. And now she was criticizing everything. Couldn't Mum see she was putting down everything we cared about? I wanted to ask why it wasn't necessary for us to live this way, but when I opened my mouth, my mum asked: 'How are you?'

And then my grandma started to talk and wouldn't stop. It was like she'd saved up all the words that she wanted to finally be rid of because the best-before date was up. She told us how she'd felt a pressure on her chest one afternoon and had felt dizzy. 'I immediately knew what that meant,' she said. 'Heart attack.'

The paramedics thought so too and took her in their ambulance.

'Have you ever driven with the blue lights on?' my grandma asked. 'It's as if the driver is Moses parting the Red Sea.'

She was checked over in the hospital. The doctors checked her body from top to bottom, from the back to the front, from left to right. They found nothing. They told her she was as fit as a fiddle.

'How can I be perfectly healthy when I have such pain?' my grandma asked. 'They didn't want to find anything because I am an old woman.'

The pain grew worse, but the doctors couldn't help her. That was why my grandma had been praying even more than usual.

My grandma laid her hands on the table and said: 'Since Christ suffered in His body, arm yourselves also with the same attitude, because he who has suffered in his body is done with sin.'

I thought: so those are the hands you used to strike my mum. My grandma wiped a tear from the corner of her eye. Mum squeezed her hand and said: 'Amen.' When she said 'We'll find a doctor who can treat you,' I knew we were done for.

10

My grandma was with us for less than half a day before she dragged all her things into my room.

Her suitcase lay unopened in the hallway because it would only fit through my door with force. My grandma took all her clothes out, pile by pile, and put everything on my bed. My mum helped her. I leaned against my desk and watched.

Then my grandma opened my cupboard. Forcefully, she shoved my clothes to one side. 'Is that all?' she asked. 'A young girl should have more clothes.' She looked worried, like if she'd discovered that all my teeth had fallen out because I didn't eat any vegetables.

'I'm not that interested in clothes,' I said, even before my mum could open her mouth. That wasn't entirely true, of course.

My grandma started putting her skirts on clothes hangers. It looked like she more or less only wore skirts. Each skirt was uglier than the next. All of them were patterned, all of them were colourful.

When she'd put away her clothes, she moved on to the rest. The rest was at the bottom of the suitcase. Piece by piece, my grandma transformed my room into a sort of shrine. In the end, I hardly recognized it.

'Try not to get worked up about it,' Mum said.

'Too late,' I hissed.

Porcelain figurines were lined up on my windowsill. I didn't look closely, but I recognized the Virgin Mary, once with Jesus and once without, and I noted a couple of angels.

There were two posters on the wall next to my bed. One had the slogan EVERYTHING YOU CAN IMAGINE IS REAL. That was a Pablo Picasso quote. The other depicted a pigeon that had been shot. It was plunging down to earth with wide-open eyes. I loved both posters. But my grandma removed the poster with the pigeon and put it face down on my desk. 'Who hangs something like that up of their own free will?' she asked.

'What's wrong with it?' I asked.

'It's tawdry.'

I told her that the artist had been a member of a street gang in the past. I told her that he'd found God and art in prison and was now a wealthy businessman, but my grandma wasn't listening any more.

'Oil landscapes,' my mum whispered. 'That's all she's into, oil landscapes and images of Jesus.'

My grandma then went on to hang a landscape next to the poster with the Picasso quote, but it wasn't an oil painting. It was a high-angle photograph of Lake Balaton. I wouldn't have known it was Lake Balaton if GYÖNYÖRŰ BALATONUNK hadn't been written across it. Which means 'Our beautiful Balaton'. Then she asked my mum for a hammer and nail. She knelt on my bed, hammered the nail into the wall and hung a wooden cross on it.

I thought she was very agile for an old, sick woman. But then I thought that she wasn't really that old, at least not for a grandma. She was sixty. My mum had just been super young when she gave birth to me.

When the cross was mounted, my grandma cleared all my books from my bedside table and put a Jesus figurine there instead. He was made of porcelain and was dragging his own cross. She laid two Bibles and a rosary next to it.

'Why did you bring two Bibles?' I asked.

'If I lose one, then I have one in reserve,' said my grandma. Then she repositioned everything again, and in the end, Jesus was standing on top of the Bibles. He looked like he was guarding them.

I needed to get out of there.

That afternoon, I went to see Lea. My grandma had gone for a lie-down and Mum had gone to work.

Lea lived nearby with her parents, but her life was the Hollywood version of mine. Number five Schöne Aussicht was like something from my dreams. The house Lea lived in was huge. It had three floors, and each floor was bigger than the flat my mum and I lived in. You were only allowed to enter the house without shoes; that's how clean it was.

'How can you tell if someone has money?' Mum had once asked me. 'By their car?' I said. Mum shook her head and said: 'By their cleaning products. People who haven't got any money clean with vinegar. The others use the lavender stuff. There's only half as much in the bottle, but it's twice as expensive.'

Of course, you could smell the lavender in the hallway as soon as you stepped inside.

Everyone had their own room in this house; Lea even had her own bathroom. There was a garden behind it, with a swing, a dog kennel and a huge pool. Lea had a proper family: a mum, two brothers and a father. Not one of those fathers who hung around at home drinking beer, but one who worked in a bank and went shopping after work in his Mercedes-Benz. He didn't shop at the discount store. He didn't look through the weekly specials. He didn't know where the milk was on special offer or where to find the washing powder. On my first visit, I'd noticed the small sticker on the letterbox: NO ADVERTISEMENTS. On Saturdays, Lea's father often did something with his two sons, and Lea went window shopping with her mum in town. Lea's mum didn't work. 'She volunteers,' Lea had told me. 'She rescues Romanian stray dogs.'

'Billie, how lovely!' said Lea's mum and spread her arms out wide. 'Come on in. You can go straight up, Lea's already waiting for you. Or would you like something to eat first? We had lamb stew with green beans for lunch.'

I thanked her and shook my head. I wondered if Lea's mum would ever stop treating us like little girls. She was forever popping her head around the door. She brought us home-made biscuits and banana milkshakes. Then she'd return to collect the dishes, and usually she'd stay for a bit to chat to us. I wasn't sure what I was supposed to think about it. On the one hand, I wanted to be alone with Lea, but her biscuits were crazy delicious.

Lea was lying on her stomach on the bed and didn't look up when I came in. She was wearing a red checked miniskirt, and her bare feet seemed to float in the air. On her right leg she wore a silver anklet decorated with small charms. Her T-shirt had slid up to reveal her tanned back. Her long, gold-blonde hair fell in thick, heavy strands over her shoulders.

'Hey,' I said and waved, and then Lea noticed me and took off her headphones.

'Hey hey,' she said, tucked a strand of hair behind her ear and smiled at me.

It was the smile. Right from the start, I'd been stuck on this smile like sugar on a child's damp hand.

'How's things with your grandma?' Lea asked and shifted over.

'All right,' I said and sat down next to her on the bed. Then I told her about the figurines and the crosses and the Bibles in my room. Lea's eyes grew larger and larger.

'She's staying in your room?'

'Yes.'

'Shit,' Lea said. 'And how long is she staying?'

I shrugged. 'Not forever, at least that's what my mum said. But who packs everything they own in a single suitcase and then stays just a few days?'

'You can live here,' Lea said. 'We have enough space.'

Lea's room was twice the size of mine and at least three times as nice. She had one of those modern beds that are really low, almost on the ground. It was white and plain and looked very elegant. Lea wanted to get away from the 'pink stuff and all the flowers'. But what I liked best was Lea's dressing table. It was made of white wood and had an oval mirror. In front of the table was a matching little stool with a dark green velvet cover. There were little pots and tubs, brushes in different sizes and hair clips.

And there was a jewellery tree, hung with necklaces, bracelets and earrings.

It wasn't that I used much make-up or liked to wear jewellery, even if I'd been able to afford it. It was the excess that fascinated me.

'Shall we go for a swim?' Lea asked.

'I don't have a costume with me,' I said.

'You can have one of mine,' said Lea, got up and opened her wardrobe. But Lea didn't have any costumes, only bikinis. The tops were a bit too big, and when I looked at myself in the mirror, I felt strange.

There was no one downstairs when we came down. In the living room, Lea pushed open the big glass doors to the garden, and the air conditioning stopped humming. The pool was still and blue in front of us. I felt the urge to destroy the calm surface with a cannonball.

Lea pulled a double lounger into the sun and spread out a large towel. Then we lay down on the soft surface. After a few minutes, Lea reached for the bottle of suntan oil. 'Lie on your stomach,' she said.

I never got sunburned. Perhaps I'd have been burned in the south, I thought, but I didn't protest. The suntan oil smelled of coconut, and Lea took her time. She spread the oil carefully over my back, and then massaged it in. I closed my eyes. Suddenly it didn't seem that bad not to be in France.

'There you are, my two beauties.'

Lea's mother's voice jerked me out of my doze. I squinted. I was lying in the shade; the sun had disappeared behind the house diagonally opposite. Lea was lying in the last little spot of sunlight on an inflatable island in the pool.

'Dinner's ready in ten minutes,' Lea's mum said and disappeared into the house. Whenever I visited Lea, I was allowed to eat with them.

The living room had a dining area, and we sat at the big oak table.

'Something light because of the heat,' Lea's mum said when she brought in the plates. There were two slices of Hawaiian toast on each plate, and a large bowl of salad stood on the table.

'Where's Dad?' Lea asked.

'He's coming later. He has to work,' Lea's mother said and heaped salad on our plates.

'Again?' Lea asked, but her mum had already turned to me.

'Billie, how is your mother?'

'Well, thank you.'

'Oh, that's a relief,' she said.

'Why, what's up?' Lea asked.

'Oh, it's just she wasn't at parents' evening,' said Lea's mum. 'And it was the last one in the old school year.'

'Mum,' Lea said.

'She had to work,' I said, but that was a lie. Mum couldn't stand parents' evenings. And because Lea's mum was a member of the parents' association, she sometimes didn't go at all. She used to go occasionally when parents' evening happened to be on an I-must-be-a-better-mum day. But usually Mum just relied on me telling her what she needed to know.

'Anyone want seconds?'

I said nothing, but Lea's mum still put another slice of toast on my plate.

After dinner she asked: 'Shall I pack the rest up for you?' and her voice went all soft.

That evening, I came home with a slice of Hawaiian toast in one plastic box and salad in another. My mum and grandma were sitting in the kitchen, drinking tea.

'What's that?' Mum asked when she saw the boxes.

'Lea's mum gave me the leftovers from dinner to take home,' I said. 'Why are you home already? Did Larry let you off early?'

Mum got up, took the boxes, and without looking inside threw them in the bin.

'Hey!'

'We don't need charity,' Mum said. Then she grabbed the car keys.

'Marika!' my grandma called out, but Mum was already in the hallway. When Mum got angry, she took the Nissan and put her foot down. She sped down the autobahn for a bit and listened to music until she'd calmed down.

'Is she always so hot-headed?' my grandma asked.

I shrugged. 'Sometimes.'

Mum had never thrown away food before. There had only been a couple of times before when she'd been so dismissive. The last time she'd been like that was when I asked her about my dad.

My dad was a mystery. I knew almost nothing about him. All I knew was that he'd left my mum when I was small. And that the white cowboy boots had been a gift from him. That day I'd learned something new: Mum definitely didn't want to talk about him. 'Some things are best left where they belong,' she'd said as she put on red lipstick in front of the mirror above the sink. But I wouldn't drop it, and Mum had exploded. 'Stop digging around in the damn past,' she shouted, and then she was gone.

Maybe my dad was a drug baron or a famous politician. But maybe he was just a very boring person and there was nothing to say about him. In any case, my mum was like a dark, bottomless lake.

My grandma took the boxes out of the bin, put the food on the plate and the plate in the fridge. Then she washed the boxes, dried them and gave them to me. 'Tell your friend that she's invited for dinner with us next time. I will cook. Hungarian.'

I had no idea my friendship with Lea would never be the same again.

11

When I came into the kitchen the next morning, Mum and my grandma were already there having breakfast. At least my grandma was having breakfast. A piece of toast with a bite taken out of it lay on Mum's plate. She was bent over the yellow pages, chewing on a pencil. There were pieces of paper lying all over the place.

'What are you doing?' I asked.

'Good morning, Erzsébet,' my grandma said.

'Sit down and eat something,' Mum said.

'I'm not hungry yet,' I said, but I sat down anyway.

'You are a growing girl, you have to eat,' said my grandma. 'Shall I make you a hot chocolate?'

I shook my head.

'Well, then you'll just stay small,' my grandma said and ripped off a small piece of her soft, white toast. She dipped the little piece into her very sugary coffee and put it in her mouth.

My grandma put sugar on everything. It didn't matter if it was tea, coffee, Hawaiian toast or salad. 'Why does she do it?' I'd asked Mum. 'Once you've got used to everything tasting sweet, you can't do without any more,' she'd replied. 'But why should she? She is old and sick.'

Mum took another bite of toast. She'd put the Hungarian salami on it, which she'd bought specially for my grandma. But my grandma was the only one who didn't touch it. 'The only thing Hungarian about it are the colours of the packaging,' was what she'd said last night after studying the ingredients and smelling a slice. Then she'd heated up Lea's mother's Hawaiian toast in the microwave.

I picked up one of the pieces of paper. Mum had written down the names and specialities of various doctors, with their phone numbers and opening hours.

After breakfast, my grandma went to lie down and my mum started making calls. After each call she made a note. I sat on the sofa and tried to read.

The morning was over by the time Mum had finished. 'It's disgusting,' she said and sank down next to me.

'What?' I asked.

'Letting an old, sick woman wait that long for an appointment.'

Worried, I closed my book.

'Three months,' Mum said. 'Most of them won't give her an appointment for three months.'

I pictured my grandma sitting here until Christmas. I pictured her eating the biscuits I'd baked, and knitting an ugly, itchy jumper for me.

'There is only one doctor who said he would see her tomorrow,' Mum said. 'There's just one slight problem.'

'What's the problem?' I snarled. I knew my mum was about to say something I didn't want to hear.

'The appointment is at four. Larry asked if I can come early tomorrow. Private party. We need to get the tables ready and all that.'

'Which means?'

'Can you go to the doctor's with her?'

I sighed.

'Please,' Mum said and took my hands. 'I'll get everything ready. And as soon as it's possible, we'll do something nice together. Lake, swimming pool, funfair, whatever you want. Just the two of us, okay? Promise.'

Of course I said yes. I was still a bit annoyed with my mum for having cancelled our holiday. But I still would have liked nothing more than to gather up the hours alone with her and put them in a bag, so I could take them out whenever I missed our old life.

We loved going to the funfair.

Three times a year the promenade down by the river transformed into a glowing rainbow of colours. My mum planned what she was going to wear the day before. She had a swing carousel dress with fringes that fluttered when she spun around, and a Frankenstein shirt for the house of horrors.

Once, Mum had had the idea of cutting out sweets in the days leading up to the fair. 'You won't regret it,' she said. 'Do you remember how good that first slice of pizza tasted after you had that stomach flu?'

That was true. After three days, I had finally been up to eating something. After five days, Mum ordered a pizza delivery to celebrate me being better.

'There you go. The first bite is … hmm …' Chocolate-covered marshmallows, candied almonds and gummy fruit snakes danced in her eyes.

*

'Absolutely not,' my grandma said when my mum told her that I'd accompany her to the doctor's. 'She's a child. And anyway, I don't want to take the bus.'

'What's the issue with the bus?' Mum asked.

'Too many germs,' my grandma said.

'But you came here on the train,' I interrupted.

'Was I supposed to walk?'

'You can wrap your scarf over your mouth,' I said.

'Am I supposed to look like a complete idiot?'

'We could ask Ahmed if he would drive her,' Mum said.

'Who is Ahmed?' my grandma wanted to know.

'Our neighbour. You saw him yesterday when you arrived,' Mum said.

My grandma frowned. She didn't seem to remember.

'He was beating his carpet.'

'Ah, the Jew,' my grandma said. 'Then I'd prefer to take the bus.'

'Ahmed is an Arab, not a Jew,' Mum said.

'That's just as bad. And anyway, I don't even know him.'

'You don't know the bus driver either,' I said.

'That's different.'

I explained that Ahmed had often helped us and never wanted anything in return.

But all she said was: 'Even a lamb can contain a wolf.' Then she picked up one of our sofa cushions. 'I can embroider something nice on this, Marika. A deer, perhaps, or a horse?'

I didn't hear the rest of the conversation. I got up, went into my room and closed the door. I'd hidden my notebook in my desk drawer. I took it out and wrote: *My grandma is the most complicated person I know.*

There was a knock on the door.

'Billie?'

I let my mum in.

'Why did you leave?' Mum asked and sat down on the bed.

'She's so rude,' I said.

'She's our guest, don't forget that.'

'She's the rudest guest we've ever had. And she doesn't like Jews. Or Arabs.'

'I know.' Mum sighed.

'And?' I asked. 'Did you choose the deer or the horse?'

Mum laughed. 'A Mongolian wild horse.'

Now I had to laugh too. I put away my notebook and sat down on the bed with my mum.

'You're all tousled, didn't you brush your hair this morning?' Mum asked, and stroked my hair.

'No,' I said.

And then Mum brushed my hair. She hadn't done that for a long time. She pulled the brush through my curls slowly and evenly; she continued brushing even after my hair had long stopped resisting.

'What did Grandma mean when she said it's an honour to be called Erzsébet?' I asked.

'Erzsébet was a Catholic saint and also a Hungarian princess.'

'But I'm not interested in princesses or the Church.'

'Thankfully,' Mum said.

'Why did Grandma say we don't have to live like this?'

'Oh, she just always knows better about everything.'

It was only later, when I thought about this sentence again, that I realized it wasn't really a proper answer.

There was another knock on the door, and then my grandma came into the room. 'What are you doing in here so long?'

'We're hiding from you,' I said, and my grandma laughed because she thought I was joking.

'You have a wicked tongue,' my grandma said. 'You take after your mother.'

'What if I took after my father?' I asked.

Mum froze mid-movement. I couldn't see her because she was sitting behind me, but I saw that my grandma's eyes went to my mum for a moment too long. But when my grandma replied: 'I can't answer that,' Mum had put on her poker face again. Her face was entirely unreadable; any card player would have been proud of it.

'I have given it some thought,' my grandma suddenly said. 'I will go with Achmed.'

'Ahmed,' I said, but she ignored me. I pictured Mum putting the car keys into his hand, enclosing his hands with hers.

'Billie can still come along,' Mum said.

'No, no.' My grandma clicked her tongue and made a dismissive gesture. It was like my mum was standing in front of me. I wondered if it was something typically Hungarian or just a habit, like when someone keeps running their hand through their hair or tugging on their earlobe. 'Your daughter is meant to enjoy her summer holidays,' my grandma said. 'Accompanying an old woman to the doctor is no fun.'

I couldn't believe that my grandma was suddenly being so nice. I almost felt bad that I'd got rid of that plastic thing.

Grandma had brought it with her and had proudly waved it under our noses. You could open any jam jar with it, it was dead simple. But I made it disappear – I didn't want Ahmed to be even more unemployed than he already was. My mum hadn't searched for it for long. But she'd bought lots of jam, like she had to make up for it.

I almost said: 'I don't mind, I'm happy to come.' But then I thought of all the things I could do the next day, meeting Lea for example, and that my grandma was right about one thing. Going to the doctor's with her would not be fun.

That evening Mum and I got ready for bed together in the bathroom.

'I wanted to translate her medical reports, but she didn't bring a single document with her,' she said as she plucked her eyebrows. I had no idea what a medical report was. Mum explained it to me.

'Why didn't she bring them?'

My mum took a wet wipe and removed her lipstick. 'She said the doctors didn't find anything anyway.'

'Okay,' I said. 'But shouldn't the doctors here know that the doctors there didn't find anything?'

'Yes,' said Mum. 'But your grandma thinks it's enough for her to say it. Your grandma is a strange person.' She turned and smiled at me, and for a moment I felt like everything was the same as always.

Since my grandma had come, we had shared the air mattress in the living room, like when I was really small. I imagined us drifting on a raft. A million stars glimmered above, and the bottom of the ocean stretched out beneath me. I'd once read that outer space was better researched than the deep sea. I lay on my back, on the border between water and air, and allowed myself to be rocked to sleep.

12

I kept wishing my grandma would disappear. I closed my eyes and made her disappear like a magician does with a rabbit. I put her in her suitcase, closed the lid, and when I opened it again, she was gone.

But with time, I got used to having my grandma with us. The days flowed into one another, and most evenings I couldn't remember which doctor she'd seen that morning.

The first doctor Ahmed had driven my grandma to was a GP. He had examined her and then sent her to an ear specialist to check out her dizziness, but the ear specialist didn't find the cause. He did, however, discover that my grandma had extremely good hearing. After that, my mum and grandma were back in the GP's waiting room. He sent her to a cardiologist, and the cardiologist did lots of tests. She wrote down the names: ultrasound, ECG, exercise ECG and Holter ECG. My grandma's heart was in great shape, but she insisted there was something wrong with it. 'It misses a beat, the rhythm speeds up, it beats too fast, it's chaotic,' she said, and so the cardiologist examined her once again. He came to the same conclusion as the first time: my grandma's heart was as fit as a young girl's.

In the third week, I lost track. I was told that my grandma went to see a gastroenterologist, an orthopaedic surgeon, a specialist in diabetes, an allergist, a neurologist and a rheumatologist, but I wouldn't bet my life on those appointments being in the right order.

Also in the third week, my mum's patience ran out. She'd never admit that, of course. But I knew anyway. 'Once you've started on the medical circuit, you never get off it again,' she said and immediately afterwards: 'I'm just going downstairs for a moment.'

After I'd waited for an hour for her to come back, I went to look for her. I found her in the Nissan.

'Driver's licence and vehicle registration please,' I said in a deep voice. Mum flinched. She had the window wound down halfway. The entire car smelled of smoke and something else, sweet somehow. On the passenger seat was the ashtray she'd made herself from aluminium foil. Inside were three cigarette butts, all just half smoked.

'Goddamn it, do you have to give me such a fright?' Mum hurriedly put out another butt. A last, thin thread of smoke twirled upwards from the cigarette. I knew my mum secretly smoked, and she probably knew I did too.

'Ha! You ran off,' I said.

'I did not,' Mum said.

'Because your mum is getting on your nerves.'

'Not true,' Mum said.

'It's fine to admit that you'd rather be lying on the beach in France now, sunning yourself and drinking a coconut —'

'I don't have to admit it, because it's not the case,' Mum said.

'Are you coming back up?'

'Yes, in a minute. You go on up.'

I sighed and headed off.

When I returned to the flat, my grandma was lying on the sofa listening to music. 'Márta Sebestyén?' I asked.

My grandma sat up. She glowed like someone had lit a candle inside her. 'How do you know Márta?' she asked, like the singer was a friend of hers.

'I like listening to Hungarian music,' I said. 'Have you heard of Ando Drom?'

My grandma shook her head.

I went to my room, pulled a CD from the shelf and gave it to my grandma.

'A Roma band?' she asked.

'Yes.'

I put the CD on, and my grandma's eyes began to glow. She immediately started tapping her foot to the beat. 'Lovely,' she shouted, and I turned it down a bit. 'I didn't know you could buy this music in Germany.'

'I borrowed the CDs from the library,' I said.

'Lovely,' my grandma said again. 'You must never forget where you came from.'

At that moment, my mum came into the living room. 'What's going on here?' she said.

'A party,' I said.

'Aha,' Mum said. 'This is the worst party I've ever been to.'

'You would know,' my grandma said.

Mum gave my grandma a dirty look.

'When do you have to be in the bar this evening?' I asked Mum.

'Not until eight,' she said.

'That's not for another five hours,' I declared. In five hours you could go to the pool, you could go and eat an ice cream in town, you could watch two films or ramble round the flea market.

'I will cook tonight,' my grandma said. 'Tell your friend that we'd like her to come for dinner.'

'You could ask us if we're okay with that,' Mum said.

'Are you okay with eating something tonight that doesn't start with "frozen"?' my grandma asked. 'You need to eat more vegetables.'

I grinned.

Mum didn't think that was funny at all. She crossed her arms and looked at us like she was about to puke.

I had no idea why, but it seemed to me like Mum got more irritable the better I got on with my grandma. I'd have preferred to be alone with my mum, of course. But it didn't look like my grandma was going anywhere soon. So I tried to make peace with the fact that she was there.

Sometimes I chatted to her for a while when Mum had gone to work. She mostly told me things about Hungary.

She told me that it was a Hungarian who'd invented the Rubik's Cube, that the largest peppers grew in Hungary ('they can grow up to fifty centimetres long'), that children and pensioners can travel on buses and underground trains for free and that Hungarian parents have to choose a name for their baby from a list.

'What sort of list?' I asked.

'A list with legally approved names that's even stricter than the one in Germany. It's published by the Academy of Sciences.'

'Is Billie on it?'

'Of course not,' my grandma said. 'That's why your name is Erzsébet.'

'Mum didn't tell me anything about a list. She said I'm called Erzsébet because you were against the name Billie.'

My grandma laughed. It sounded a bit like a dog barking. 'Your mother does what she wants anyway. That's why it's a good thing we have laws.'

Sometimes I tried to find stuff out about my mum. Once my grandma said: 'Your mother wanted the best for you. She wanted you to have a better life in Germany.'

'A better life?'

My grandma nodded. 'Yes, education and… what's it called?'

I didn't have a clue what word she was looking for.

'More social participation. That's what they call it on the television.'

We were silent for a while.

Then my grandma said: 'Your mother always wanted to leave. That's why she ran off.'

'To Germany, or what?'

'First to Budapest. I almost died with worry. She was only fourteen.'

'What? Didn't you look for her?'

My grandma clicked her tongue. 'She wouldn't have wanted that.'

'Why not?'

'When Marika's father died…' my grandma began. She looked at her hands and remained silent. Finally she said: 'If you remove a piece of the puzzle, then the picture isn't right any more.'

'And what did she do in Budapest?' I asked.

'She wanted to be a dancer.'

I pictured my mum. Her arms and legs were much more graceful and long than mine. I saw her diving from the ten-metre platform, I saw her taut body. Whenever she dived into the water, the film in front of my eyes rewound. Then she flew back up, back onto the platform.

'And then what happened?' I asked.

'You'd best ask her that,' my grandma said. She picked up her sewing things. She'd already finished the head of the Mongolian horse.

13

I called Lea to invite her for dinner, but part of me wanted her to be busy. Lea had only ever been to our flat once. She hadn't said anything about how we lived, but I'd seen the pity in her eyes.

And suddenly I'd felt embarrassed.

About the fact that we didn't have any money. About the fact that there was rubbish lying everywhere outside. We called the area outside our housing block the scrap graveyard. People used it to dump everything they no longer wanted. Televisions, fan heaters, mini ovens. They even chucked stuff over the parapet. That's why it was so dangerous to walk along there. It was one of the few bans my mum had issued. Once a mattress had hurtled towards us as we looked up. The mattress had large rusty red stains on it, like someone had died on it. Mum had said: 'That's quite possible.' And then: 'The next time it might be a person falling from heaven.' She laughed, but it had made me think of Uta and Heinz.

Lea was free and agreed to come over.

And from then on we were busy with the preparations. My grandma wrote a long shopping list. It was so long that there was no way Mum and I could carry everything home on foot. So we took the Nissan.

'What does she need all this stuff for?' I asked my mum as we searched for vanilla pods and cloves.

'When your grandma invites someone for dinner, she doesn't do things by halves,' she said.

And that was true.

My grandma was in the kitchen for four hours. She cooked and baked at the same time, and in the end the smells wafted through the entire flat.

When the doorbell rang, my grandma had just put the last bowl on the kitchen table and wiped her hands on her apron. Her cheeks were red, and her forehead gleamed damply as she held out her hand to Lea. 'Welcome,' she said in German.

'Köszönöm,' Lea said.

My grandma put her arm around Lea's shoulders and led her into the kitchen. Then she presented all the dishes she'd made. 'All the dishes...' she began in Hungarian, then nudged me with her elbow and said: 'Can you translate?' and I translated: 'All these dishes are Hungarian specialities.'

We sat down.

My grandma took Lea's plate first. She piled the food on it, then she filled the remaining plates.

Then she lowered her head, folded her hands and said: 'Bless us, O Lord, and these, Thy gifts, which we are about to receive from Thy bounty. Through Christ our Lord. Amen.'

The starter was töltött tojás, stuffed eggs, along with cucumber salad. By the time we had finished these, my grandma already knew Lea's favourite subjects, what she wanted to be when she grew up, what political party her parents voted for, and if she liked cooking, had ever been to Hungary, had any siblings, believed in God or had a boyfriend.

Or at least my grandma thought she knew. I made sure the

two of them got on famously. I replaced all the embarrassing questions with harmless ones. And I gave my grandma the kindest answers.

Mum kept her mouth shut. Only once could she not keep it together, choking with laughter. She choked so badly that my grandma reached out and slapped her hard between her shoulder blades. The piece of potato flew through the kitchen.

After dinner we moved into the living room, and my grandma poured a schnapps for everyone. 'To Hungary!' she said and raised her glass.

'To Hungary!' Lea said.

'To Hungary!' I said.

Only my mum said nothing.

'Why are you not joining in?' my grandma asked.

'I am not raising my glass to Hungary,' Mum said, and crossed her arms in front of her chest.

'Hungary is your home,' my grandma said. 'What's wrong with raising a glass to your homeland?'

'I don't have a homeland,' Mum said. 'I only have my child.' She drank her schnapps and reached for the bottle.

'You're talking rubbish, Marika,' my grandma said. Her tone was harsh. Then she took the bottle from my mum's hand.

'Can Billie sleep at mine tonight?' Lea asked. I looked at her in surprise. We hadn't talked about it. 'My parents aren't home tonight,' she whispered in my direction, but no one was paying us any attention anyway.

My grandma and my mum were arguing with one another, and when I asked: 'May I?' Mum looked over briefly and said: 'Yes, yes, no problem.'

*

Lea's parents had gone out to a charity ball. Lea said the ball was something to do with Romanian dogs.

We sat on the white leather sofa, ate sweets and drank Coke. Lea had sent her brothers upstairs. They were playing in their rooms with chocolate-smeared mouths and pockets full of gummy bears.

I'd quickly stuffed the sweets into my backpack at home. I knew Lea's brothers were crazy about unhealthy stuff because they never got any at home. 'The poor little things,' Mum had said when I told her about it, and then she'd put some extra chocolate bars into the shopping trolley.

The television was on, but we weren't watching.

'Do your grandma and mum argue often?' Lea asked.

'It's got worse the last few days.'

'It's quite cramped at your place. I could never live like that. No wonder you get on each other's nerves. You can always come here if you can't stand it any more.'

'Thanks,' I said and started fiddling around with the sofa. It had silver buttons in a gap between the cushions and the armrest. Depending on which button I pressed, either the headrest or footrest moved, whirring quietly. The whirring sounded like a cat purring.

'Do you know how much longer your grandma is staying?' Lea asked.

I shook my head.

'At least you're almost a proper family now. And your grandma is a really good cook.'

Something was wrong about Lea's words, but I didn't know exactly what.

It was only later that I realized the thing with Lea was only a normal friendship at first glance. My friendship with Lea was like a house with stairs that didn't lead anywhere, and with doors that had an abyss behind them.

That night Lea moved in closer to me, like she always did. When I stayed with her, we always slept in the same bed, in the same position: Lea lay behind me like we were Siamese twins. I liked it. I liked her scent, her warm breath at the base of my skull and the heaviness of her arms on my body.

But that night I pushed Lea's arm off me. 'It's too hot,' I said and moved away a little.

At some point I woke up because I was thirsty. Lea was no longer lying next to me. I didn't put the light on as I went down the stairs. The kitchen door was half open. Lea and her mum were sitting at the table. I hesitated and remained standing in the darkness.

'... stank,' I heard Lea say. 'And in the end, they were both completely drunk and argued. It was awful.' She giggled.

'That's because of the polyester clothing. It's not surprising,' Lea's mum said. 'You don't need to go there again. I prefer it if she comes here anyway. It's probably better for her too.'

I didn't need to listen to any more to know who they were talking about. I went back upstairs, got dressed, packed my backpack, and that was it.

I was standing outside our block of flats when I realized that I wouldn't go up. It was the middle of the night. I couldn't tell my mum what had happened. I couldn't tell her Lea had been mocking us. I couldn't tell her I'd lost my best friend. I knew it would break her heart.

14

It was late morning when I unlocked our front door.

Last night, I'd had no idea where to go. At first I rang Luna's doorbell. Nothing. Then I rang Ahmed's doorbell. He opened the door and let me in without asking a single question. Then he handed me a cup of tea and waited for me to start talking when I was ready.

When I told him what had happened, he said: 'That sucks. We have a saying: A gold saddle doesn't turn a donkey into a horse.' Ahmed got up, fetched a sheet and put it on the sofa. He gave me a pillow and a blanket. 'Have a little rest.' Then he went back into his bedroom.

I stared into the darkness with open eyes. I kept picturing Lea and her mum sitting in the kitchen. I kept hearing what they said. But then I heard Ahmed whispering in the next room. His prayers lulled me into a deep and dreamless sleep. When I woke up, the sun was shining into the room.

After I went back to our flat, I stood in the hallway and listened. I couldn't hear anything. There was a low hissing from the kitchen, but otherwise it was completely quiet. Usually my mum and grandma talked loudly to one another, and usually the television was running in the background.

'Where is she?' I asked my mum, who was frying fish fingers in the kitchen.

'In hospital,' she said. 'Lunch is ready.'

I sat down and put my legs on the other chair. 'What happened?' I asked.

'Billie, take your feet down!'

For a few days now, Mum had ended all her sentences with an exclamation mark. If I ate some chips, she said: 'Use a fork!', when I read late at night, she said: 'Turn the light off!' and before we went to church with my grandma on Sundays, she said: 'Put on some long trousers!'

I took my feet off the chair.

'She fainted this morning,' Mum said and shovelled fish fingers onto my plate. 'It was probably all a bit much for her. All these appointments and then standing in the kitchen for hours cooking. In this heat!'

I cut up a fish finger. The bottom was too dark and left an oily print on my plate.

Mum didn't eat anything.

'I heard a thud. And then she was lying on the floor next to the bed. She was just lying there, not moving.'

I put a fish finger on Mum's plate.

'Did you drive her to hospital?' I wanted to know.

'That would have been better. The paramedics took fifteen minutes to get here. Fifteen minutes!'

'Why didn't you go with her?' I asked.

'Because I wanted to wait for you.'

'Are we going to visit her later?' I asked.

Mum took my hand. 'Will you come with me?'

I nodded. I didn't understand everything my mum did, but I understood that she needed me now.

They'd taken my grandma to the university hospital. We were standing under an archway. Huge grounds opened behind the archway like a fan. Mum twirled around and then turned the plan of the hospital in her hand. The woman at the information desk had given it to us and marked the correct building with her biro. She might as well have given my mum a blank sheet of paper. Mum couldn't read maps. So she threw the plan into the rubbish bin. I protested, but she just set off. It took ages for her to accept that we wouldn't get anywhere with this approach, of course.

At some point she stopped walking, pulled a packet of cigarettes from her handbag and lit one. I couldn't believe it.

'What's the matter?' Mum asked, and the smoke billowed from her mouth. 'Don't tell your grandma.' She threatened me with the cigarette. Then she asked: 'Do you want one too?'

I stared at her. 'That's a joke, right?'

'Yes. You'd better not have said yes.'

Mum stepped on the half-smoked cigarette with the heel of her shoe. I knew no one who could walk in high heels for as long as my mum. I remembered the three half-smoked cigarette butts that had been in the home-made ashtray on the passenger seat.

'Why do you only smoke half of them?'

'That's freedom, Billie.' Mum smiled. Then she said: 'We need to ask someone where we need to go. This is unbearable.'

We walked into the nearest building. Mum used her friendliest voice to speak to an older man. His hair was almost grey and he wore rimless glasses and a long white coat. He looked like a doctor from a television programme. There was a bunch of biros in his breast pocket. It turned out that we were already where we wanted to go. We had accidentally gone into the correct building. My mum called it intuition; I thought of the expression of the broken clock being right twice a day, but I said nothing. My mum wouldn't have understood it anyway. The doctor accompanied us to the ward with CLINIC FOR INTERNAL MEDICINE 1: CARDIOLOGY on the glass door. Before he could leave, I pointed to his breast pocket and asked: 'What are you going to do with all those biros?'

The man laughed. 'I lose at least one a day.'

'I always lose mine too,' I lied.

He was nice. Whenever I thought a man was nice, I imagined how it would be to have him as a father. I imagined how it would be to have someone to chat about my mum with. Then the doctor took out one of the biros and held it out to me. 'Here you go,' he said. 'All the best for your grandma.' I put the biro in my backpack, and I got a nice warm feeling in my chest.

The room my grandma was in smelled clean. I'd never entered a room that smelled so clean. My grandma was lying on her back with her eyes closed. Her folded hands rested on the covers, which she'd pulled up over her chest. A drip was coming out of her left hand and led to a bottle hanging from a metal stand. Clear fluid dripped from the bottle into my grandma's body. When I leaned over her, my grandma suddenly opened her eyes. It gave me such a fright that I clawed my fingers into my mother's arm.

'I'm not dead yet,' my grandma said.

'Very funny,' said Mum.

I thought my grandma looked dead. Her face was almost as white as the pillow under her head. But I thought it best not to say anything. I felt my mother's elbow in my side even before I opened my mouth. Mum leaned down to my grandma. She kissed her cheeks, first left, then right, and sat down on the edge of the bed.

'What did the doctor say?' Mum asked, and bit off a piece of her fingernail.

'Are you still doing that?' my grandma said. Then her voice grew gentle. 'You shouldn't worry about me so…' She shrugged her bony shoulders. 'I have only spoken to the nurse so far…'

My mum's mouth turned into a thin line, and a crease developed between her eyebrows. That was her this-is-taking-too-long face. That was her expression when the traffic light wouldn't turn green or if I took too long in the supermarket to choose a flavour of jam.

'Did you tell her that you want to speak to a doctor?' Mum wanted to know.

'Yes, but she just smiled.'

'Perhaps she didn't understand you properly,' I said.

'Of course she understands me. She's Hungarian. Her surname is Szabó.'

'Did she say when she was coming back?' Mum asked.

'In a moment – that's what she said.'

On the list of phrases my mum hated, 'in a moment' was right at the top. 'In a moment' could mean five minutes or thirty-five. She jumped up. 'I am fetching the doctor now!'

'Marika, sit down! They have a lot to do here.' My grandma's understanding was like a faulty light bulb. You never knew when it would flare up or go out again.

Mum sat down again, this time on one of the two chairs at the table at the end of the bed. I sat on the other one. There was a tall birch tree outside the window. Its trunk forked into nice thick branches. There was nothing much else to see. The other two beds were rumpled but empty. My mum and my grandma talked quietly. I imagined climbing right to the top of the birch tree, so high that my grandma's bed was just a tiny little speck. My arms and legs grew heavy. A fly landed on my naked thigh, but I was too dopey to brush it off.

I was woken up by someone coming into the room. A tall woman came over to my grandma's bed. Her hair was blonde and tied back in a ponytail. She held a folder in her hands. She looked through some papers. Then she looked at us and smiled. 'Zsuzsanna Szabó,' she said and shook our hands. 'I'm the consultant.'

Mum introduced us, and her cheeks reddened. When the doctor turned to my grandma, my mum whispered: 'How can she not have seen who the woman is? Her badge says Dr! I thought your grandma had heart problems. I didn't know she had a problem with her eyesight as well.'

The doctor spoke with my mum for a long time, but the only thing I heard was that my grandma was supposed to stay in hospital for a few more days. When I heard these words, I pictured Mum and me drinking a cocktail in the sun. I saw us sharing an ice cream sundae. I saw us finding cool relief in the shopping centre and pressing our noses against the windows of the expensive shops. I didn't realize you couldn't switch on your old life like you could a light.

I sat down on the ground outside. The sun was already less strong, but the cement was warm. It was only now that I realized how cool it had been in the room.

'Do you want to stay here?'

I heard Mum's voice. She'd bought a few things for my grandma from the kiosk. She leaned down towards me and waved a magazine. There was a planet on the front. 'Is that for me?' I grabbed the magazine, but my mum was quicker.

'You can read it later. Come along.'

I jumped up and lurched. A thousand tiny stars flickered in front of my eyes. There was a pressure on my ears like I was sitting at the bottom of the ocean. My mum's voice sounded far away. There was a rustling sound, then I tasted something sweet on my tongue. Dextrose. I felt Mum's arm under my armpits, and the darkness slowly disappeared.

Since my grandma had moved in with us, my mum had been prepared. Her handbag was better equipped than a first-aid box. Anyone out and about with her needn't worry if they had a nosebleed or a stomach ache or felt dizzy.

In the past, being ill had been like the weather: it came and went. We didn't address it. If Mum had a cold, she went to work anyway. 'Do you know what it means if you pay too much attention to illness?' she'd asked me once. 'It means you are giving death an inch… and you know where that leads.'

The bus was full, and we had to stand. It smelled of exhaust fumes and sweat.

'I miss our Nissan,' Mum said and buried her nose in her upper arm.

'Me too,' I said and breathed through my mouth.

'We could go on that outing I promised you tomorrow. Just the two of us,' Mum said.

That was the best thing I'd heard her say in a long time.

15

Our lake was hidden in a forested area. It was too far from our block of flats to walk. We had to drive a section on the autobahn. I wound down the window and stuck my head out. I liked it when the hot air blew into my face and I almost couldn't breathe. My mum was singing along to a tune on the radio, and it sounded very off-key. When I held my hands over my ears, she sang even louder and even more off-key.

The forest swallowed the sound of the autobahn. We couldn't hear anything except the wind in the trees, the birds in the air and the insects over the surface of the water. I couldn't believe we were the only ones there. It was like the lake belonged to us. You weren't actually allowed to swim in it, but we didn't care. We put our stuff down on the water's edge and slipped into the lake.

Back when we'd discovered the lake, the huge sign had been unmissable. You weren't permitted to bathe, swim, barbecue or camp. Also prohibited were: dogs, football, bicycles and fire. 'Why is everything that's fun not allowed?' I'd asked. 'Because most people are already dead before they die,' Mum had said, slipping out of her blue espadrilles and calling: 'First in the water is the winner!' Later I understood that there was always someone prepared to destroy nature for a bit of fun. But we'd never have done that. Mum was one of those

'Don't-you-dare-drop-that-wrapper-here' people. Mum thought most forbidden things were an invitation to self-reflect. And that was why she'd made several rules. We never applied sunscreen before we entered the water: 'The fish can't leave the lake.' We never took any plants away with us: 'Every plant that is picked is missed by another.' We never spat our chewing gum on the ground: 'Birds can suffocate from it.'

We swam to the other side, climbed up onto the wooden jetty, had a rest and dried off in the sun. When our stomachs started growling, we swam back, and my mum unpacked our food. It was a feast. Pasta salad with peas and sausage. There were rolls I could dig my fingers into and pull out the soft centre. There were cold chicken drumsticks with chilli sauce. For afters, we had chocolate cake.

After we finished eating, we dozed in the shade. Branches snapped in the wood; a frog croaked somewhere. I lay on my stomach and Mum lay on her back and protected her face from the sun with her straw hat.

'Your grandma simply didn't teach me,' Mum said.

'What didn't she teach you?' Sometimes my mum's thoughts just got stuck somewhere in her head. Only part of it made it to her mouth.

'To be a family.'

I thought of what Lea had said, and I felt a pain in my heart. 'But we are a family. A small one.'

'Yes, we are.' Mum felt for my hand.

I said nothing. I realized of course that my mum meant more than two people when she said 'family'. It must be nice to know more than one person who you love. You'd just have to go to the next-door room, where your brother, sister or father would be. There would always be someone who had time.

'Why didn't she teach you?'

Mum shrugged. 'She wasn't able to. Did you know I almost got married when I was your age?'

'What?' I sat up and removed Mum's hat from her face.

'Hey,' she said and covered her eyes with her arm.

I held her sunglasses out to her. 'Who?'

Mum took the sunglasses. 'Someone from the village. Whenever he picked me up on his moped, the "Radetzky March" was playing. He had attached the cassette recorder to the handlebars himself.' She smiled.

'Did he propose to you?'

Her smile disappeared. 'No. At some point your grandma said, "I've invited his parents to dinner."'

'Why did she do that?'

'Because she wanted to talk about the engagement.'

'I thought he didn't propose?'

'He didn't. But my mum thought he would be a good catch.'

'Did you want to get married?'

'Of course not!' Mum said. 'What do you think? I didn't want to feed children, pigs and chickens for the rest of my life.'

'So the moped guy isn't my father?'

Behind her sunglasses, Mum rolled her eyes. 'No, he isn't.'

'Who then?'

'One who also didn't know how to be a family.'

I took my notebook and a biro from my backpack and wrote that down.

'What are you doing?' Mum asked.

'I'm gathering information.'

'Information?'

'About my father.'

'Show me,' she said. I quickly closed the notebook. Mum sighed.

'Everyone has a family. What's so hard about it?' I asked.

'Once you've been free, it's hard to give that up again,' Mum said.

'Is that why you ran off when you were fourteen? Because you wanted to be free?'

Mum stared at me.

Shit, I thought. I shouldn't have said anything.

'How do you know that?' But I didn't need to reply. Mum already knew. 'It was obvious your grandma couldn't keep her mouth shut,' she said, and her eyes filled with tears.

I looked down at the ground. I'd often seen my mum angry, but I'd never seen her cry. 'I'm sorry,' I said.

Mum wiped the back of her hand across her face. 'It's about the principle,' she said. 'It's my past. Not hers. Who knows what lies she's told you.' She jumped up.

'Wait,' I said and held her arm tight.

She hesitated, but then she sat back down again. And then I told her what I knew. I spoke fast so she couldn't interrupt.

'She didn't tell me much,' I said at the end. 'Will you tell me the rest?'

'Okay,' said Mum. 'Okay.'

I found out that my mum had been enrolled at the state dance academy in Budapest. She said she'd run away from home to start a new life.

'I wore a yellow dress that summer too, but the buttons weren't very nice.'

I looked at the puddle of yellow material lying next to me.

'When my father died, my mother was really angry. She was angry at God, at the doctors, at me.'

'Why was she angry at you?'

'Because I reminded her of him.'

I remained silent and waited for her to continue.

'She held all the anger inside and it poisoned her. She didn't have any words for it. So she used her hands. Sometimes also a belt or a wooden spoon.'

I heard the slap of a hand against a cheek, I saw a wooden spoon break on impact with a shoulder, I saw red marks on my mother's thighs. It felt like an iron fist had clenched around my heart.

My mum paused and folded her hands. 'But if you dance, then your body is yours.'

She told me how she'd run off the night of her fourteenth birthday. She'd packed her backpack long before and hidden it in the garden.

But when I wanted to know how she'd managed all alone in Budapest, she smiled. 'I told them I was sixteen. I got a job at the opera.'

'As a dancer?'

'No, as a coat check girl.'

'Oh,' I said. 'And where did you live?'

'In a house right next to the opera. Almost everyone who worked at the opera lived there. Musicians, dancers and actors. I got lucky, there was still one tiny room available.'

My mum was allowed to watch every performance for free. When she wasn't in the dark theatre studying the dancers' movements or checking the audience's coats, she spent every free minute dancing. She danced in secret in the mirrored hall where the dancers practised.

'At some point the dance teacher caught me. Then he taught me. With his help I managed to pass the entrance exam and get a scholarship.' Mum's cheeks turned pink.

I pictured my mum dancing through the flat to music only she could hear. I thought about how I'd laughed because it looked so strange. I was five and had no idea about ballet, but now I realized she must have trained for a very, very long time.

Mum began to hum a melody. '*Swan Lake*,' she said and clasped her hand to her heart. 'I was the prima ballerina, I was Odette and I was Odile.'

She looked at me questioningly.

'Odette is the white swan, Odile the black swan. Perhaps there will be a performance on the telly. Then we can watch it together.' She took my hand.

'Why did you stop dancing?' I asked.

'Life got in the way,' she said and stroked my hair. 'Shall we go for another swim?'

That's what we did.

Our outing to the lake was like taking a last deep breath before someone pushes your head underwater.

16

Three days later, my grandma was back. I moved out of my room for a second time. As I walked past carrying my duvet and pillow, I gave my mum a dirty look. 'Why did you go back in the first place?' she asked. 'You're just making life hard for yourself.'

My grandma had brought two things with her from the hospital: a bad mood and a pillbox filled to the brim. Some pills were pink, some yellow. Some were as big as a fingernail, others so small you could swallow them without water.

'How do you know which pill to take when?' I asked my grandma, who was sitting in the living room, sewing.

'Sweetie, if you depend on it, then you remember things like that.' My grandma hardly ever called me by my name any more. Instead she said 'Sweetie' to me. She'd simply stolen the word from my mum. She'd taken it and put it on like a dress that didn't fit her.

When Mum and I lay on the air mattress that evening, the moon hung big and round in the sky. It shone straight at us.

'Are you still awake?' I whispered.

'Yes,' Mum whispered back.

'What did the doctor say?' I asked. I hoped my grandma would be well again soon. The quicker she was well, the quicker she could return to Hungary.

'Her heart seems healthy. The fainting probably has nothing to do with it. But the doctor said she doesn't have enough red blood cells.'

'Is that why she's in pain?' I asked.

'I don't know.' Mum sighed. 'But she's been given so many pills we could open a pharmacy.'

Mum pulled me close, and I nestled my head on her shoulder.

The next morning I was woken up by Mum kissing me goodbye. She smelled of toothpaste and coffee. Even before the sun had come up, she carefully pulled the door shut behind her. I'd dreamed about a vampire, I'd dreamed it taught me to fly. Then I realized the vampire was my grandma. That same moment, it turned into a bat and disappeared into the night.

I rolled out of bed. I was so drowsy I almost ran into the door frame. The light was on in the bathroom. My grandma was already awake. She was standing in her white nightie between the sink and the toilet, the pillbox in her hand. She dropped a couple of pills into the toilet and flushed.

'What are you doing?' I asked.

My grandma flinched and dropped the pillbox. She slowly turned towards me. 'What do you mean?'

'Why are you throwing your pills away?'

'You gave me a fright. That's why they fell down,' my grandma said.

'But you just threw them into the toilet!'

'I didn't. What made you think that?' she said, and her lips narrowed. 'Please help me pick this up.'

I bent down to sort the pills into the box again.

'Go back to bed,' my grandma said when we were done.

When I woke up for the second time that morning, my head was throbbing and I wasn't sure what I'd seen and what I'd dreamed.

Mum had left me some money and a shopping list in the kitchen. She'd written *Don't forget to look through the brochures* on the list, with a heart next to it. I put the list and the money in my trouser pocket.

Outside on the walkway I met Ahmed. He was on his way to boxing practice. 'I heard your grandma was in hospital. How is she?' he asked.

I told him what my mum had said.

'Just because her heart looks healthy, it doesn't mean it is,' Ahmed said. He lifted his sports bag onto his shoulder. 'Let me know if you want to come along to training one day.'

When I opened our letterbox, the brochures tumbled towards me. There was a postcard right at the back. The sea and a palm tree-lined beach on the front with the slogan BELLA VITA! I turned the card around. On the back just three words: *I'm sorry. L.*

I couldn't decide if I should rip the card in half or hang it up with the others on my cupboard. My wardrobe was full of evidence of the holidays Lea had taken with her family. I put the postcard on my desk.

Late afternoon, Mum got back from work and was in a bad mood. That made three of us.

Mum plopped down on the sofa, removed her earrings and kneaded her earlobes. They were all red from the clips. Then she took off her shoes and wiggled her toes. 'Aah,' she said. 'Madam

Naff was there today.' All the guests my mum couldn't stand shared a surname: Naff.

'What happened?' I asked and sat down next to her.

'You know I always ask the guests if the food was good.'

I nodded. I knew Larry cared what his guests thought of his food. If they didn't like it, they got something else instead at no extra charge.

'So Madam Naff eats everything up. Her plate looks as if she's licked it clean. While she's fawning all over her guy, she says: "We just spent our honeymoon on Hawaii. I ate the best burgers of my life there. They were made with crabmeat. Have you ever eaten a crab burger?"' My mum mimicked Madam Naff's voice. 'But then I realized: Madam Naff was actually Madame Poor Little Sausage. Her guy was staring at my tits the entire time.'

My grandma appeared in the doorway and stared at the low-cut top my mum was wearing. Then she looked in my direction. 'You should buy her a bra,' she said and sat down. She ran her hand over her skirt several times, like she wanted to iron it. 'It is wrong to allow her to run around like that.'

I needed a moment to understand that she meant me. She spoke about me like I wasn't really there, like I was a photograph in her hand. I looked down at myself, saw my white tank top and the two tiny mounds.

'She's still a child,' Mum said. 'Do you remember? You said it yourself. She doesn't need a bra yet.'

'She is fourteen.' My grandma said 'fourteen' and it sounded like an accusation.

'I know how old my daughter is.'

'Did you forget that you were just a couple of years older?'

Red blotches formed on Mum's chest. 'Do you want to argue?' she asked. And then: 'Remember: we have an agreement.'

'What agreement?' I asked, but no one paid any attention.

My grandma clicked her tongue. 'All right. I just don't want her to ruin her life.'

'Like me, you mean?' Mum asked.

My grandma shrugged weakly, like she was exhausted from all the shrugging. 'I just meant you should have stayed. Just this once you shouldn't have run away.'

'Stayed where?' I asked, but I seemed to have become invisible.

'You were the one who couldn't stand him,' Mum said.

'Yes, but at least he took care of you,' my grandma said.

'I can take care of myself. You were just jealous,' Mum said and her voice grew louder. I knew what was coming next if my grandma didn't immediately shut her mouth: an explosion.

'I just wanted what was best for you. But you ruined your lives. And for what? For this? Is this better than a life in Hungary? Look around you. It's a disgrace!'

'At least I'm free!' Mum shouted.

My grandma laughed, but it was a bitter laugh. 'Free? What does that even mean? You could have had a good life. You had a chance and you didn't use it.'

'We *have* a good life!' Mum stood and picked up her shoes.

'Where are you going?' my grandma asked.

'Away!' Mum said.

My heart skipped a beat.

'Do you know what your problem is? You always run away. Running away is your solution to everything.' My grandma's eyes were glistening with tears.

Mum pressed the shoes to her chest. 'If you hadn't beaten me back then, I wouldn't have run off.'

'Beat you? I never beat you. If anything, I gave you a little slap!' Now my grandma started shouting too.

I looked back and forth between the two of them. I thought about the belt and the wooden spoon. I thought about what Mum had said, that lies weren't allowed.

'She's lying, she's lying again,' I said.

'I know,' Mum said. 'She beat me.'

Now they both looked at me.

'No,' I said. 'That's not what I mean. She's not taking her medication. She says she takes it, but I've seen her flush her pills down the toilet.' All of a sudden I realized. 'She doesn't want to get well again at all,' I said.

My grandma said nothing. Her silence was like a loaded weapon pointed directly at my mum's heart.

Mum immediately put both her hands up in the air. 'Billie, what are you talking about?' she said.

'I saw it,' I said stubbornly.

My mum stared at my grandma. 'Is it true, Mother?'

It was the first time I heard her call her mother 'Mother'.

'That's outrageous,' my grandma said. 'I don't have to put up with this.'

'Oh God,' Mum said and covered her face with her hands. 'Oh my God.'

'Now look what you've done,' my grandma suddenly shouted and grabbed me roughly by the upper arm.

'Everything was fine until you came along,' I shouted back.

And then my grandma raised her hand.

'Let her go!' Mum jumped between us, mad with anger. From the corner of my eye, I saw her stumble. Then she staggered. Then she fell.

Mum fell very quickly and in slow motion.

Mum fell, and her head smashed against our glass coffee table and then onto the floor. Her head smashed against the corner of the table like my grandma's pillbox on the edge of the toilet.

She didn't bleed, and she didn't scream. She just lay there, quite still. Her sequinned top glimmered like the sky had lent her its stars.

17

I sat next to Mum and held her hand. I held her hand until the paramedics arrived. I was convinced she'd get better again. I just needed to believe. That was all.

The paramedics asked what had happened. I told them while my grandma sat on the sofa, her hands in her lap. She was shivering despite the heat.

One of the men held a clear mask over my mum's face. The other shone a small lamp into her eyes. Then I had to let go of her hand, and they put Mum on a stretcher. I asked if I could come, but the paramedic shook his head. 'In cases like this we're not allowed to take relatives with us,' he said. His tone was calm, but his movements were fast. I had no time to ask what he meant by 'cases like this'.

From the walkway I heard the sirens, which slowly disappeared. Mum and I sometimes imagined what was happening when we heard an ambulance. 'Always be careful, sweetie,' she'd say and take my hand.

Now I had to take care of my mum. I thought about the fastest way I could get to her. On the bike? The university hospital was too far away, and anyway, I didn't know if the bike was still where I'd left it. I thought about who apart from my mum had a driver's licence. My grandma didn't, Luna didn't, but Ahmed did!

I knocked next door. I knocked once, twice, three times. I held my ear against the door, but inside everything stayed quiet. I ran back into our living room.

'Do you have any money?' I asked my grandma, who was still sitting in the same spot. She didn't reply. I grabbed her shoulders. 'Do you have any money? For a taxi?'

She slowly shook her head.

In the kitchen I searched for Mum's purse. I brushed everything off the kitchen table in one sweep of my arm. The purse fell on the floor. It had been lying under the brochures. There were only coins inside. I didn't know how much it would cost to take a taxi to the hospital, but I knew it wasn't enough.

At that moment, the doorbell rang. I was sure it was Mum. In my imagination, she'd be wearing a bandage around her head, would smile at me and give me a hug.

But it wasn't my mum. It was two police officers. They introduced themselves. Then they asked me for my name.

'I'm Erzsébet. But everyone calls me Billie.'

'Listen,' Mum had once said. 'If you get lost, you first have to give the name on your ID card, okay?'

'Is there anyone else in the flat apart from you?' the policeman asked.

I nodded. 'My grandma.'

'We would like to speak to you. Can we come in?'

Everyone knows that's not a real question when the police ask if they can come in. They hold up their ID badge and a moment later they're sitting in your flat.

'My grandma doesn't speak any German. She's Hungarian,' I said as I led the two of them into the living room. Then

I offered them something to drink, because that's what I've seen people do on the telly. 'But I only have tap water,' I said.

The policewoman smiled. She was very pretty. Her face was delicate and gentle. I imagined she had pets, maybe a baby cat and a guinea pig, which she stroked in turn when sitting in front of the telly in the evenings.

I put two glasses on the table.

'One of the neighbours called us,' the policewoman said and carefully sat down on the stool next to the sofa. 'An argument could be heard, and a loud crash.' She observed me closely. My grandma held her head lowered and constantly twisted the ring on her left hand.

And then I tried to tell her what happened. I was so nervous that the words just tumbled out in a jumble. I told her a bit from the middle, then a bit from the beginning, then a bit from the end. In the end, even I didn't really understand what had happened.

Then the policewoman asked for my mum's name. When I said it, my grandma raised her head. And then she went completely mad. She made a sound that reminded me of an animal, but I couldn't think which one. Her teeth chattered, her body seized up. When she tried to stand up, she collapsed. She fell back on the sofa, wide-eyed, her hand pressed against her chest.

The policewoman jumped over to my grandma. She helped her to lie down on the sofa and pushed a pillow under her legs. The policeman asked where our phone was. And then the ambulance came for the second time that day. I didn't ask if I could go with it.

'She'll be all right,' the policewoman said when the paramedics had left.

'And what about me?' I asked.

The policewoman leaned over to her colleague. 'We can't leave her here alone.'

The policeman rubbed along the side of his nose. 'What about your father?'

'I don't know him,' I said.

'Do you have any aunts or uncles?'

I shook my head.

'No one except your mum?'

'No,' I said quietly. 'Can you please take me to my mum?'

The policewoman chewed her lower lip.

'Please!' I repeated.

'All right,' she said. Her colleague looked at her in surprise. 'It's okay, my shift is nearly over anyway.'

It was my first ride in a police car. The radio crackled a few times, but we drove without the siren or blue lights, so it was almost like sitting in a normal car. When we stopped outside police headquarters, the policeman got out and said goodbye.

Then the policewoman opened my door. It looked like a polite gesture, but I knew the back door was locked and could only be opened from the outside. 'You can sit in the front,' she said.

When we drove off, the policewoman switched on the siren and the blue lights.

'Thank you,' I said. I knew my mum would like her.

The woman at the reception desk searched for my mum's name. Then she told us where to go. The policewoman led me down the corridors confidently, like she was leading me through her flat.

Mum was on the neurological intensive care ward. There was a bell. A woman opened and asked for our names. When I gave her my last name, she immediately knew who I was. 'Please wait a few minutes,' she said. 'The consultant is still in the operating theatre, but he'll be with you in a moment.' I wanted to wait with my mum, but the nurse shook her head. 'I'm sorry, but you'll need to speak to the doctor first.'

'Why can't I see her?' I asked.

'Let's wait, Billie,' the policewoman said and gently held my shoulder.

The nurse accompanied us into the waiting area. We sat down on plastic chairs. I could smell the disinfectant and the rubber gloves, I could hear the machines in the rooms quietly beeping and gurgling. I tried to imagine me putting my arms around my mum in a minute. But the image kept blurring in front of my eyes. The clock on the wall ticked. I counted in the rhythm of the second hand to calm myself. Then the ticking simply stopped and I started to count my heartbeat. The policewoman had leaned her head against the wall. Her eyes were closed, but I could tell from her breath that she was still awake.

Then the doctor finally arrived. It was the never-without-my-biro doctor who'd accompanied us to my grandma. He had a lot of biros in his coat today too. If someone is constantly losing their biros, I thought, then it must be because they're so busy keeping an eye on important things.

He took us into his office and closed the door. Then he said we should take a seat. I asked him about my mum, and he asked about my relatives. I didn't reply. Instead I said: 'I want to see my mum. What's the matter with her?'

The doctor put his hands in front of him on the desk. His fingernails were short and clean. I heard the policewoman moving around on her chair. I saw the delicate beads of sweat on the doctor's hairline. I felt everything going in the wrong direction. I saw the glass fall, but I couldn't do anything about it.

'Your mother came to the emergency department with a subdural bleed.' He said it like she'd simply walked in.

'What does that mean?' I whispered.

The policewoman rested her hand on mine. It was as light as a bird.

'That means that her brain was damaged in the fall and that the injury in her head bled.' The doctor didn't look at me. 'We operated on her immediately, but she didn't make it. I'm sorry.'

There was a whirring sound in my ears like I was underwater. But my body just carried on breathing. Air streamed into my lungs and out of my mouth again. I didn't even have to make an effort.

The policewoman and the doctor talked to one another; I saw their mouths moving. The doctor gave me a glass of water and put a small white pill in my hand.

At some point my body stopped shaking. Small weights hung themselves on my muscles and pulled my body down; fur grew over my heart.

At some point I saw myself sitting in the waiting area. The policewoman got up a few times, went outside and came back in. 'I've called someone who will take care of you,' she said. 'Someone from the CPS.'

When I heard child protection services, I thought of abused children and parents who drank too much. I thought of Mum's great fear of the CPS. I knew that in her nightmares, a woman would ring our doorbell because she'd found out that my mum was a bad mum. When Mum woke from such dreams, she pulled me close and buried her nose in the nape of my neck.

'Can't I come to your house?' I asked.

The policewoman smiled. 'I'm afraid not. I'm not allowed. I haven't been trained for that.'

I didn't know what she meant. I liked her. She was nice. What did she need training for? Then I remembered Mum's words. She'd said that nowadays you needed a degree for everything.

The policewoman hugged me goodbye. When she let me go, she looked me in the eye and said: 'You'll be all right.'

'Thank you,' I said.

'If you don't know what to say, you either say no or thank you. Never just say yes,' Mum had drummed into me.

The woman from the CPS was waiting in the corridor. I'd only ever met someone from the CPS once in my life. That was when I'd gone to school in my pyjamas in primary school. Three days later the CPS had rung our doorbell. 'Because of pyjamas! Can you believe it?' Mum had said. She'd worked late that night, and I'd had to get ready by myself. I'd combed my hair, poured cornflakes and milk into a bowl, washed my face, cleaned my teeth, taken my backpack and headed out. It was only at school that I realized I hadn't got dressed. When I got home, my clothes were still in the bathroom. Mum had laid them out for me the night before.

'I almost got into a lot of trouble for that,' my mum had said and sighed.

*

The woman from the CPS came over to me. She had a clipboard in her hand. She looked at it.

'So you are Erzsébet.'

She said *Erz-she-beht*.

I nodded and she introduced herself.

'I was told that you are alone. No father, no siblings, no other relatives?' she asked.

The way she said it sounded awful, but it was the truth. I was alone. I pictured my grandma in her cell. I pictured her embroidering forests, lakes and mountains on pillowcases for the other prisoners. Maybe she could get out early for good behaviour. Either way, I never wanted to see her again.

The woman from the CPS stared at me.

'No other relatives,' I said.

'Is your father dead, or do you not know who he is?'

'I don't know who he is.'

I'd never considered that my father might be dead. The social worker wrote something down.

'Is it a possibility that one of your friends might take you in?'

I thought of Lea's postcard. It was still lying on my desk. 'No.'

The social worker sighed. 'Then I will take you for now,' she said.

And she did.

Then I realized.

My life had broken into two pieces. Into one before and one afterwards. Before, my mum had been the answer; afterwards, she was the question.

18

The light in the walkway didn't work. Coming home felt like I'd never been away. At the same time it felt like I'd been gone for ages. I unlocked the door and went straight to my room. I grabbed my pillow that I'd put in the cupboard and sat down on my bed. Then I buried my nose in the pillow until the social worker appeared in the doorway.

'Hey, don't you want to pack?'

I didn't want to pack. I wanted to stay here. My body felt so heavy that all I wanted was to fall onto my side and never get up again.

The woman from social services sat down next to me. 'I get that you don't want to go,' she said.

I was sure she didn't get it. 'That's just a trick,' I whispered.

'A trick?' she asked.

'Yes, to get me to go back. But I want to stay here.'

Now the woman from social services crouched down in front of me and laid her hands on my thighs, almost like she was going to propose to me. 'It's not a trick. But you shouldn't be alone now. Someone needs to be there for you and check on you. Come on, I'll help you pack,' she said and stood up.

I kept my gaze lowered. I couldn't look at her. I knew that my eyes were black holes that sucked up every caring gaze, leading it straight to my heart whether I wanted or not.

The social worker opened the doors to my cupboard and put clothes on my bed. She left the room and returned with a toothbrush.

And then I packed my backpack, like I was going to spend a few days on holiday or with friends. When I was almost done, there was a knock on the door. Luna and Ahmed were outside. They immediately saw that something wasn't right.

I was a plant without earth.

I was a snail without a house.

I was a beetle that had landed on its back.

The social worker appeared behind me. 'Who are these people?' she asked.

'My neighbours,' I said.

'What's happened?' Luna asked.

I couldn't speak. But I didn't have to. The social worker did it for me.

Then Ahmed and Luna hugged me so tightly that my bones cracked. Luna wiped tears from her face. Ahmed wanted to know why the police had been there, but the social worker was in a hurry.

'One moment,' Luna said. She disappeared into her flat and came back with a bundle of money. It was the banknotes from the porcelain bowl. 'Here,' she said and stroked my back. 'You need it more than me. You didn't choose this journey.'

When we were in the car, the social worker said: 'When we lose someone we love, we sometimes don't know who we are for a while.'

I looked out of the window. All I could see was my own reflection. I was still holding Luna's mother's money in my hand. I couldn't believe she'd just given it to me.

'Some children simply stop speaking. Others get aggressive. You need to give yourself time,' the social worker said.

I rested my forehead against the cool glass. It vibrated gently against my head. I couldn't understand how I'd landed in this car, but I realized that from now on everything would be different. I put the banknotes into my backpack. I held onto it like it was a buoy and the car was the open sea.

The children's home was on the edge of the city next to a park. The social worker parked the car right in front of the entrance. A stone staircase led up to the door. Inside, we were greeted by a woman who looked like my German teacher. She had grey, shoulder-length hair, a double chin and rimless glasses. She seemed soft and firm at the same time.

'I'm Mrs Geiger. I'm the one who will take care of you and the others. Come, I'll show you your room.'

As we walked up the stairs to the first floor, I heard the social worker drive away. The gravel scrunched under the tyres of her car. She was probably on her way to another child already. There were so many children who no longer had anyone. The entire stairwell was full of them.

Mrs Geiger stopped. 'Before you leave here again, we take a photograph to remember you by. We find a foster family for almost everyone. For you too. You'll see.' Then in front of one of the white wooden doors in the corridor she said: 'This is where you'll be. You'll share the flat with Marlene. She's in the room right next to you.'

Off a living room with a kitchenette was my room. The wooden floor creaked under our feet. There was a bed, a cupboard, a chest of drawers and a writing desk. The furniture was painted white, and a net curtain fluttered in front of the window. Mrs Geiger closed it, like she was scared I'd run off as soon as she left the room.

I laid my backpack on the bed and sat on the edge. I thought of Luna's mother, whose whole life had fitted in a handbag.

'Get some sleep now,' said Mrs Geiger. 'We'll sort everything else in the morning.'

Then I was alone.

I opened the window again, lay down on the floor, and looked up at the sky. In the deepest corner of my heart I sensed that I should get up and go to bed, but gravity pulled me down and I couldn't move.

19

One day after my mum died, the thing with the hair started. My hair fell out as if it had decided to move on. It came out in big chunks.

When I woke up on the floor, the sun was shining in my face. At first I didn't know where I was, but then I remembered everything. I saw Mum lying on the floor. I heard the bang, I felt her hand in mine. I saw the policewoman, the nurse, the doctor, the social worker and Mrs Geiger. The pain dug into my heart and took my breath, but the sun just carried on shining.

I got up and looked around my room. High ceiling, a mirror, two windows. A big bed. A Bible on my bedside table. I remembered that the social worker had mentioned something about youth welfare services being run by a religious organization. I opened the cupboard door and the drawers of the chest of drawers, but the room held no secrets. A couple of empty hangers dangled from the clothes rail; there was a woollen blanket on the top shelf. The chest of drawers contained towels and sheets.

There was a knock on the door. It was a boy. His hair was dark and messy, and his eyes shimmered like smooth stones. 'Hi, I'm Marlene,' he said with a soft voice.

'Marlene?' I asked, and then I realized the boy was a girl.
She nodded.

'I'm Billie,' I said.

'Cool name. You don't look like an American?'

'And you don't look like a girl.'

I felt myself blush. Sometimes my words were like wild animals I'd like to have tamed. But Marlene laughed, ran past me and sat down on my bed. I sat down next to her. 'Wherever you slept, it wasn't in here,' she said, tugging at a corner of the pillow.

I shrugged and looked at my feet.

'How old are you?' she asked.

'Fourteen. And you?'

'Seventeen.'

'How long have you been here?' I asked.

'Not that long. I ran away from home when I was fifteen. Since then, I've been here and there.'

I thought about what Mrs Geiger had said, that there was a foster family for almost everyone. Perhaps the 'almost' had something to do with Marlene. I wanted to ask her why she'd run away, but I didn't dare. Perhaps it was a secret. But if Marlene had secrets, her family history wasn't part of it.

'I kept losing it. My finger was always on the trigger.' Marlene rolled up the sleeve of her denim shirt. The scar went from the middle of her upper arm to her elbow. It was red, raised and ragged at the edges. I'd never seen such a long scar.

'May I?' I asked.

'Sure.'

I carefully ran my finger over it. 'Who did that?'

'My mum,' Marlene said.

I stared at her. 'Your mum?'

Marlene nodded.

'Why did she do that?'

'I was cutting veggies in the kitchen, and her new boyfriend touched my bum. My mum saw it and then… rip.' With a pretend knife, Marlene cut her arm.

'Oh,' I said.

We stayed silent for a while.

Then Marlene asked: 'Do you also have issues with your mum?'

'No,' I said.

'There's nothing about her that bothers you?'

I thought about it. 'No,' I said once more, but Marlene heard the hesitation in my voice. 'Perhaps the fact that she left me alone,' I said.

'Did she run off?'

'Not really,' I said. And then I made an idiotic gesture that was supposed to mean my mum was dead.

Marlene got it straight away. 'Oh,' she said. 'And what about your dad?'

'My mum never told me anything about my dad.'

'Then you don't know him?' Marlene said.

I shook my head.

'Did you never want to know who he is?'

'Yeah, of course, but my mum always made a secret of it.'

'That's more than most here have,' Marlene said. 'That's a chance. You should look for him.'

'Maybe he's dead. Or a dick.'

'Maybe. But either way, he must have been important to her.'

I thought about all the conversations Mum had cut short before they even properly began. I thought about the white cowboy boots he'd given her that she wanted to wear until they fell apart. I thought about what Mum hadn't said at the lake. I had no time to think about it any more.

Marlene's thoughts didn't seem to stay in the same place for long. 'Come on, I'll show you my room,' she said.

The first thing I saw was the punchbag hanging from the ceiling in the middle of the room. There were clothes on the floor, the bed was unmade, the sheets were colourful.

'Do you want to give it a try?' Marlene passed me the red boxing gloves that lay on a chair. I took the gloves, but I didn't know who to be angry at. 'That will come,' she said, and put the gloves to one side.

I saw nothing that might have revealed who Marlene's family was. There were no photographs, no postcards, nothing.

'Do you miss your family?' I asked.

'Sometimes,' Marlene said without looking at me. And then she said: 'I'm sorry your mum isn't alive any more.' She was silent for a moment. 'If you feel lonely, you can come and sleep here with me. And you can always use the punchbag. Always. Even if I'm not here, okay?' She hesitated before she continued. 'But usually I'll be here.'

No one knew better than her that the children's home had a revolving door. Most went out and straight back in because the foster parents had imagined everything quite differently. Marlene looked me in the eye, and I felt like crying. I knew that look. The children in the stairwell looked the same way. It was the I-know-what-being-lonely-feels-like look.

*

That same afternoon, someone from CID came to the children's home. They wanted to ask me some questions about my mum's death. The officer wasn't wearing a uniform but a white shirt and a tie. His hair was greying, he had piano-player's hands, and he smelled of aftershave. I couldn't picture him shooting anyone in the leg. I couldn't even picture him driving a police car. And I certainly couldn't imagine that anyone in the world was frightened of him. He had probably been employed specifically to talk to girls like me.

We sat opposite each other in Mrs Geiger's office. She'd given us a bottle of lemonade. I drank a sip. The lemonade tickled my nose and made my eyes water.

'I need to record our conversation,' the officer said and pulled a small black device from his briefcase. He rolled up his sleeves to the elbows and laid his arms comfortably on the table. 'We need to know what happened. We need your help with that.'

'Okay,' I said.

'Good.' He cleared his throat. 'Did your grandma live with you?'

'Yes.'

'Was it temporary?'

'What does temporary mean?'

'Temporary means that it was only for a certain period of time.'

'Yes, she was only supposed to stay with us until she was better.'

'What illness did she suffer from?'

I shrugged. 'Something was wrong with her heart.'

The officer thumbed through a stack of papers. I recognized the writing from the university hospital. I didn't understand why he'd asked me if he could simply have read it. He looked up. 'I would like to speak about the day your mother died.'

My stomach lurched briefly like when we shot over little hills in our Nissan and I felt like I was falling.

'Please tell me everything that happened. It is important that you also tell me the things you don't think are important. Take your time.' The policeman leaned back. Perhaps he wanted to create space for my thoughts.

I started to talk. But the more I thought about what had happened, the more uncertain I grew. The more I tried to tell the truth, the blurrier the film in my head became. I knew words were like bullets. But I kept missing.

'So there was an argument. What about?' the policeman asked.

'But I already told you.' My T-shirt was stuck to my body.

'Listen, I'm sorry, but I do need to ask you more questions. All right?' This time he didn't wait for my reply. 'So, what did you argue about?'

'My mum and my grandma spoke about the past. But my mum never really wanted to speak about it.' And then I suddenly remembered the thing about the pills. 'I stuck my nose in,' I whispered.

'How do you mean?' the officer asked, and his gaze rested on me.

'I told my mum that my grandma had thrown away her pills.'

'What exactly happened there?'

'I watched her flush her pills down the toilet.'

'When was that?'

'That morning. I woke up early and wanted to use the bathroom. The door was open a bit, and I saw her flush her pills down the toilet.'

'Did you confront your grandma about it?'

'Yes. I asked her why she was throwing her pills away. She said she hadn't been.'

'Why do you think she was throwing her pills away?'

'I don't know.'

'When did you tell your mum about what you saw?' the officer asked.

'While she was arguing with my grandma.'

'How did your mum react?'

'She was livid. And she wanted to leave.'

'And what did your grandma do?'

'She said that it was all my fault. She attacked me. My mum jumped onto the sofa; my grandma grabbed her. Then my mum lost her balance. And then she fell off the sofa.'

'Thank you, Billie.' The officer tidied the stack of papers on the table and put them in a cardboard folder.

'What's going to happen to my grandma now?'

'We will question her, and then we'll see.'

I was sure they'd put her in prison. If it hadn't been for her, my mum would still be alive.

'Please call me if you remember anything else.' He pushed a business card across the table towards me. I put it in my trouser pocket.

I took a long look at myself in the mirror in my room. But it felt like I was looking at a stranger. It was like this stranger had taken the place in this life that wasn't mine any more. I took a second mirror to help me look at the bald spot I'd felt. It was as large as a coin and just as round. My scalp shimmered through pearly white. It looked like hair had never grown there.

20

When Mum made a plan, her eyes glittered. Once she said: 'Put on your prettiest dress and pack your suitcase.' We took the bus and got out at the casino to win a million with some change.

We didn't win, of course. But we still went to the airport and looked at the big departure board. I read the names of places I'd never heard of. Bogotá, Baku, Brisbane. If my mother didn't know which country the city was in, then she simply made one up until we could check in our atlas at home.

In the children's home, the plans Mrs Geiger made for us were stuck on the inside of our room doors. There were sixteen other children living here. Most of them were younger than me. From waking to bedtime, the plans divided our day into small sections.

We were meant to go shopping together, cook and eat, take trips to the zoo and to the museum and sit in a circle to discuss our problems. We were meant to work in the garden, harvest vegetables, exercise and talk to a serious woman who kept pushing her glasses back up the bridge of her nose, nodding and taking notes in a black book.

I couldn't stand the plan Mrs Geiger had made for me. I didn't want to speak to anyone. White boxes in my plan meant that I was allowed to be alone. Then I lay in my bed. I stared at the ceiling or out of the window and sometimes I fell asleep. My mum was the main character in all my dreams. I lost her a million times. But the good dreams were even worse. As soon as I woke up, reality washed over me like a wave.

When I didn't turn up to my appointments, Mrs Geiger came to my room. She'd sit down on the edge of the bed and say: 'It's not good for you to sit around here alone.' I knew that was true. But the truth was that I didn't care because there was nothing that would have been good for me. So I might just as well have got up. And obviously I realized I couldn't spend the rest of my life lying down. I'd heard about a man who refused to get up for months. At some point the skin on his back disintegrated, and his muscles disappeared like the water from a puddle when the sun shines on it. They had to heave him out of the bed. He couldn't even move his toes any more.

Mrs Geiger didn't get up until I did, though. I didn't hold it against her. She felt responsible. The children's home was her universe, and she was the sun.

My only glimmer of light was Marlene. Sometimes we sat in the park together and shared a packet of cigarettes. Marlene was the only one who left me alone, who I could sit with in silence. Perhaps that's why I liked talking to her.

'I'm dissolving,' I said.

'What do you mean?' Marlene asked and chucked a large piece of bread to the ducks in the pond. The bread hit one of the ducks on the head, and it dived under. I remembered the words of the song: *Ducks are a-dabbling / Up tails all!*

'Did I kill it?' Marlene asked.

'No, ducks are tough,' I said, although I wasn't sure. But then thankfully the duck reappeared and continued swimming like nothing had happened.

'I'm losing my hair,' I said and lowered my head.

'Oh,' Marlene said. 'Have you been to the doctor about it?'

'No, I can't be bothered.'

I hadn't told anyone about it so far. I realized that soon I wouldn't have to. Everyone would see it. Then I wouldn't just be the girl without a mother but also the girl without hair.

'Do you think it'll grow back?'

'For sure,' Marlene said and squeezed my hand.

That same afternoon, a few days after the social worker brought me to the children's home, I decided to call my grandma.

Mrs Geiger was in her office. I knocked on the half-open door.

'Billie, come in.'

Mrs Geiger took off her glasses. They dangled from a purple cord around her neck over her large breasts.

'What can I do for you?'

'I would like to call someone,' I said, and hoped she wouldn't want to know who. I stared at the phone on Mrs Geiger's desk.

'Of course. Can you give me five minutes?'

I waited outside by the bookshelf. My eyes skimmed across the spines of the books. One book was taller and narrower than all the others. I pulled it out. It was so heavy I needed both hands. I sat on the stairs and started looking through it. It was almost all photos, hardly any words. The people in the photographs weren't doing much. They were sitting in their messy living rooms, dining rooms and kitchens, lying on sofas and beds, spending time in the garden. Most of them wore oversized T-shirts and jeans. Some women wore dresses made of shiny material and other dresses looked like curtains. Their hair was badly dyed and stringy, like they hadn't washed it for days, or exploded in curls around their heads. In some of the photos it was summer, in some it was winter. Children played with each other, indoors and outdoors. In one of the photos a couple got married in front of a big American flag. There were images of babies, cats and pigs. People appeared, disappeared for several pages, and then came back with other people. In a way I couldn't explain, they all belonged together. I pushed the book back. It felt wrong putting it there. I knew I'd come again to fetch it.

'Do you like reading?' Mrs Geiger asked.

I jumped and turned around. Then I nodded.

When I'd started school, my mum had taught me that I should always say yes if someone asked me if I liked to read. 'The Germans are obsessed with books. A book under your arm is the ticket into their world.' On our next trip into town, we counted the people who were reading. They sat in trains, in buses, at the lido, on park benches and in cafes. They even had their noses stuck in books in lifts and queues. Later, when I had a library pass, I'd asked my mum why she didn't read anything except the special offer leaflets in our letterbox and the words on the back of shampoo bottles. She shrugged and said that it was too late for her.

'You can borrow books any time. Just enter your name on the list,' Mrs Geiger said.

I rang my own number from the phone in her office. It rang and rang. I pictured Mum picking up. She'd ask me where the hell I was. Then I pictured myself picking up the phone, imagining that I was in two separate places at the same time, one part caught in a parallel universe while Mum and I carried on living in our world. I'd heard such a thing was possible. But no one picked up. It just carried on ringing.

And then Marlene disappeared. She disappeared the day the wig turned up. The wig lay like a hairy, extraterrestrial creature on my pillow, and I immediately knew it was Marlene's goodbye gift. A delicate pain went through my chest.

During lunch, Marlene had got up and gone upstairs. 'Headache,' she'd said and pocketed the apple that lay next to her plate. I'd have liked to tell Mum that everyone got an apple after dinner. 'An apple as pudding?' she'd have asked and laughed. Fruit wasn't pudding for us. Eating fruit was important if you didn't want your teeth to fall out one day, but pudding was chocolate and marshmallows, gummy snakes and Starbursts.

When I went to see Marlene later, she was gone. The punchbag was there where it always was, the gloves lay on her bed, which was made, and the smell of her shower gel still hung in the air. Marlene had gone out of the door and wouldn't be returning.

In my room, I put on the wig and looked at myself in the mirror. My new hair was blue. Angel blue. Smurf blue. Ocean blue. The sides came down to my chin and the fringe came down to my eyebrows. The wig was a perfect fit. I barely recognized myself. 'Thank you,' I whispered to the stranger in the mirror, and she smiled back at me.

Then there was a knock at the door. It was Mrs Geiger. She looked at me. 'May I come in?'

I stepped to one side.

'Your mother's funeral will take place in three days' time,' Mrs Geiger said. 'You will be freed from all activities that day, of course.'

'Okay,' I said, and my legs tingled. I imagined my mum lying in an open casket with her hands folded. I knew dead bodies were ice cold, even in summer. I didn't know if I'd manage to give Mum a kiss.

'Your mother's friend called us,' Mrs Geiger said. It took a moment for me to understand she meant Lea's mum. We hadn't spoken since the thing in Lea's kitchen that night.

'How does she know I'm here?'

'It seems your friend went to your house, and when she realized you weren't there, she asked your neighbour.'

I nodded.

'Your mother's friend's association is going to cover the costs,' Mrs Geiger said. 'There's an emergency fund for such situations.'

'What costs?'

'For the funeral.'

'Oh,' I said, because right then I remembered Mum's words. 'Do you know how expensive funerals are, even if they only put you in a shoebox?' she'd asked, and then she'd said: 'But don't you worry. At some point I'll die here all alone in this flat, and the cats will eat me up.' Sleepily, I'd said, 'But we don't have any cats,' because Mum had woken me up. 'That's not the point, Billie,' she'd replied. 'It's just something you say.' Sometimes Mum wandered around our flat in the dark at night, like she was searching for something. I lay in my bed and heard her sighing. Sometimes she banged her knee or her arm. Then she swore.

I didn't know why she couldn't sleep. But I knew night-time made everything worse. 'If it wasn't for you, Billie, I would have no one,' she said when I asked her why she constantly walked around.

I almost told Mrs Geiger that Lea's mum could stuff her money up her arse, but I felt my mum deserved a nice funeral. She deserved to have her coffin decorated with flowers. And if I had to swallow my pride to make it happen, then I would just have to.

'She's also offered to take you in,' Mrs Geiger now said.

'What?'

'Yes, they really are generous.'

'I need to think about it,' I said.

'Don't think about it for too long. Very few get an opportunity like that.' Mrs Geiger stood up.

I thought about it the whole night.

I knew Mrs Geiger was right.

I thought about the holidays Lea's family went on. Holidays in paradise. Holidays where you actually travelled. I thought about freshly cooked meals and about bubble baths in the big tub. I thought about the beautifully decorated Christmas tree that was put up in the living room at Lea's house from the first week of Advent. My mum had never put up a Christmas tree. 'I'm not going to watch a tree die,' she said. Instead we always drove out to the forest on Christmas Eve, lit a lantern and put it underneath our favourite tree.

Mrs Geiger was right, but I couldn't do it.

It was because of the pity. I imagined Lea's mum collecting me in her big black car that smelled of leather and lemon.

Maybe she'd apologize for what she'd said, but maybe not. Either way, she'd pull me in close to her soft, large chest, wrap her arms around me and say something like: 'Why didn't you call me straight away? We would have picked you up the first day.' She'd take me in like one of her dogs. She'd stroke the top of my head and look at me, full of pity.

My mum had once said: 'Pity is like a bed you lie in. You never get up again, because it's so comfortable.'

I definitely didn't want her pity.

And I didn't know if I could forgive Lea. But either way, I had to make sure my mum got a lovely funeral.

21

My mum was already there when I arrived at the cemetery. It was cool inside the chapel. I stared at the coffin. It was closed; a bunch of sunflowers lay on the wooden lid. I laid my hand on the spot where Mum's heart would be. I thought about how often I'd cuddled up to her in bed and listened to her heartbeat. I knew I'd never get closer to her again than now, with my hand on her coffin. I knew I had to say goodbye, but I couldn't. My body was being tugged; my stomach was churning. I felt dizzy, and I sat down on a pew. I closed my eyes, and when I opened them Luna was sitting next to me. 'It gets better eventually,' she said quietly and put her arm around my shoulders. Her fingernails sparkled like a starry sky.

'Thank you for coming,' I whispered.

She waved it away. But I knew it didn't feel natural to Luna to go to a funeral.

'Is Ahmed here too?' I asked. If Mum could have sent the invitations to her own funeral, Ahmed would definitely have had one.

Luna nodded. 'He brought a juniper branch for your mother. Juniper is a symbol of eternal life.'

Mum had once said Ahmed would make a woman really happy one day. At this moment, I was that woman, because he'd brought something so beautiful for my mum.

'Is your grandmother still in hospital?' Luna asked.

'Maybe,' I said. 'But maybe she's already in prison.'

'And how is it going in the children's home?'

'It's not a home.'

And that said it all.

When we went out, Luna took my hand.

The sky was white and the heat wrapped around me like a coat. Luna had tied her hair back and there were beads of sweat glistening on the back of her neck.

Ahmed was standing a little apart under a tree with Lea's family. When he saw us, he came over. Lea's mother followed him. Ahmed hugged Luna, took my hands, looked into my eyes and asked me how I was doing.

'Billie is very brave,' Lea's mother said. 'She's coping really well.'

'He asked Billie,' Luna said and rested her arm around my shoulders again.

The sun was setting on Lea's mother's face. 'And who are you?' she wanted to know.

'I'm Luna. Billie's neighbour.'

'Ah, I might have guessed,' said Lea's mother.

Ahmed said nothing. Then he said: 'It's wonderful that you made this possible.' Ahmed always managed to create harmony. Lea's mother tucked a strand of hair behind her ear and smiled.

Then the vicar came over to us. He leaned over to Lea's mother and said something quiet that I couldn't hear. Lea's mother recoiled, like he had bad breath.

When I was little, Mum checked every night if I'd brushed my teeth. 'Breathe on me,' she said. Sometimes when I'd just eaten some crisps, she'd pinch her nose with two fingers and say in a Mickey Mouse voice, 'Go and brush your teeth.' When I came out of the bathroom, she'd shower me with kisses. I was sure the vicar's mother had never checked if he'd cleaned his teeth. And now it was too late. She was probably dead.

He turned to me. 'Would you like to say a prayer for your mother at the grave?'

'No thank you,' I said.

'No?' he asked, surprised.

I shook my head. I didn't know how to pray for my mum. I only knew how to pray for people who were alive. Or for things I wanted. Suddenly, I thought that maybe it had been wrong to pray for all those things. Thinking about it, the things I'd asked God for seemed trivial. I hadn't kept a single one of them.

The hole in the ground for Mum was deep. 'What if she wakes up and no one hears her?' I whispered.

'The doctors would definitely have noticed if she were still alive,' Luna whispered.

'Things like that don't happen in Germany,' Lea whispered.

'I didn't ask you,' I said to Lea.

When Lea had arrived at the cemetery, she'd hugged me, but she hadn't looked me in the eye. She told me about her holiday and how she'd argued with her brothers. That's when I realized things would never be the same again. The thing in the kitchen was one thing, but the other was that I'd lost my mum and she hadn't.

'Billie, I wrote to you that I'm sorry,' Lea said now.

'What exactly are you sorry for? That you think you're better than me?' I got louder and everyone stared at me.

'Billie, calm down please,' Lea's mother said.

'Think of the donkey with the golden saddle,' Ahmed said.

'Your mother is being laid to rest,' the vicar admonished. 'You should show a little respect.'

I stared at him. Was he serious?

The vicar started praying; he prayed so hard, like he wanted to pray away my anger. Then the coffin with my mum in it was lowered into the grave.

I concentrated on the lizards. They zoomed back and forth between the tombstones. I saw one without a tail and wondered how long it would take to grow back. I imagined growing a new heart because the old one had shattered into a thousand pieces.

Lea and her family bowed their heads; only Lea's little brother had his head tilted back and was looking at the sky. A flock of birds flew by. They flew so slowly and lazily that it wouldn't have surprised me if they'd plummeted down on us.

When the vicar sprinkled holy water on the coffin, I felt a very strong tug low down in my tummy. I clenched my teeth.

When he threw earth onto the coffin, something warm and wet trickled from the centre of my body and ran down my legs.

When he said: 'From the earth you were taken, to the earth you shall return, but the Lord will raise you up,' I realized it was blood.

I stared at my red finger and pressed my legs together. I thought I could stop the blood like stopping a nosebleed. I couldn't believe I was getting my first period here. I wanted to be invisible, but everyone was staring at me like I'd burst into flames.

Lea's little brother asked: 'Is she dying now too?'

'It's just her period,' Luna said loudly, popping a bubble in front of her face with her gum. I was still standing there without moving. I wanted the blood to disappear back where it came from. 'As soon as you start bleeding, you'll have nothing but trouble,' Mum had once said.

'Come with me,' Lea's mother said and pushed me by the shoulders towards the chapel. She gave me a pad and waited outside a cubicle. I sat on the toilet, looked down and couldn't believe what my body was doing.

'Did your mother tell you why women bleed?' Lea's mother asked through the door.

'Yes,' I said. I pulled off the backing and stuck the pad in my underwear. It felt weird.

'Listen, it's important that you know your first period is a good thing.'

'Okay,' I said, but I wasn't ready. Not for my period and definitely not for advice from Lea's mother.

Lea's mother gave me some paper towels by the sinks, and I wiped the blood off my thighs. My dress was a bit stained, but I didn't have any spare clothes.

'Let's forget about the stupid stuff from the other day,' Lea's mother said. 'It'll be nice to have you with us.' She reached out her hand like a mother when she crosses the road with her child.

'Yes, sure,' I said. At that moment, I didn't care that I was lying.

When we got back, everyone was praying hard. Or maybe they were just pretending. In any case, they were looking down, and I was thankful for that.

In the end, we threw flowers into the grave. My rose hit the coffin with a dull thud. Mum would have felt sorry for it.

At Mum's grave, I'd kept looking round for my father. But when the guests had said their goodbyes and he still hadn't arrived, I realized he wouldn't simply appear in my life.

22

One day after my mum's funeral, the summer got weaker. It was like someone had adjusted the dimmer switch. The nights grew cooler, and the water was emptied out of the pools. School would go back in a week.

I kept dreaming about my mum. There was one dream that kept coming back. I was standing on the ten-metre platform; the surface of the water glittered beneath me, and my mum was standing on the grass. Then I jumped. As I fell, I saw that the pool was empty. I screamed for my mum but she'd disappeared. I knew that in a few seconds, my body would burst like the melon someone had once thrown from the eleventh floor.

It was time to go home. That afternoon I went to get the picture book. When I arrived downstairs, Mrs Geiger's door was closed. She was on the phone. I took the book off the shelf and put it in my backpack. I noticed the pieces of paper and brochures lying on the windowsill next to the bookshelf. I picked up a city map and a bus timetable and stuck both of them down the front of my jeans. In my room, I packed my things and checked that my house key and Luna's money were still there. I took one of the banknotes and put it in my trouser pocket. Then I shoved the backpack under the bed. The whole thing took just a couple of minutes. I took a closer look at the bus timetable. I couldn't wait too long. The later it got, the fewer buses would head in my direction.

When it was growing dark, I set off. The air was nice and cool, and it smelled of earth, cement and rain. But it felt like I was separated from it by an invisible pane of glass.

In my trouser pocket I found a cigarette. The paper was crumpled and had burst open in one place. Bits of tobacco were sticking out. I lit it and inhaled deeply. But smoking alone seemed pointless.

I wondered how many 'buts' were in store for me. Perhaps this was my life now. Obviously I realized a 'but' life is not a real life. Luna would say it was a life with the handbrake on.

The bus stop was in a road just behind the children's home. When the bus came, I got in right at the back. The bus driver ignored me.

Our block of flats was visible from far away. The lights were still on in lots of the flats. I remembered the picture books in Lea's youngest brother's room. One of them showed the inside of a house. The people who lived in it ate, slept, washed and played in all of the rooms. No one lived alone.

I stood outside our block for half an hour. I'd spent my entire life in there. I stood in the car park and couldn't go up. Everything around me was silent. But the blood rushed in my ears. I sat down on the ground.

'Billie?'

I turned around. Uta. Her T-shirt hung loosely over her body. She'd grown thin since the last time I saw her.

'What's the matter, sweetie? Why are you sitting out here?'

I didn't know what to say. I didn't know why I was sitting there.

Uta put the plastic bags she'd been carrying down on the ground and sat down next to me. 'It's hard to lose someone you love,' she said.

I made a fist. Small stones from the tarmac pressed into the skin of my left hand. I hated the fact that everyone thought they knew what was going on. I couldn't stand another person pretending they understood me. I jumped up. 'How would you know?'

Uta didn't look at me and nodded towards the plastic bags.

'So what?'

'Those are Heinz's clothes.'

'Why are you carrying his clothes around with you?'

'I wanted to throw them in the charity bin. But I can't do it. Stupid, right? They're only clothes, and he didn't want them any more anyway.' Uta looked at her hands and twisted her wedding ring. 'Heart attack,' she said, and then: 'Bang, dead.'

Uta wiped her hands across her face. She suddenly looked very tired. I was surprised I wasn't relieved to hear this news. I just felt really empty. I didn't understand why she was sad, but I thought of what Mum had said about love and didn't ask. Instead I sat back down again.

'Don't you want to go up?' Uta asked.

I shook my head.

Then she said: 'The first time is the hardest. It's easier the second time.'

My eyes filled with tears.

'Shall we go together?' Uta asked and held out her hand.

'Okay,' I said and wiped my nose on my T-shirt. Then I took her hand.

'Yuck,' Uta said and smiled.

When I entered our flat, I took a deep breath and inhaled the smell of our home into my lungs. From there it spread all through my body, and it felt good, and it hurt. All at the same time.

My mum's cowboy boots lay in the hallway. They were in the way. I didn't make it to the living room. I stared at the shoes. Suddenly I realized Mum wouldn't be coming back. Her shoes lay exactly where she'd taken them off after work.

I sat down on the floor, right next to the boots, and cried. I cried and thought of my mum, and cried and thought about all the things she'd done and said and all the things she hadn't done and hadn't said.

Once, in the park, a stranger had approached us because I wasn't wearing a hat. It was so cold that I was jumping on the frozen puddles to test if the ice was hard enough.

'She's a clever child,' Mum said to the woman. Then she turned to me and asked: 'Is your head cold?'

'No.'

Mum shrugged. 'No cold. If cold, then hat.'

I remembered that my mum's German wasn't yet the bee's ankles, as she'd have said.

My mum didn't let trivial things hold her back. But sometimes the things that others thought trivial were a big deal for her.

Once, we'd been at the playground. Apart from us, there was just one little boy and his mum. When he finally dared to go down the slide, he kept wanting to do it again. At some point his mum said to him: 'If you don't come now, then I'll go without you.' When my mum tapped the woman on the shoulder from behind, I already knew what was going to happen. My mum interfered. Most people don't like it when others interfere. 'He was three, Billie,' she told me later. 'How can you threaten to leave a three-year-old behind?'

I sat next to the shoes and cried, because I knew my mum would never have wanted to leave me alone. I couldn't bear the thought that she'd realized she was doing it anyway. I'd have liked to have told her how awful it was that she had to go, but that I would manage. It would have been okay to lie.

But the worst thing was that I had forgotten the last thing she'd said to me. I simply couldn't remember.

When I had no tears left, I had thoughts like: there's a big mould stain on the ceiling. The caretaker wanted to remove it months ago. The next rent payment would be due in three weeks. And I had to hide from Mrs Geiger and social services. It wouldn't be long until they found me. Then I thought of Uta. I'd have liked to ask her what she missed about Heinz. I'd have liked to ask her if she was relieved. Just a tiny bit. 'Men always make you cry. We cry when they are there, we cry when they're gone. When you find one who makes you laugh, then you've hit the jackpot, you understand?' Mum had once said.

It was only when my stomach started growling that I got up. The kitchen cupboards were almost empty, but right at the back I found some spaghetti and tomato sauce, all in one packet. I put a pan of water on the stove.

Then I sat down at the kitchen table and stared at the purple diamond pattern. I couldn't remember us ever having a different tablecloth. The colour had faded, and the plastic was always a bit sticky, even if you'd just wiped it.

I'd eaten alone a thousand times. But this time it was different. Nobody prepares you to lose your mum at the age of fourteen. There was no lesson in the curriculum where you learned to wake up alone and go to bed alone because your mum was dead.

'School is overrated,' Mum had once said. 'But you still need to go. It's your ticket to a better future.'

My future? I thought. I had better things to do than go to school.

My blue hair gleamed in the morning sun. I'd hung it over the globe on my desk. Blue on blue. Seventy-one per cent of the Earth's surface was covered by water, and I'd never seen the sea. I took the wig and put it on. I looked at the strange girl in the mirror of my wardrobe.

I sat down at my desk and took my notebook out of the drawer. I opened it and then I closed it again.

I couldn't write.

In the kitchen I filled a bowl with milk and tipped in the cornflakes. I was just about to start eating when the phone rang. I thought about whether to answer it for so long that it stopped again. I sat down on the sofa and waited for the phone to ring again. But it stayed silent. Not many people called us. Mum's bosses. They were probably wondering why she hadn't turned up to work. I couldn't bear the thought of them thinking my mum was unreliable. I had to tell them. Then there was Lea and my grandma. I pictured my grandma praying the rosary in her cell, begging God for forgiveness for what she'd done to us. She didn't deserve any cake. She didn't deserve someone smuggling a nail file into prison baked inside a cake. I couldn't call Lea. Not after everything that had happened between us. In any case, she'd tell her mum I'd run away from the children's home. I suddenly thought about calling my dad. What if he'd heard about Mum's death? What if I'd missed the opportunity to meet him because I hadn't answered the phone?

After I'd eaten the cornflakes, I drank the sugary milk from the bowl and thought how nice it would be to have a cat. During the day, she'd let herself fall from the kitchen table, from the sofa and from the cupboard and would always land on her feet. At night, when I had a bad dream, she'd lie next to me purring until I fell asleep again.

23

I immediately sensed that someone was there. I'd just got back from the shops. I'd only bought what I absolutely needed. I was sure I'd need Luna's money for more important things than food. There were other ways to get hold of food.

And then I spotted my grandma's small brown shoes. They were sitting tidily in the hallway. My heart missed a beat, and my legs started to shake. I couldn't control them.

'There you are,' my grandma said. She was holding a kitchen towel and a wooden spoon in her hands. She came towards me and stretched out her arms.

I froze.

'I've made soup,' my grandma said and lowered her arms. 'Soup is good when you're sad.'

I wanted to reply, but as soon as I found the words, I lost them again.

'What's happened to your hair?' my grandma asked. 'Why are you wearing that ugly thing?' She pointed the wooden spoon at my wig.

I pulled the wig from my head.

And then my grandma finally kept her mouth shut, but not for long. 'What is that?' she asked as I unpacked the shopping in the kitchen.

'Soup,' I said.

My grandma shook the packet. 'There's powder in there.'

'You can make it into soup,' I said.

'That's horrible,' she said.

'You don't have to eat it.' I filled the kettle and tore open the packet.

'Leave that,' my grandma said. 'Eat my soup.' She raised the lid. A whole chicken was floating in the soup between carrots and celery. My grandma took a ladle and filled a bowl. 'Sit down,' she said.

'No.'

'I told you to sit down.'

'No.'

'You're to do what I tell you!' My grandma banged her fist on the table.

'You're not my mum,' I screamed.

'I am responsible for you now, Erzsébet. It is my job —'

'I don't care. You're to blame for Mum's death.'

My grandma slumped down on a chair. She pulled off her headscarf and covered her face with it. 'It was an accident,' she said.

'Is that what you told the police?'

My grandma nodded.

'And then?'

'Nothing.' She removed the headscarf. 'I was in the hospital until this morning. Then they discharged me.'

I couldn't believe my grandma wasn't in prison.

My grandma pushed the bowl towards me. 'You need to eat.'

'I'm not hungry.' I got up. 'Do you see all this?' I asked. 'This is our kitchen table. The tabletop was dirty and one of the legs was wobbly when we found it. Mum worked on it and now it's a good table. But you never sat at this table. Do you see the photograph on the fridge? We were at the zoo. We pretended that I was younger so I didn't have to pay the full price. It was a nice outing. But you weren't there.'

My grandma stayed silent. Her rosary lay on the table in front of her.

I wondered when exactly God had abandoned us.

My grandma sat on my mum's chair. Then she lay on our sofa and looked at our moon.

Why had God taken my mum from me and sent me my grandma?

I ran into my room. I pushed my desk chair under the door handle and brushed all my grandma's things to the floor with a swipe of my hand. Then I dropped onto my bed. I decided not to leave my room until my grandma had returned to Hungary.

The problem was that there were things you just couldn't do in a room that only contains a bed, a cupboard, a desk and a chair. I couldn't eat bread, drink Coke, make a phone call, go to the toilet. And if you can't go to the toilet, then a few hours can feel like a lifetime. Then you immediately think you have to go even if you don't actually need to.

'Erzsébet, please come out,' my grandma said a couple of times and knocked on the door. I put my hands over my ears. The door handle went up and down, but I could only hear the blood rushing through my skull. I sat on my bed for hours. When my stomach started to growl, I ate a chocolate bar. I had a box full of sweets and crisps hidden under my bed.

But at some point I really did need to go. I waited until I couldn't hear any more noises from the other rooms.

My grandma was lying on the sofa sleeping, buried under the bedclothes I'd thrown into the hallway. On the table next to her was a small box of pills. They were sleeping tablets. The soup was still on the stove in the kitchen. The kitchen towel hung tidily on the back of the kitchen chair. My grandma's apron hung from the nail in the wall. I thought of how my mum had cleaned the flat. I pictured her clearing the nail polish bottles, the brochures and everything else from the kitchen table.

I realized my grandma had never left. She had always been there. First in my mum's head and then in our flat. I took a Coke from the fridge. Then I crept back to my room.

I was woken by the doorbell the next morning. I didn't move for a moment, but I didn't hear any footsteps in the hallway. Why didn't my grandma go to the door? When I came into the hallway, she was standing by the living room door with her arms crossed, looking at me.

'Why are you not opening the door?' I asked.

'I wanted you to come out of your room first,' she said. 'I know how curious you are.'

Mrs Geiger and social services were outside the door. They'd been quicker than I expected.

'Billie, you're only fourteen,' Mrs Geiger said. She tried to sound like a mother, but she didn't know my mum had never sounded like that. 'You can't —' Then she saw my grandma. 'Who is that?'

I told her.

Mrs Geiger and the woman from social services looked at each other. The woman sighed. 'Kind of the police to tell us,' she said and flicked a bit of fluff off her sleeve.

'Tell you what?' I asked.

'Who are these people and what do they want?' my grandma asked.

'The prosecutor didn't tell us that they clearly aren't conducting criminal proceedings against your grandmother, nor that there is someone who can care for you,' the social worker said.

'And what if I don't want to stay with my grandma?'

'I'm sorry, but there are only limited spots we can place you.'

'And besides, you didn't want to stay with us anyway,' Mrs Geiger said and forced a smile.

Her smile said: *We searched for you for nothing.*

It said: *You're wasting our time.*

I had lied to them. It was evident that she was annoyed. I didn't hold it against her. She must have understood that I wasn't planning to move in with Lea's family.

'What exactly is going on here?' my grandma wanted to know, and tried to push me out of the way.

'I have a father,' I said.

'Are you in contact with him now?' Mrs Geiger asked.

I shook my head.

'You said you didn't know who he is,' the social worker said.

'Yes —'

'If your mother didn't put his name down on your birth certificate, officially, then there is nothing we can do. Then he is unknown,' the social worker explained.

I had no idea where my birth certificate was or what it said. My mum had a box she kept her papers and letters in. Sometimes she threw letters in the bin without opening them first. 'Most things resolve themselves,' she'd said and shrugged. Sometimes she was right, sometimes she wasn't. And sometimes a second letter came from the same sender. Or a third. I decided to look for my birth certificate as soon as the two of them had left.

'What about your grandma?' Mrs Geiger said. 'Does she know who your father is?'

'You're to tell them who my father is,' I said to my grandma in Hungarian.

My grandma looked at me sceptically. Then she crossed her arms. 'I already told you that I don't know.'

'She says that she doesn't know, but I'm not sure if that's true,' I said.

'Well, that would be a private matter,' Mrs Geiger said.

'Yes, then there's nothing we can do,' the social worker confirmed and took a business card from her bag. 'But if there are any problems with your grandmother, then call us.'

And that was it as far as she was concerned.

When they were gone, I tore the business card into lots of little pieces and let them rain down from my window.

24

My mum didn't have her own room, but she did have her own cupboard. The cupboard was made of shiny dark brown wood and looked like a treasure chest.

There was a part I was allowed to look in and a part I wasn't allowed to look in. The allowed part was at the bottom. As well as all sorts of other stuff, this was also where the box with all the paperwork was. The non-allowed part was behind the two top doors. Obviously I wanted to know what she kept in there.

'Everyone needs a bit of privacy,' Mum had said. And: 'Don't force me to hide the key.'

I'd never forced her to do that.

I waited until my grandma fell asleep. Mum had once claimed that my grandma snored louder than ten Siberian lumberjacks. I hadn't believed it, but it was true: I could hear her from my room. And because the walls were thin, Luna probably heard her too.

On tiptoe I sneaked into the living room.

I stood in front of the cupboard and stared at the key. I knew it was wrong to open the top doors.

Suddenly I was sure my mum could see from up there what I was planning.

I thought it couldn't do any harm to make the sign of the cross and ask for forgiveness. 'I'm sorry,' I whispered, and wasn't sure if I meant God or my mum.

When I turned the key in the lock, it grated loudly, and I held my breath. But my grandma didn't wake up. She just grunted and then turned on her side, and the snoring grew quieter.

The secret compartment contained bedding. Pillows, sheets and linen, folded carefully, edge to edge. What was this? I couldn't remember us ever using these things. A sort of round bag made of fleece lay on the other side. It was quite large, and heavier than it looked. I took it into my room, and decided to look for my birth certificate first. Right at the bottom of the cupboard, I found the book where my mum kept all sorts of papers.

I emptied it out on my bed in my room.

The first thing I picked up was an envelope. My mum had written on it. It said *All My Tears*. I ripped it open and banknotes tumbled towards me. I had to laugh. I couldn't believe I'd forgotten all about our winnings. I hid the money in my cupboard. Then I carried on looking.

I found old payslips, car documents with chewing gum stuck on them, our rental agreement and a whole pile of letters from government departments. I had no idea what they were about. Then I discovered a plastic folder containing something that looked like a certificate. I took a closer look. There were several pieces of paper in the folder: certificates from an adult education centre for successfully completing German courses. The centre was in a town I'd never heard of. I looked it up in my school atlas. It was a small town. It was right in the north of Germany. There were no larger cities nearby. Why had Mum taken an adult education course in that place? I looked at the date on the first certificate. One year after my birth. I'd never asked my mum where we had lived when we came to Germany. I'd never even thought it might be somewhere other than here. And my mum had never told me different.

At the very bottom of the pile of documents I found my birth certificate. It had been issued in Hungary, but behind the original was a German translation. On both of them it said FATHER UNKNOWN. The thought suddenly crossed my mind that maybe my mum hadn't known who my father was. Perhaps she wasn't sure and hadn't wanted to admit it.

After I'd looked through everything in the box, I opened the bag. A strange smell wafted towards me as I unzipped it. It smelled somehow like old cloth; it smelled like powder mixed with a small amount of sweat. It smelled like my mum hadn't opened this bag in a long time.

The bag contained a tutu.

I ran my fingers over the white tulle. It was quite stiff. I took the tutu and put it on my desk. I pictured my mum wearing it. She must have looked beautiful. I wiped the tears from my face and lay down to sleep.

The next morning my grandma knocked at my bedroom door. 'Breakfast,' she said, and then: 'I'll put it outside the door for you.' There was a piece of bread with cheese on it, a fried egg and a cup of hot chocolate. At first I didn't want to touch it, but my stomach was growling. It was definitely better then eating gummy worms and chocolate bars all day. When I'd finished, I tidied the papers spread across the floor back into the box. The birth certificate was no use to me, but I still hid it in my cupboard together with the German-language certificates.

Then I took the tray back to the kitchen. My grandma was sitting on the sofa sewing. When I walked past her, she looked up. She opened her mouth like she wanted to say something, but then she seemed to change her mind.

I waited the whole day for my grandma to leave the flat. I wanted to look in the cupboard one more time. I wanted to clear out the bedding. Perhaps my mum had hidden some love letters in between the sheets she'd tied up with a red ribbon. Or fake papers. Or a weapon she'd used to kill my father with. The more I thought about it, the crazier my ideas became.

When my grandma finally set off to the supermarket, I took out the bedding, item by item. Then I spotted it.

The box was made of the same wood as the cupboard and was square; the sides were about as long as a large ruler. It wasn't very high and was leaning against the back of the cupboard. It was almost invisible.

In my room, I pushed open the lid.

There were no love letters in the box. No weapon either. The box contained half a bottle of perfume, a seashell, a torn photograph, a receipt and a CD.

The perfume smelled like someone had taken paradise and put it in a bottle. I pictured palm trees, colourful flowers and exotic fruits swimming in it. I didn't recognize the perfume; my mum had never worn it. It smelled expensive. I didn't dare put any on.

The seashell looked like a normal seashell. It was neither big nor small, and you could probably find it on any beach. I only knew shells from the one-euro shop. They had various mixtures of shells in jars there. Some of them were varnished. The shells gleamed so much; I couldn't imagine they'd ever had a living creature inside them. Not a single grain of sand trickled out of them. But when I listened to the shells, I could hear the faint rushing of the sea. I used to think shells grew on the seabed. I imagined mermaids decorating their flats with them. 'We know less about the sea than we do about the moon,' Mum said when I told her about it. 'Perhaps the mermaids are just good at hiding.'

I saw my mum in the photo. She was younger and had a different hairstyle. I almost didn't recognize her. That was also because of her expression. She looked like a child that had lost its parents in the supermarket and then suddenly finds them again. Mum was standing in a garden, in front of a red shed. She was holding a baby in her arms.

There were no photo albums that my mum had stuck photos in and there were no baby photos of me where she'd written next to them how much I weighed and how tall I was. 'You had dark green eyes and lots of hair,' Mum had once told me when I asked what I'd looked like as a baby. When I'd wanted to know why there were no photos of us, my mum bent down to me, took my face in her hands and said: 'You can't hold on to moments, Billie. A photo is just a photo. It never shows reality.'

Around my mum's shoulders was an arm, but I couldn't see who it belonged to. Someone had torn the photo. The arm was in a leather jacket. I immediately knew it was my father's arm. Someone who liked cowboy boots would also wear a leather jacket. I took a close look at the arm and tried to work out what sort of person my father was. Obviously it didn't work. You needed more than an arm.

Next I looked at the receipt. There were expensive things on there. Much too expensive. We couldn't afford salmon and avocado. Not even at the beginning of the month.

The CD my mum had kept in the wooden box was a Miles Davis album. And that almost drove me crazy. I'd always thought Mum didn't like jazz. I immediately checked if the album in the box was mine. But my Miles Davis CD was on my shelf with my favourite things. I'd listened to it around 3,567 times, I recognized each piece in my sleep. But I'd only ever once turned the music up really loud. Mum had immediately rushed into my room. 'What is that?' she said, and it sounded like an accusation. Before I could reply, she said: 'Turn that off!'

'Why?' I asked.

'Can't you see that my ears are bleeding?'

'But —'

'I never want to hear that again, do you understand?'

I hadn't understood, but I never listened to the album without headphones after that. Why did my mum own a Miles Davis CD, and why on earth had she hidden it so well?

My grandma was the only one who could tell me something about all these things. I had the key to my mum's cupboard. Maybe my grandma had the key to her head.

25

The only thing was that we didn't speak about my mum. We spoke about neither her death nor her life. At least not for a long while. But my grandma spoke with her eyes. She cried a lot at night. I could hear her when I lay awake in my bed.

During the day, she cooked. And when she wasn't cooking, she was baking. I ate goulash and Esterházy slices, lecsó and dumplings, rakott krumpli and túrógombóc. My grandma's food reminded me of the evening Lea had eaten at our place. The memories made me sad, but the food still tasted better than spaghetti with tomato sauce or frozen pizza.

When I told Luna that my grandma spent her entire day in the kitchen, she said: 'She has lost her child. And she can't even lay her to rest. She's cooking to stay alive.'

When I told Ahmed that I spent almost my entire day in my room, he said: 'You've put yourself in prison, and your grandma is running around free outside.'

After that I left my door open.

It took less than a minute for my grandma to sit down next to me on my bed. She took my hands. She took them carefully, like they might break. 'I promised your mother to take care of you,' she said. 'I promised to take care of you if she should die.'

'When?' I asked and wiped away my tears.

'When you were born,' my grandma said.

'Why did you promise her that?' I wanted to know. I thought about all the things my mum had told me about my grandma. I thought about everything that had happened.

'You are my granddaughter,' my grandma said.

'But you don't even like me,' I said.

My grandma sighed. 'That's not true. I don't actually know you.' She got up. She was almost in the hallway already when she turned back to me. 'Will you help me make bejglis?'

'What are bejglis?'

My grandma smiled. 'Did your mother never make any?'

'She made pancakes. The best pancakes.'

'Bejglis are a delicacy in Hungary. You can fill them with poppy seeds or walnuts,' my grandma said. 'They're usually eaten at Christmas.'

'I like walnuts,' I said and got up.

Before my grandma started baking, she got everything together that she needed. She fetched the eggs, butter, milk and yeast from the fridge and the rest from the kitchen cupboard. She put the ingredients on the table, plus a set of kitchen scales I'd never seen before. Then she tied an apron around her waist. 'Now we can start,' she said. 'First we measure everything.'

I weighed the flour, the icing sugar, the butter, walnuts and the raisins and put them all onto plates. My grandma stirred the yeast and some icing sugar into the lukewarm milk and then stirred that mixture into the flour, salt, butter and eggs.

While she stirred, she started to sing.

I couldn't believe these sounds were coming from her. Her

voice was like a summer breeze before a storm, like a final hug, like a love letter without a lover.

I knew the song. It was 'Szerelem, Szerelem' by Márta Sebestyén. 'Szerelem' means love.

'I sang it so often for your mother when she was small,' my grandma said, and tears dripped into the dough. She dabbed her eyes with her apron and covered the dough with a damp tea towel. 'Now we'll make the filling.'

We heated up water with icing sugar, and I added the ground walnuts.

My grandma took a spoon and tried it. 'The nuts from my tree are better. Did you know that we have a walnut tree in our garden in Hungary?'

I shook my head.

'Your mother always climbed up it when she was sad.'

'Was she often sad?' I asked. I imagined Mum with her bottom lip stuck out and her arms crossed sitting in the tree and refusing to come down.

'When Márton died, she was up there almost all the time.' My grandma went silent and crushed biscuits with a glass. 'Please take the pan off the stove.'

I did what she said, and she stirred in the biscuit crumbs, the raisins and some lemon zest. It smelled like a cake shop, and I was sure all the neighbours would ring the doorbell in a moment to find out what was happening in our flat.

'That needs to cool down, and when the dough has risen, we can continue,' my grandma said. 'I'll have a little rest.'

An hour and a half later, my grandma removed the tea towel from the bowl and stuck her finger in. 'Very good,' she said. 'The dough needs to feel as firm as an earlobe.' Then she dusted the work surface with flour and rolled out the pastry until two rectangles lay in front of us. I brushed the pastry with the filling, and my grandma showed me how to roll up the pastry sheets. She brushed the bejglis with beaten egg and laid a clean tea towel on top.

'Do we need to wait again?' I asked.

My grandma nodded. 'Yes. And later when we've brushed the bejglis with egg white one last time before they go in the oven, we'll have a cup of tea, all right?'

'Okay,' I said.

My grandma put the kettle on and I drew a pattern in the flour on the work surface. Then we sat opposite each other at the table and sipped our tea.

'I didn't want it to happen,' my grandma suddenly said.

I raised my head and looked her straight in the eye. For the first time since my mum had died, I looked right at her. I saw her face, the wrinkles on her forehead and around her mouth, the eyes that reminded me of my mother's.

'I didn't want it to happen,' my grandma said and I heard: 'I'm sorry.' Then she said: 'Your mother was my only child,' and I heard: 'I loved your mother.'

'But you hit her,' I said, and a big lump formed in my throat.

My grandma put the spoon to one side. 'It's complicated,' she said.

I didn't understand what was complicated about keeping your hands to yourself.

'Sometimes you do the stupidest things out of love,' my grandma said.

I couldn't stand these fortune cookie replies.

'Do you admit that you flushed your pills down the toilet?' I asked.

My grandma didn't look at me. Then she nodded.

'Why?'

'I wanted to stay here and fix everything. I didn't want your mother to send me away because I was better.' Her voice quivered.

'Why didn't you admit it right away?'

She shrugged. 'I suppose I was afraid.'

'When you're afraid, you can't do the right thing.'

'You sound like your mother,' my grandma said and drank her last sip of tea. 'Your mother always had nice words.'

Later, I ate a piece of bejgli straight from the baking tray. The sweetness spread through my body and comforted me. While I ate, my grandma tidied up the kitchen. She washed the dishes and wiped the work surface and the table. Then she stuck the supermarket receipt on the spindle. I hoped she hadn't been to one of those supermarkets where a trolley full of shopping cost almost as much as a yearly bus pass. I glanced at the receipt, and then remembered something.

First I ran into my room to fetch the birth and language certificates. Then I ran into the living room and fetched my mum's wooden box from the cupboard. The receipt was faded, but the address of the supermarket was still recognizable. I searched for the place in my atlas. It wasn't far from where my mum had taken the language classes. There were one and a half years between levels A2 and C2. A1 was missing.

I put the wooden box on the coffee table in the living room, right under my grandma's nose. 'These are things my mum kept. I don't know what they mean.'

My grandma put her sewing things to one side, and I put the photograph on her lap.

'Is that my father's arm?' I asked.

'Are you joking?' my grandma asked and shook her head.

'Is it him?'

'I have no idea. It's just an arm. I never saw your father. Your mother never introduced him to me. And he never bothered with you.'

'She lived in the north of Germany, right?' I asked.

'Your mother didn't leave an address when she disappeared.'

I didn't understand what my grandma was saying. 'I thought she went to Budapest to become a dancer?'

'That was the first time.'

'She ran away twice?'

My grandma nodded. 'And it was a stupid idea both times. But that was your mother. A dreamer.'

I crossed my arms. 'Well, she did dance *Swan Lake* as the prima ballerina.'

My grandma raised her eyebrows. 'Is that what she told you?'

I nodded.

My grandma sighed. 'I saw that you found her tutu. But a tutu doesn't make you a prima ballerina.'

'Why should she lie to me?' I asked.

'Who knows. Out of habit. She lied constantly.'

I thought of my grandma's lies, but I chose not to say anything.

My grandma handed back the photograph. Then she started rummaging around in the box. 'What is all this stuff?' she asked, holding up the perfume, then the CD and then the receipt.

'I thought *you* would know.'

'I know less about your mother than you might think.' My grandma went silent for a moment. 'She had secrets. Like everyone else.'

26

Obviously I'd thought about looking for my father. At night I lay in bed and wondered who he was. It was like my mum had taken a piece of me with her. Sometimes I wasn't even sure if I was still there. Then I switched on the light and looked at myself for minutes on end in the hand mirror I'd put on my bedside table.

I hadn't planned on finding my father in the beginning. The matter was more an idea or a possibility. But then it turned out that my grandma had made her own plans. A few evenings after I'd shown her the box, she opened the cupboard in the living room and said: 'School starts again tomorrow.'

I had no idea how she knew that.

'I have a surprise for you.' My grandma pulled out a piece of checked fabric. 'I have made you a new blouse,' she said and held it up against my chest. 'Try it on.'

The blouse fitted perfectly and my grandma clicked her tongue in contentment. 'It looks great on you.'

I looked like a clown. I didn't tell my grandma that, of course. Instead I said thank you and then I said: 'I'm not ready to go back to school yet.'

'What?' she asked. I repeated what I'd said.

'Yes, yes,' my grandma said. 'What does that mean, you are not ready?'

'It means that I don't want to go.'

My grandma stared at me. 'And what do you want to do instead? Sit around at home and get on my nerves with your constant questions?'

'I want to write.' The moment I said it, I realized it was true. That was exactly what I wanted to do.

'And what do you want to write?'

'Stories.'

'Stories?' My grandma sat down and started shifting her rosary from one hand to the other. 'What sort of stories?'

'I don't know yet.'

'Absolutely not,' my grandma said. Her cheeks went red. 'One wants to dance, the other wants to write. What did I do wrong? You are going to school tomorrow.'

'And if not?' I asked, and I took a few careful steps backwards. My grandma had become quite loud.

'Then we'll just go back to Hungary sooner.'

I couldn't believe what I was hearing. 'We? Who's we?'

'You and me. I need to sort out a few matters first.' When my grandma saw my face, she said: 'Did you imagine I would leave you here alone?'

'No, I thought you were staying here.'

My grandma shook her head. 'I am old. Hungary is my home.'

'And Germany is *my* home,' I protested.

'You are Hungarian,' my grandma said. 'And you are young. When you are young, you quickly adapt.'

'I don't want to adapt.'

'That's how you see it now, but we will have a good life. There are just a few little things that need repairing in my house, and once I have given notice on the flat and the custody —'

'You can't even speak German,' I said and crossed my arms. 'How are you going to manage all that?'

'Don't you worry,' my grandma said. 'Do you remember the doctor?'

'Which doctor?'

'Zsuzsanna Szabó.'

Shit, I thought.

'Her son helps Hungarian refugees. She has given me his telephone number. She really was very kind.'

'But you're not a refugee,' I said. 'Refugees can't go back to their home country.'

'You don't need to take that so literally,' my grandma said. 'I am fleeing from Germany. I want again to at last eat good salami. And in any case, the air is much better in the countryside, you will see.'

'Have you even thought for one second what I want?' I asked. Then I left my grandma sitting there and went to my room.

I spent the rest of the evening on my bed. My grandma only came in once. She sat on the edge of the bed and took my hands. Then she said: 'I see how sad you are. It will be good for you to get out of here. It will be good for you to take care of the animals. You will find new friends. And the Hungarian schools are good.'

'I already have friends,' I said.

'That Lea girl?' my grandma asked.

I nodded.

'She's not the right one for you anyway.'

When my grandma was gone again, I pulled out my notebook from underneath my pillow. I wrote: *My grandma understands and doesn't understand.* Then I turned to the next page. I wrote: *The story of my mother.*

I pulled the box with Mum's things out from under my bed and took each item into my hands again. Then I wrote down everything I knew. When I got to the bottom of the page, I realized I had quite a lot of information.

I had place names and a photograph.

I had time and a car.

And I had no reason to stay here.

27

I was twelve when my mum decided I was old enough to learn to drive a car. 'Your legs are long enough now,' she said.

Mum gave me theory lessons on the car park in front of our block. She explained where the brakes, the accelerator and the clutch were. She taught me that cars coming from the right always had priority, unless I was faster. She explained how fast I was allowed to drive on which road and which gear I should use there. And she showed me her favourite songs to listen to while driving. There were songs for the night and songs for the day.

Sometimes we played I spy. But when you're sitting in a parked car, then I spy gets boring pretty quickly. So we modified the game. Mum slipped a CD into the player, reclined the passenger seat and put up her feet on the dashboard. Once the music started, she closed her eyes. Sometimes I guessed what my mum was seeing and sometimes I didn't.

She saw country roads that wound through dark green forests. She saw mountains and rocks that glowed red in the sun. She saw the Hungarian Puszta with its fields and steppes and the wind that blew.

I always saw the sea.

For the practical part, Mum drove to the supermarket car park with me one Sunday evening.

'Off we go,' she said, and pressed the car keys into my hand. I didn't feel at all ready. I pressed the clutch and turned the key in the ignition. The engine bubbled and I dug my fingers into the plush steering wheel cover. My mum rested her hand gently on my T-shirt, exactly in the place where my heart was beating.

'Breathe in, breathe out. You can do this.'

I took a deep breath in and out. I wanted to set off. I took my foot off the clutch, and in the same instant the car jumped forward and the engine died. I had no idea what I'd done wrong.

'You said I can do this.'

'Yes, but not on your first attempt.'

'How many is it going to take?'

'How should I know? Maybe forty-two times.'

I said nothing. I felt deceived.

Mum took hold of my chin and turned my head gently in her direction. 'It takes a while for the body to learn what the head is telling it. But at some point it becomes second nature. You'll see.' She smiled.

'Are you sure?' I asked.

'I'm sure,' she said.

And Mum was right.

Almost right, at least.

Everything went smoothly the second time around. I drove out of the car park like I'd been born with a gearstick in my hand. I waved to my grandma in the rear-view mirror. She couldn't see me, of course. My grandma was lying in the living room on the air mattress and our block of flats lay behind me in the rising sun.

On my first attempt I'd stalled the Nissan and then I'd almost run Luna and Ahmed over. I'd adjusted the rear-view mirror and put on the white sunglasses I'd found among my mum's things. The cowboy boots were on the back seat, together with all the other stuff I'd taken. If you're planning on living in a car, then it's not enough to just take your toothbrush, although a toothbrush is a good start. I'd taken my swimming costume too, just in case. I didn't know yet where I was going to shower along the way, but I knew there were a lot of perverts who liked nothing more than watching you.

I'd turned the key in the ignition and let the clutch come up, just like Mum had taught me. The Nissan jumped forward and then stalled. I turned the music louder and closed my eyes. I imagined Mum's hand on my back. I breathed in and out. Clutch, first gear, accelerate, biting point. The Nissan started rolling, but before I could even think about changing gear, there was such a loud bang that my heart almost slid into the footwell.

When I opened my eyes, I saw Luna and Ahmed. They were right in front of the bumper. Luna was rubbing her hand. I wound down the window. 'Are you crazy?'

'Damn hard bodywork,' Luna said and grinned.

'I almost ran you over.'

'We almost missed you,' Luna said. Then she opened the passenger door and dropped into the seat.

Ahmed got in the back. He was holding his prayer mat like a newborn. 'We wouldn't let you go alone,' he said and leaned back.

'Off we go,' Luna said and wrapped a strand of hair around her finger. Luna's hair was almost blonde again. It just had a slight tinge of pink. I ran my hand over my wig. A few hairs were sticking up. 'Are we off now or what?' she asked and drummed her fingers on her thighs.

But I didn't set off. I couldn't. I'd had a plan. The plan was to drive alone.

Luna was chattering, and Ahmed was unfolding a map. I pictured Luna's head doing crazy things and me having to protect her from herself. I pictured having to stop constantly so Ahmed could unfold his prayer mat. I clutched the steering wheel with my hands.

'What is it?' Luna asked.

I didn't know what to say. She'd given me her mum's money without a second thought. I didn't want to hurt her feelings. But I couldn't sit here forever.

'I need to be alone,' I said. Speaking the truth was harder than any lie. I didn't dare look at Luna and Ahmed. Both of them had a good reason to want to get away from here.

At first they said nothing. Then Ahmed said: 'But you're only fourteen. You will get lost and then someone will rob you out in the sticks.'

'What's anyone supposed to steal?' I asked. 'My toothbrush?' I thought of how my mum had said almost the same things when she left our front door open at night to let some air in.

'I get you, sweetie,' Luna said. 'It's okay.' And then she said to Ahmed: 'Come on, let's go.'

I knew that if Luna had learned one thing in her life it was not imposing on others. That made it much worse. 'Wait,' I said to Luna.

'Yes?'

I pulled the bundle of money from my trousers and gave it to her. 'I found our winnings,' I said. 'And I know you need the money.'

Luna gave me a kiss on the cheek. 'Come on, Ahmed, let's go party,' she said, and winked at me.

'I will pray for you, Billie,' Ahmed said, opening the door, and I thought that God had quite a lot He'd have to do with me.

And then I was alone.

28

'You're always alone in the end,' Mum once said. Our forest walk finished near the cemetery. 'In the end, the only thing that takes care of you is nature,' she said and stumbled over a tree root. Her heel broke off and she swore in Hungarian. 'Crap shoes.'

The cemetery was no ordinary cemetery with gravestones. People were buried under trees here. Each had their own tree, and on each tree there was a small sign with a number on it.

After Luna and Ahmed had disappeared, there was no one left to hold my hand. There was no one left to tell me what to do.

I wasn't sure if Mum had been right. I didn't know if this was a beginning or an end. Perhaps it was both together. The only thing that was clear was that I wasn't used to being alone. For a brief moment I even wished that my grandma was here with me, and of course that was stupid.

Luna and Ahmed had barely got out of the car when I started talking to myself. I looked at the road with one eye, and with the other I looked at the little compass Ahmed had forgotten. I'd stuck the compass onto the dashboard with chewing gum. The little needle quivered around the big N. I looked at the compass and said: 'I'm like a migrating bird that's lost its way.' I felt stupid as soon as I said the sentence.

I stopped the car and took my notebook out of my backpack. I turned it around and drew a bird on the first new page, and then I wrote the sentence about the migratory bird. Underneath I wrote a second sentence: *I am one who has lost her mother.* Obviously that didn't fill the page; there was still so much space that I suddenly felt quite dizzy.

I'd calculated that I could make it to the coast in around twelve hours. This wasn't America, and I wasn't Sal Paradise. I wouldn't need months to drive from one side of the country to the other. Another advantage was that I didn't need to steal a car first. I had one. And I wasn't just driving into the blue. I had something to do. I needed to find my father.

But I hadn't factored life into the equation – I should have known something always gets in the way. That same day, I realized it would take longer. The journey would take me more than seventy-two hours.

I stuck my notebook behind the sun visor and set off again. I drove onto our autobahn and then straight off again. My legs were shaking and felt like jelly. Driving 120 kph with Mum felt different from driving 120 kph by myself.

I stopped at the side of the road and took a few breaths in and out. Ahead of me were fields on the edge of the forest, behind me was the city; the autobahn lay in between. I ate a chocolate bar and pulled out my notebook again. I wrote: *The Nissan is a rocket, and I am an astronaut, but without training.*

I decided to take smaller roads instead. No one cared how fast or how slowly I drove on those roads. I could drive at sixty or a hundred and ten. But everyone still sounded their horn at me anyway. I hadn't thought about traffic lights. They never stayed green, and I put my foot down when I should have braked, and braked when I should have put my foot down.

I drove until I got tired. I had no idea how long I'd been travelling. The radio in the Nissan didn't work. Some idiot had torn off the aerial. And the clock was broken too. I decided to buy myself a watch at the next opportunity. But fortunately there are lots of opportunities to serve God in the countryside. Every village had a church and almost every church had a clock.

So I carried on driving.

In the next village, I realized I'd only been on the road for two and a half hours. How come I was so tired already? I thought about stopping there and then and going straight to sleep. But I might as well have stood on the village square with a sign around my neck that said *I'm an underage runaway who's stolen their mother's car. Please arrest me!*

As the village disappeared behind me, the country road went through a forest. The leaves sailed from the trees, and the sky was blue and wide. Autumn did everything it could to make it as easy as possible for me.

I stopped the Nissan in a hikers' parking area and then I walked into the forest. I stopped at a raised hide. I climbed up the ladder, and because the rungs creaked beneath my feet I hurried. The high seat had a door. I knocked just in case, but there was no one there.

It was dim and warm inside, and it smelled of wood. The sun shone through the gaps in the wooden panels, and the floor was clean, like someone had recently swept it. I laid my coat on the floor and sat down. The leaves rustled above me, and a bird sang somewhere. Otherwise it was quiet. I took out my notebook and wrote: *Nature doesn't care where I am. Nature doesn't care if I even am.* Then I curled up on the lining of my coat like an embryo.

When I woke up, I was cold, and I had no idea how long I'd slept. On the way back to the car, I realized I'd forgotten to lock it. But the Nissan was still there. It was the most beautiful heap of junk I'd ever seen. I dug around in the glove compartment for a CD, pushed it into the slot, turned up the heating and drove off. Janis Joplin sang that freedom was just another word for having nothing left to lose, and because Mum had once said exactly the same thing, I wondered if she'd stolen her other sayings too.

I thought about what Mum had said to my grandma during the argument. 'At least I'm free!' she'd said, and I wondered what she'd exchanged her freedom for. What had my mum given up? And why? Had it been worth it? And why did my grandma not seem to be able to understand her? 'What does that even mean?' she'd asked. Now at least Mum had nothing left to lose. But what's the use of being free when you're dead?

Once, when I was still small, I'd dreamed that my mum died. When I'd woken up, Mum had hugged me tight. It was a real bone-breaker of a hug. 'I don't want you to die,' I said and pressed my damp face against her. And my mum had whispered: 'One day I will die, Billie. That's the way it has to be. Mothers always go first. No mum can bear to lose her child.' Perhaps she'd seen my horrified face; in any case, she quickly added: 'But by then you'll be big and won't need me any more.'

I switched off the music. The car sounded good. No strange noises. Suddenly I thought I could drive all the way to Hungary in it. I didn't know how many kilometres it was to the border, but I knew Budapest was very far away.

My stomach was growling. I tried to unwrap a sandwich from the foil, but when I almost came off the road, I stopped by the side of the road with my hazard lights on and laughed at myself. If I carried on like this, I wouldn't arrive until Christmas. And I wasn't sure if I'd recognize my father's garden in the snow. Everything looked different with snow.

I started scoffing the sandwich and drank the Coke in huge gulps. When I needed to burp, I burped my grandma's name. She'd probably already notified the police, although I'd left her a note telling her not to worry. I'd just shoved the last bite into my mouth when there was a knock.

A man knocked on my window like on a door: *Knock, knock, knock.* I hadn't seen him coming. I was startled and choked so badly that tears shot into my eyes. I remembered what Ahmed had said. I wound the window down a little bit.

'Do you need help?' the man asked.

'All good, thanks,' I said and forced myself to breathe slowly.

His clothes were all the same colour, green or brown or something in between. A gun was slung over his shoulder. I'd never seen a hunter except on the telly.

'Are you sure everything's all right?' he asked and looked past me into the car. His gaze travelled over the pillows and the blanket, over the sweets on the passenger seat, the books, my clothes and Mum's things. He wouldn't have known the things belonged to my mum, though, even if I hadn't put them into a sports bag. 'Are you living in here?' he asked.

'No!' I said. 'We're just moving house.'

The man crossed his arms in front of his chest. They were strong. You could see that despite his coat.

'I recognize a runaway when I see one.'

I wondered if he'd call the police or the CPS or whoever. But then he shrugged and said: 'Well, you'll have your reasons…'

'No one does anything without a reason.' He was starting to get on my nerves.

'Either way, you should be careful. Some guys might not mean well when they see your doe eyes.'

I stayed silent, and he stared at me. I counted the seconds in my head. I got to four. Four seconds is a heck of a long time. It seemed quite likely that he was a pervert. I let my sunglasses drop from the top of my wig onto my nose.

'Can I see the gun?' I asked, and I wound down the window a little bit more. I felt that someone who might be a pervert shouldn't run around with a gun.

The hunter removed the gun from his shoulder and held it out to me. I touched the barrel. The metal was smooth and cool.

'Feels nice,' I said. I imagined how nice it would be to have a gun to protect me. I pictured myself pulling the gun into the car in a single movement. I pictured myself driving off so fast that the wheels spun. But then I pulled my hand back and asked: 'Can I have it?'

Then he laughed. 'Are you mad?'

'I might well be,' I said.

'No,' he said when he'd calmed down. 'Of course you can't have it.' He touched his hat and turned to leave.

'Excuse me?' I asked.

'Yes?'

'Could you tell me what time it is?'

He looked at his watch. 'Almost four.'

'Oh,' I exclaimed, because I'd slept so long.

'Did you miss an appointment?' the hunter asked.

I thought of Mrs Geiger's plan on my room door, and then I shook my head. 'There are no appointments in the place where I'm going.' I only said it to make it true. And I said it especially loudly.

The hunter laughed. 'Sounds like a nice place.'

'Yes.'

'Well then, have a good trip,' he said, and then he walked off. I watched in the rear-view mirror as he grew smaller.

I drove for a while without thinking, and most of the time I just drove straight ahead. I'd mapped out my route. I had only covered a small part.

There was a difference between driving in circles on a supermarket car park and driving to the coast on real roads with real traffic signs. I knew roughly what most of them meant, but I was sure all the other drivers knew what to do. So I stuck with them and didn't worry about it.

As the sun went down, the air grew cooler and damper. It smelled good, of forest, meadows and water. Better than in the city. I wound the window down to let the wind blow in my face. I considered whether I should drive at night too. But the right headlight was still broken, and the weather looked like it would get foggy. I hadn't thought about where I'd sleep. I knew I'd sleep in the car, but not where I might park the car. I tried to imagine what it would be like to sleep in the forest. But the trees had faces at night and whispered to each other. I tried to imagine how it would be to sleep in a village, in a car park or in the entrance to an abandoned house. But people weren't good at minding their own business. They'd probably call the police and then this journey would have been pointless.

So the forest.

I continued until the world ahead of me began to blur. The trees on the side of the road were just shadows against the whiteness, and the nothingness right in front of me seemed endless. I needed to find a place for the night right away. Even now it was almost impossible to see where the forest began and where it ended. But then the country road suddenly twisted straight through the forest. I just had to take one of the forest tracks and turn off it.

I parked between the trees and switched off the engine. It was too early to go to sleep, but I still locked all the doors, at least all except the passenger door, pushed the driver's seat as far back as it would go, and took off my shoes. I put a pillow behind my back and the blanket over my legs. I dug out the candle I'd brought along, and the lighter. Then I put the burning candle in a cup and put the cup on the dashboard.

It was as quiet as a church in the car. The silence flowed through me like I wasn't even there. The Nissan locked the world out, but I couldn't escape the world in spite of that.

I opened up my notebook and wrote: *I am the inside of the forest. I am the night. I am the fog.*

After a while I felt cold. I switched on the engine and turned the heating all the way up. But as soon as I switched off the engine again, the cold returned and crept through the passenger door into the car. I thought the passenger door fitted our life perfectly. It more or less worked, but you constantly needed solutions for problems that others didn't have. I'd never wondered why we lived the way we did or if my mum was to blame. I'd never wondered whether we might have had a different life. It was simply the way it was. Suddenly I thought that our life was like a painting hanging right in front of my nose. I was too close. When you're too close, then you see all the details, but you don't see how they fit together.

I took the sports bag with all my mum's things and removed one item after the other. I put the photo of my mum with me in her arms in the candlelight. Mum looked happy. I'd never seen her so happy. Sometimes she was happy, sometimes she was unhappy, but neither for very long. She'd barely been happy when she was already on her way to being unhappy, and vice versa. It was like Mum's heart had had a defect. It couldn't beat at a normal pace; it was always beating a bit too fast.

After three hours, my teeth could have chattered because of the cold, but I didn't let them. I clenched my jaw tightly. It's pointless to chatter your teeth if there's no one to hear you and run you a hot bath.

I wrote: *Freezing to death is a nice death. You just fall asleep.*

I checked my trouser pocket for the hundredth time that day. The money was still there. In the dim candlelight, a big soft bed with a thick duvet appeared in front of me. But I knew I wouldn't find a hotel that didn't ask questions.

I put on all the clothes I had with me on top of each other, and started the engine once again. Then I leaned back, put my hands under the blanket and waited for sleep to come.

But it didn't.

Instead the thoughts did.

I wrote: *I miss you. Where are you?*

I missed my mum so much that I wrapped one of her T-shirts around the pillow. I held it to my face and breathed in deeply although I knew I shouldn't. It was my birthday in a few hours. I realized it would be the loneliest birthday ever. Either way, I might as well start feeling lonely now. It made no difference.

My mum had always woken me up with a chocolate cake on my birthdays, and I was allowed to miss the first lesson. There had always been a single sparkler in the chocolate cake, regardless of how old I was. And each year Mum told me how she'd looked into my eyes for the first time. 'You weren't planned,' she said. That was all I knew about my conception. 'But I loved you from the first second.'

She told me that as a baby my eyes had been green, as green as the lake in our nature reserve when the sun shone on it.

'You had a special gaze. You were wise from the first moment. Much wiser than me.'

My mum always took the day off on my birthday and I was allowed to choose what we did. It had always been my big dream to drive to the sea. But of course I knew Mum needed me to wish for something she could actually do. And I didn't disappoint her.

Once I'd wished to go to a furniture store. We walked through the aisles and pictured how we'd furnish our flat. My mum was obsessed with the bedrooms. We got into the biggest and softest bed we could find.

Then a saleswoman appeared and said: 'You can't just lie here.'

'Why not?' Mum asked. She'd crossed her arms behind her head and pulled the covers up to the tip of her nose. Her shoes were next to the bed. My mum would never get into a bed with her shoes on. Before the saleswoman could reply, Mum continued: 'We are testing the bed. How am I supposed to buy a bed I haven't tested first? How am I supposed to know whether the little one won't get backache?'

It was clear as day that we weren't going to buy the bed. Not this one and not a different one.

The saleswoman said: 'This isn't a hotel.'

My mum said: 'Oh really? The service is better in a hotel. Come on, Billie, we're going.'

I was allowed to choose something from the odds and ends section. I chose a notebook. It was dark blue and had a starry sky with silver glitter on the front. An astronaut floated among the stars and underneath it said LOST IN SPACE.

A year later, on my eleventh birthday, I wished for a visit to the planetarium. Shortly before we set off, Mum handed me a package. 'A birthday without a surprise isn't a proper birthday, right?' she said, like every year.

The T-shirt was grey, and a blue circle represented outer space. The word NASA was written in white letters in the circle.

I fell into my mum's arms. She stroked my hair and tucked a strand of hair behind my ear. 'Maybe you'll be an astronaut,' she said with a smile. 'Just in case your career as a writer doesn't work out.'

That evening, when we sank back into the cushioned chairs in the darkened room, I knew something exciting was about to happen. The black dome above our heads slowly filled with stars and planets, and I was sure I'd never seen anything as beautiful in my life.

'I've only ever seen that many stars in Hungary,' Mum had said, and her whispering was so loud that the other visitors turned to look at us.

I buried my nose in my mum's T-shirt one more time. I was like an addict, and the smell of Mum was my opium. I smelled our washing powder, I smelled Mum's deodorant and a little bit of her sweat. I breathed in Mum's skin, I breathed in my home and I cried. Then I fell asleep.

At some point I was woken by a bang. The T-shirt was still on my face. I was confused, I knew nothing, but I clearly wasn't dead. Blood rushed in my ears, and my body trembled. I didn't move and listened into the dark. But everything stayed silent. I remembered Luna's hand on the bonnet. But who'd bang on my car in the middle of the night in a forest? I stared out of the window. The fog had lifted a bit, and it was windy. Perhaps a branch had fallen on the car, or a pine cone. But the longer I thought about it, the more uncertain I became whether the noise might have only been in my head. I was so cold I could barely move. My body was completely stiff. Perhaps it had woken me before I froze to death. I had no idea how many more times I'd sleep in the car. I didn't just need a watch, I also needed a sleeping bag.

29

As soon as the sun came up, I set off again. I'd looked closely at Ahmed's map as soon as there was enough daylight. The route to the sea looked much longer than on mine, but this was probably because the scale was smaller. Each tiny village and country lane was shown.

I was starving, but when I thought of the chocolate bars on the passenger seat or the eight-pack of salami sticks, I felt sick. I wanted a proper birthday breakfast. I wanted freshly squeezed orange juice and soft rolls with butter and honey, and I wanted hard-boiled eggs with salt and mustard.

I passed a few bakeries and cafes. The lights were on in some of them. I could have just gone inside. But as soon as I pictured myself sitting there, I saw an overweight elderly lady with a perm and an apron. She'd hand me a sticky laminated menu. She'd also give me the feeling that she knew more about me than I did. That's how it was in the countryside, I knew that from my mum. 'But in the end it doesn't matter where you are,' she'd said when I asked her if she preferred living in the country or in the city. 'Most people don't care about you. Most look and only see themselves.' Then she'd hugged me and said: 'But I care about you. I see you.'

Now there was no one to see me any more.

Now everyone just saw a girl with blue hair and too-big

sunglasses. And that was more noticeable in the country than in the city. That was obvious.

I followed the next signpost to the autobahn. I wanted to eat in a place where no one asked any questions. Shortly before the slip road, I dug my fingers into the plush cover of the steering wheel, and then I put my foot down. For a moment I closed my eyes, and a prayer shot through my head. But it was just a reflex, like when the doctor taps your knee. I knew I couldn't rely on God. The second my mum breathed out for the last time, God left me hanging.

I drove to the nearest service station.

The site was large and confusing. I parked in front of a red brick building and got out. It smelled of exhaust fumes and frying fat.

In the restaurant, I sat down at a table by the glass front. Then I waited to be served. At the table in front of me was a mother with a little girl. The girl was wearing a tulle skirt covered with sequins. The skirt reminded me of Mum's tutu. The girl's blonde hair was elaborately plaited and wrapped around her head.

The mother was drinking coffee and reading a magazine, while the candyfloss girl was wiping ketchup on the window. She was using a chip as a paintbrush. She kept dunking the chip back into the puddle of ketchup on her plate. She painted a sky with clouds, a moon and lots of stars. But at some point the chip got squishy, and the girl now used both hands to paint the outlines. When she was done, she wiped her hands on her skirt, inspected her artwork and smiled. The people at the neighbouring table watched and whispered. And then the girl's mother looked up. She first went pale, then red. She jumped up fast, like someone had set fire to her chair. She grabbed the girl's arm and turned her towards her. The child tried to get out of her grip and started to cry. The mother let the child go, pulled one serviette after another from the holder on the table and tried to clean the window. But she made everything worse. The starry sky disappeared, and the window looked like someone had been shot right in front of it. The girl screamed like crazy, and the mother bent down towards her.

Then she hit her.

She hit the girl twice in the face, first on the left cheek, then on the right. I heard the smack, I heard the sob, and then everything happened at the same time.

Suddenly I was the girl.

Suddenly the girl was my mum.

Suddenly I had the girl in my arms.

Suddenly there were two men blocking my path. Almost at the same time, the mother came running over. The girl screamed 'Mama!' and the mother opened her arms.

And then I ran.

I ran straight across the car park. I just wanted to get away, but I couldn't find the car. Where the hell had I parked the Nissan?

At some point I turned around, but the two men had disappeared. I flopped down on a bench. I had a stitch and no idea what had happened. I must have run to the other side of the service station. Everything looked completely different. Next to me was a lorry park, and in front of me was a petrol station. Diagonally behind, on the edge of the forest, was a low, flat-roofed building with colourful neon signs on it. The building was painted mint green, and the windows were framed in red. When I got closer, I saw the sign above the entrance. One letter after the other, lit up in red: D-I-N-E-R. The letters blinked in time with the rhythm of my heart.

I pictured the pancakes, the burger and the milkshake on my table before I'd even gone through the door. I knew I'd landed in a magical place.

The place was empty except for an old man and the waitress. The old man was pretty ancient. He had his bony back towards me and was bent over in a booth. I heard him stirring his drink with a spoon.

I didn't see the waitress at first. She stood motionless behind the counter. When our gazes met, she didn't acknowledge my greeting, just smiled. Her smile was heavenly. It was the icing on the cake. I'd never seen such a beautiful woman in my life. The walls were covered in ads for household appliances and cocoa. She looked like she'd simply stepped out of one of them. She wore a yellow skirt, a red sleeveless blouse and a white apron over it. The apron had lace around the edges. She'd tied her dark hair back in a tight ponytail.

Of course I knew she lived somewhere and that she cut her toenails in her flat and all that stuff. But I couldn't imagine finding her anywhere but here. Here, the seats and stools were covered in red leather, the floor was tiled in black and white, and there was a jukebox in the corner.

I sat down and studied the menu. When the waitress came and poured me some coffee without asking, I ordered a feast. She didn't take notes, and I wondered how she could remember it all.

It didn't take long for the food to come. The waitress put everything down on my table, and then returned to her spot by the steaming coffee machine behind the counter without a word. Perhaps she was mute, or didn't speak any German.

I scoffed the lot. I wanted to lick the plate. When I'd sucked the last bits of the milkshake from the glass, I waved to the waitress to show I wanted to pay. But she didn't move. Only when I got up to go to the counter did she nod towards the corner where the man sat. I had no idea what she was trying to tell me. But then the man turned around. I hadn't been wrong, he looked as though he was a thousand years old from the front too. He said a single sentence. He said: 'It's on the house,' and winked at me. It was a nice wink, not like those Heinz gave. I looked back at the waitress, but she just shrugged. I didn't object to it being on the house, so I didn't ask any questions.

The old man got up and shuffled over to the jukebox. He fumbled awkwardly in his trouser pockets for a coin. He pushed it into the slot, and a moment later a song began that I didn't recognize. But my English was good enough. A woman's voice sang the chorus: '*Happy Birthday, Billie Blue.*'

Okay, I made up the bit about Billie Blue, but the rest is true, even the thing about it being on the house. I had no idea how the man knew it was my birthday. It's quite possible that he was crazy and did the same for everyone. But it didn't matter either way.

In any case, when I stepped outside, I was pretty calm. Perhaps this was why it was easy to find the Nissan again. I opened up my notebook in the car. I wrote: *God is a skinny old man, and he didn't forget my birthday.*

Of course I knew the old man wasn't really God. God didn't just sit around in a diner. On the other hand I had no idea what He did all day, so how could I be one hundred per cent sure?

30

The longer I drove, the simpler it was to be on the road. I tried not to think. I didn't think about the fact that the Nissan might break down. I didn't think about the fact that I might not find my dad's house. I didn't think about the fact that our winnings might be used up at some point. I locked all the 'what if' thoughts into a box and threw away the key. There were still enough other thoughts left over. Sometimes I thought about my grandma and how she was probably already going mad with worry. Then I pictured her praying her rosary with shaking hands. I pictured her putting an extra spoonful of sugar in her tea to calm her nerves. I tried to shake off my feelings of guilt and looked at the road, the houses, the trees and the sky instead. I was so far away from home already, but still much too close. Occasionally I looked at the compass. The compass had led Ahmed to God; hopefully it would lead me to the sea. But until that was the case, I had a few things to organize. I didn't want to drive to a city, but cities were the best place to organize things.

I'd never stolen anything as big as a sleeping bag. Even when it was rolled up, it would be hard to hide. It wouldn't fit into my backpack or under my sweatshirt.

I thought of Lea. She'd have had an idea. She always had one. I'd learned my best tricks from her.

*

It had all started with the lipstick.

I never told anyone about it. I didn't want Mum to find out. She'd have been ashamed of me.

'Come on, let's go to the shopping centre,' Lea said.

We were sitting in her room and flicking through one of her magazines. I didn't feel like going to the shopping centre. The heat was making me sluggish, and I was thinking about the book that lay open on my bed.

'You can read that under the covers with your torch tonight,' Lea said, took my hand and pulled me up.

We sat right at the back in the bus. Lea drew a heart on the backrest of the seat in front of us with a felt tip, and wrote a B and an L in the middle. At that moment I felt like we were Thelma and Louise; at that moment I believed we'd be friends forever.

'Only very young and very old people believe in eternity,' Mum said when I told her about this belief.

Now I knew she'd been right.

Now I know Lea loved me for being different and that she hated me for it at the same time.

For some reason, Lea had believed I loved danger. But she was the one who enjoyed walking out of a shop with a bag full of things. I just wanted to make my mum happy with the lipstick. It was her birthday, and I was too old to paint her a picture. That was all.

Anyway, we were sitting on a bench outside a department store. Lea looked me in the eye. That look was enough to make me do anything. I was helpless to resist. And so I knew I wouldn't just be watching today.

'Are you excited?'

I nodded. I couldn't hide things from Lea.

'Stealing is like magic. The magician does two things at the same time, but the audience only sees one of them.'

'Which one?' I asked.

Lea smiled. She tucked a curl behind my ear, and her hand brushed against my cheek. Her touch was cool on my warm skin. 'They only see what the magician wants them to see. They only see the distraction.' She reached behind her, put on her sunglasses and smiled. It took a moment for me to understand. Her hand on my face. Her hand in my hair. I felt the pocket on the front of my T-shirt. It was empty. Lea gave me back my sunglasses. 'Ready?'

I nodded. I told myself it was only a small lipstick, not a bank robbery. I told myself Mum had earned this lipstick. I told myself what Lea said: it's not so bad stealing from rich people. But the truth was that I didn't want to disappoint Lea.

She told me what I was supposed to do. I would distract the saleswoman first, then she would. 'You go in first,' said Lea. 'I'll join you in five minutes.'

In the make-up department, I asked a saleswoman what eyeshadow would go best with my eyes. 'Blue,' she said. She bent down and started searching.

I looked around for Lea and spotted her by the shelf of ladies' perfumes. Everything about her was delicate. She looked perfectly innocent. Her hair was very soft, much softer than mine. Her legs were long and her wrists thin. They were so thin that she'd lost the bracelet I'd given her for her birthday. Her eyes were blue, but only the left one had three tiny golden flecks in the middle. If I was oil, then Lea was fire.

The saleswoman stood up and turned back to me. 'Let's start with this one,' she said and pointed to a little tin. Then she took a brush and started applying the colour to one eyelid. When I looked at myself in the mirror, a stranger stared back at me. It looked like someone had given me a black eye.

'I'm looking for a perfume for my mother,' Lea said. She stood behind us, and when we turned around, she smiled at the saleswoman. Quickly, before the woman could reply, I said: 'It's all right, I'll take it. Thank you very much for your help.'

I took a few deep breaths. I looked around. No one was looking at me. The saleswoman was showing Lea several perfumes. And I slipped a lipstick into my pocket. It was dead easy. Then I went to the till with the eyeshadow.

We met outside. Lea pulled two bottles of perfume from her backpack and handed me one. 'This is for you,' she said.

I hesitated.

'It suits your type.'

I sprayed it on my wrist.

'Syrian rose, magnolia and cedarwood.'

Lea was right. I liked the smell.

'Did you get the lipstick?' she asked.

It was still in my pocket. I pulled it out. The case shone black.

'Good choice. Chanel is really expensive.' Lea gave it back to me.

'How expensive?'

'34.95.'

My heart jumped. For 34.95 we could almost fill an entire trolley at the discount store. I could go to the pool ten times. Mum could fill up the Nissan with petrol and drive 500 kilometres.

We'd have made it to Italy. There was no way I could give my mum this lipstick. She'd immediately know what was what. I was angry with myself. Why had I stolen the most expensive lipstick?

'Wait here,' Lea said, and when she came back: 'Close your eyes and open your hands.' The lipstick was unremarkable and the case was made of cheap plastic.

'4.95,' my friend said and grinned.

It was perfect. I didn't ask if she'd bought or stolen it.

When Mum opened the lipstick a few days later, she was as delighted as if I'd given her a new car. She danced around the flat. She painted her lips red. Then I was covered in kisses. With each kiss, she called out my name. I laughed, and Mum carried on until I was covered in red marks.

I thought about whether I should simply buy the sleeping bag and the watch. But petrol was expensive and the tank was almost empty. I pictured myself simply driving off at the petrol station. I pictured myself being chased by the police with sirens and flashing lights. I'd turn up the music full blast, fire off three warning shots from the open window and disappear across the meadows and fields. The only problem was that the hunter hadn't given me his gun and that the Nissan was only a Nissan.

I followed the signs to the town centre.

And then I saw the case on the side of the road. It was a case for transporting musical instruments. It was in a pile of bulky waste. I had no idea which instrument the case was for, but that didn't matter. It was big enough. I stopped. The case looked used and the shoulder strap was torn. It was perfect. I put it in the boot.

The department store was almost empty, and I had all the time in the world. I could look around in peace and quiet. No one suspected a person who moved around a department store like it was their own living room.

I smiled at the salespeople and they smiled back.

I asked a salesman where I could find sheet music and he told me. I took the escalator to the right floor and then asked again.

Then I went to the camping department.

When I'd finished doing what I wanted to do, I got in the queue at the till with the sheet music in my hand. It was so easy. Department stores like this made things easy for a girl like me.

31

I bought myself a soft ice cream in the pedestrian precinct. It was so ridiculously small that I finished it in about ten seconds. Then I pressed my nose against the windows of the expensive shops. They were displaying winter coats, gloves and scarves. The mannequins looked very elegant. I liked one coat in particular. It was dark green and had a fur collar. The mannequin was also wearing red leather gloves and a red hat. I imagined how it would feel to wear the coat and daydreamed.

The houses on the other side of the street were reflected in the shop windows. So were the people who trickled past. Suddenly I saw a figure behind me that looked familiar. Before I could even think clearly, I knew. It was my mum. I turned around, but she was nowhere to be seen. I felt hot and cold at the same time. I put the instrument box down. Then I slid to the ground. I clenched the box between my legs and clasped it with both arms like it was a boyfriend. I sat like this until the sweat on my forehead had dried.

In the car I removed the sleeping bag from the packaging and rolled it out. It was filled with down. The label said it was suitable up to minus 18 degrees. I could have spent a summer night at the North Pole in it. I put the alarm clock on the passenger seat. It had been impossible to steal a watch. All the watches were displayed in glass cases and double-locked. But the alarm clock was made of cheap plastic and had been in a cardboard box on a shelf. It seemed to be made to be lost while camping. No one would shed a tear for it.

Ideally I'd have already crawled onto the back seat. Ideally I'd have curled up in the sleeping bag like a kitten in its mother's fur. But I hadn't showered for three days, and the sleeping bag was my bed now. And there's nothing better than getting into bed after a shower. I had no idea how I was supposed to get one. But then I remembered that Mum and I had showered in the swimming pool a couple of times when our warm water had been switched off. We hadn't paid the bill in time. Every decent city had a swimming pool. I just had to find it.

First I moved the Nissan. I parked it in an official car park, but with the passenger door so close to some bushes that no one could see the broken door. Then I stuffed my swimming costume, some clean clothes, a towel, shower gel and my notebook into my backpack.

I asked a few people the way to the swimming pool. Some sent me in one direction, the others in another. There were probably two swimming pools.

The pool I got to looked like a spaceship from the outside. The roof gleamed silver, the building was round and made of glass, and the inside was brightly lit.

In our swimming pool, you could simply step over the turnstile if the ticket seller was on a cigarette break. And in winter, when the pool was closed, you could sneak into the indoor pool through the supervisor's entrance.

But this was something else. The entrance hall was enormous, and there were four ticket windows. There were cameras above each one. There was also a shop to buy bikinis and other swimming things, and a cash machine. I got in the queue. When the ticket seller named the entrance price, I almost felt sick. I immediately started translating the amount in my head. I converted it to petrol, lunch and books.

'But I just want to shower,' I said. 'Is that cheaper?'

The ticket seller just laughed at me. She laughed so loudly that people turned around to look at us. My cheeks were burning. I knew she deserved the finger. She deserved for me to just turn around and leave. But I thought of the warm water and the sleeping bag. And so I didn't give her the finger but a banknote.

My mum would have felt ashamed of me. But it had always been important to her to be clean. Most expensive shower in the world or not.

This was my very personal beginning of the month.

And if I had to pay a heap of money, I might as well have a bit of fun. After all, the spaceship wasn't a normal swimming pool but an adventure pool. At least that's what it said on the big sign near the main entrance.

There were so many pools that I could barely decide which one to jump in first. There was one with salt water, one with fresh water, one with a lagoon and a waterfall, and one with waves. Some were warm, some cold, some were square, some were round. Huge palm trees stood around the pools, and there was even a sandy beach in front of one of them. Water slides wound their way through the palm trees like the arms of an octopus. There were wooden huts with straw roofs everywhere. People on bar stools sat in and outside the huts and drank real cocktails.

I looked for diving platforms, but there weren't any.

I walked around in a circle beside the glass frontage until I ended up back where I started. The black outlines of birds were stuck on the windows and the screech of parrots could be heard in the air. It came from loudspeakers. They hung from the palm trees. I wondered how many birds had slammed into the windows so far. Could birds die from a bleed on the brain?

I sat on a sunlounger and opened my notebook. I wrote: *I have landed in a fake paradise.* Then I jumped into the saltwater pool and waited for the waves.

I'd shaved off my last tuft of hair before I left home. The good thing about having no hair was that there wasn't much to do when you got out of the water. The bad thing was that people stared at you. They thought you were either a freak or a cancer patient.

A gong sounded and then the first waves rolled in. I breathed out and let myself sink to the bottom. I opened my eyes. The water surface above me danced and glimmered.

And then I saw my mum for the second time. She floated right next to me in her white bikini and smiled at me. A billion air bubbles hung in her hair. When I reached out my arm towards her she moved away, like she'd been taken by a current. I pushed myself off the bottom of the pool and surfaced. I blinked. Then I spotted her disappearing among the other bathers by the edge of the pool.

I ran so fast that I almost slipped on the wet tiles. Then I was right behind her. I gripped her shoulder and she turned to me.

The woman in the white bikini looked at me in alarm.

I'd never seen her before.

I immediately let her go and raised my hands apologetically.

The encounter left a pressure inside me that I couldn't explain. It radiated from my heart into my whole body. It didn't matter how often I went down the slide or which pool I jumped into. The pressure was still there. It only let up in the shower.

I stood in a cloud of steam, and the hot water hammered against my body. The room was full of women. Their voices and laughter echoed from the walls, but I was completely alone.

The water washed everything away. The chlorine, the dirt and all the questions disappeared into the drain. I knew they'd come back, but for the moment everything was okay.

I showered for an eternity. I showered without worrying about the water or electricity meter. I showered for so long that my skin squeaked with cleanliness, the skin on the surface of my hands and feet swelled, and I was as wrinkled as a prune.

That evening I spoke to my mum.

I was cuddled up in my sleeping bag on the back seat, writing in my notebook.

I wrote: *I am a caterpillar in a cocoon.*

I was too tired to drive any more, so I'd just stayed in the car park in the town. I'd fixed foil to the windows for privacy. I always had a roll of foil in my backpack. You never knew when you might need it. Lea had shown me the trick with the aluminium foil. 'If you line your handbag with it,' she'd said, 'then the anti-theft device doesn't work any more.'

I pulled the sleeping bag up to the edge of my nose and talked to my mum like she was lying next to me.

I said: I know you're here with me.

I said: I know your heart can't rest. Why should it be any different now than before?

I said: I know you were in the trees and in the old man in the diner and in the shop window and in the woman in the white bikini. But I also know people can suddenly go mad.

I asked: Will you show me, because I want to settle the matter with Grandma.

I said: Please give me a sign.

And then it started to rain. The rain pelted steadily onto the roof of the car, and it sounded like music. It was the best lullaby my mum had ever sung for me.

32

The next day, I woke up feeling rested. When I removed the foil, the sun warmed my face. I knew I'd manage to travel a long way today.

I changed my clothes and cleaned my teeth. After all, I wasn't a homeless person. At the same moment I realized Mum would have been annoyed by that reasoning. 'Have you ever had a homeless person breathe on you?' she might have asked and crossed her arms in front of her chest. 'No? Well, how do you know they haven't cleaned their teeth?'

I only stopped three times.

The first and second time I just went to the toilet and bought some food, and the third time I filled up the car with petrol and called my grandma. And if I hadn't done that, I truly would have missed something.

It rang three times, then there was a crackling sound on the line. At first I thought my grandma had picked up the phone, because I could hear her voice. I was about to say something, but then I realized she'd recorded a message on the answering machine. Since when did we have an answering machine?

The message went something like: 'Billie, if you hear this, please come home. What were you thinking?' Then Luna's and Ahmed's voices came on. Ahmed said: 'We shouldn't have let you go on your own. Please call us!' And Luna said: 'Ahmed, we're not her babysitters – don't do anything stupid, sweetie, and please be careful!'

When my grandma started to sing, I hung up. It was simply too embarrassing. But also sweet in a way. I breathed in and out a few times and then called again. I told the answering machine that I was fine, that everything was going well, that they shouldn't worry about me, and that I'd be in touch again soon.

Then I carried on driving.

Since I'd set off, I'd been waiting for the world to change. And then the change had simply happened without me having noticed.

The countryside was flat and endless in front of me. The road led directly to the horizon, and sheep grazed in the distance. I stopped at the side of the road and got out. I took a deep breath. It smelled different, fruitier. Then I lit a cigarette. It was so windy that it took me three tries to light it. It was my first cigarette since I'd set off. There was no other car to be seen far and wide. I took my time to smoke. Then I put my notebook on the bonnet. I wrote: *I am driving into nowhere. If I carry on driving, I'll fall off the edge of the earth. And that's all right.*

I drove until the twilight laid itself in front of my eyes like a blue veil. I stopped in a village and parked in front of a primary school. The next day was Sunday, and I didn't have to worry. The building was old and beautiful. Colourful paper hands were stuck to the windows.

I decided to take an evening walk. A stream ran through the village. I walked along its banks. There were benches everywhere. I liked the fact that the mayor had thought about the children, the old people, the pregnant ladies and the sick. All the houses were red brick. It looked orderly in a good way. Smoke rose up into the sky from some of the chimneys. I thought that I'd like to show my mum how pretty the houses here were. But then I remembered that she must have known that.

I wandered on to the middle of the village. There was a church on a small hill. If you went up the steps from the street, you found yourself in a sandy courtyard. From there more steps led up to the entrance. I sat on the steps and wrote: *Perhaps I was never closer to God than now.*

I stayed sitting there until the first stars twinkled in the sky. There were more now than I'd ever seen in the city. I wondered if there were as many as in the grasslands of the puszta. Soon the entire sky was twinkling. It looked like God had thrown sequins around.

Back in the car, I took Mum's things out of the sports bag. I took each item into my hands and looked at it for a long time. I waited for them to start speaking to me.

I had no idea how to find out where my mum had lived. I looked at the photograph with the garden shed for the hundredth time but it could have been taken anywhere. The only thing I knew for sure was where she'd gone shopping and where she'd learned German. I removed the adult education certificates from the plastic sleeve and sniffed them. I don't know what I expected, but they smelled of nothing but old paper.

I closed my eyes. Then I pictured my mum in a classroom. The room has lots of windows and in front of one window is a big tree. The teacher comes in and greets the students. Everyone opens their books. The teacher asks what they did at the weekend. My mum puts her hand up and her bracelets jangle gently. The teacher calls on my mum: 'Yes, Marika?'

And then I knew what I had to do.

33

I turned the music up full blast and wound down my window. The morning air was mild. Large puffy clouds gathered in the sky. I didn't see any forests. I thought about what this sort of countryside was called. In my mind's eye a page from my geography book appeared. I saw a map of Germany divided into various regions. Moorland. It's called moorland. I kept holding my hand out of the window, feeling the air against it. I drove for hours without a break.

And then I saw the town sign.

The towns had had odd names for a while. They ended in -um and -oh and -ook. I took another look at the map to make sure. And yet I could have named the town in my sleep.

I was in the right place.

But before I looked for the adult education centre, I wanted to see the sea. It was no problem finding somewhere to park. If this area had one thing, it was space.

I didn't need a map to find the North Sea.

It was like something was guiding me in the right direction.

I followed a paved path. It ran behind the dunes at first and wound its way between them. The dunes blocked the view of the sea, but I could smell it. It smelled of salt and fish and seaweed. I walked faster and faster, it went uphill for a bit, and then I saw the beach. It was empty; only a few people were walking their dogs.

The blue-grey sea lay before me.

And because the rushing really was a bit like our autobahn, I started to cry.

First I just sat down in the sand.

But then I took all my clothes off except my underwear and ran into the water. It was cold, and I held my breath. But after a minute or two I'd got used to it. I went so far into the water that my toes only just touched the bottom. Then I waited for the next wave and let myself be carried. I dived under, and surfaced again, and it was like I was a million years old, like I was the water, the salt and the sand all at the same time.

It felt like coming home.

I swam out a bit further, and when I turned around, the people on the beach were tiny. Suddenly I heard the sound of an engine. A boat was coming straight towards me. There were two men on deck waving in my direction. They wore orange hi-vis jackets and looked like paramedics. When the boat got very close, I saw what was written on the hull. Three red letters. I had no idea what the letters stood for, but I realized it was a lifeboat.

Shit, I thought, and a moment later two strong arms pulled me out of the water as easily as if the ocean had made me weightless.

'Are you mad, girl?' one of the men shouted, and the other one wrapped a blanket around my shoulders. The blanket shone like gold. I looked like an astronaut, but the luxury version.

'Why?' I wanted to ask, but out came 'W-Wh-Why?' because my teeth were chattering so badly.

'Were you trying to kill yourself or what?'

'No!' I said.

'You swam out way too far,' the other one said.

I shrugged. 'I would have made it back.'

'This is the North Sea, not your bath,' the first one said. 'The currents are unpredictable, especially with an outgoing tide.'

'I'm a good swimmer.'

'You're not from here, are you?' the man asked, but it didn't sound like a question, more like a statement. We'd almost arrived at the beach. An ambulance was already waiting there, and nearby there were groups of people with worried expressions on their faces.

'No,' I said and raised my hands. 'I'm fine, really.' But the two of them handed me over like a parcel and I couldn't do anything about it.

The paramedic was nice. He examined me, took my temperature and blood pressure, and then he wanted to know where I lived and where my parents and my clothes were. I told him what he wanted to hear. He accompanied me to where I'd left my things, and then he left me. 'You were lucky,' he said as he left. 'Someone on the beach saw you and called the emergency services.' I almost asked him where the adult education centre was, but then I left it. Attention was sticking to me like old chewing gum to a shoe anyway.

On the way back to the Nissan I thought about where I might shower. I had no idea if there was a swimming pool here or not. Until I thought of something, I'd carry around the salt on my skin like a trophy. My skin looked like the ground in the documentary about Africa I'd seen once. Tiny salt crystals hung from the little hairs on my arms. I licked one arm. I was sad that I didn't have a hard-boiled egg.

I was hungry. I didn't have much money left over. I'd spent most of it on petrol and food. I fetched what I had left from the car, and then headed to the town centre. I knew from my mum that supermarkets threw away the best food. Everything ended up in the big rubbish containers. They threw it away because no one wanted it one or two days after the best-before date. 'A container is the final resort, but it is a resort,' Mum had once said. 'You just need to make sure that the packaging is not damaged.'

I was lucky. The containers were full to the brim. I traipsed around three different supermarkets and stuffed the loot in my backpack.

In the car I sat in my living room. The living room was in the front, the bedroom at the back. I laid out kitchen roll on the passenger seat, lit the candle, and then I ate. There was a baguette, green olives stuffed with feta, pumpkin soup and cherry yogurt for dessert. The baguette was quite hard already and the soup was cold, but it still tasted good. I'd even found an opened bottle of Coke.

Later, when I lay in my sleeping bag on the back seat, I heard the sound of the sea. I'd opened the back window a tiny bit, and the clean, salty air streamed in and mingled with the stale air in the car.

I lay on my tummy, the notebook in front of me. And then I wrote: *Hey, Mum, can you hear the sea?*

34

The adult education centre didn't look the way I expected it to. The building was unremarkable and modern.

I'd woken up early. When I woke up, I was too excited to fall back asleep. I felt like someone had put popping candy in my blood. I knew it wasn't very likely that I was going to find the person who'd taught my mum, but I had to try. I entered the building through a sliding glass door. Then I followed the signs to the 'administrative office'.

The door was open a little bit. I knocked and went in.

A young blonde woman with a polo neck sweater and glasses was standing by the photocopier. When she saw me she said 'Hello there' and put the stack of papers to one side.

I explained my request. I concentrated on not saying anything I might later regret. Then I laid Mum's certificates on the counter. The woman took a close look, and then she exhaled loudly. 'That's a long time ago,' she said. 'I've only been working here for a short while.' She stayed silent for a moment. Her index finger rested on her mouth. I could already hear myself saying 'It's not that important,' but then she said: 'I'll see what I can do. Have you got enough time?'

I nodded twice. And as a precaution I said: 'But unfortunately I don't have any money.'

The woman laughed and waved her hand to show that this didn't matter.

There was a waiting area in front of the counter. I sat down in a green armchair in the corner. A clock ticked on the wall opposite. Apart from that, it was completely silent. No phone rang, no one knocked, no one walked down the corridor.

I closed my eyes.

The ticking grew louder and louder.

And suddenly I smelled the disinfectant, heard the bleeping of the machines, then the doctor came. I could see his biros quite clearly.

I gripped the armrests of the chair like the chair was a boat and the floor the sea. I breathed in the rhythm of the clock until my heart slowed. Then I took my notebook out of the backpack and wrote: *I am everywhere at the same time, I am inside and outside myself.*

When the secretary returned, I'd waited half an hour. She handed me a piece of paper and a map of the town. She'd written a name and an address on the paper in pencil. She'd made a cross on the map.

'It could be that your mother was in Edda Kruse's class. Why don't you go and see her? She retired a long time ago and is probably home.'

'Thank you,' I said. 'How did you find that out?'

'I asked a colleague. He looked in the old files. Mrs Kruse had a German class at the time. Maybe you'll be in luck.'

When I was in the corridor, I searched for a gift in my backpack. I knew the secretary hadn't had to do that for me. She could easily have asked me lots of questions. But I had nothing I could have given her.

I pulled a page from my notebook. I didn't need to think much. The words just flowed out of me. I carefully folded the piece of paper and wrote her name on the front. Then I popped it in the letterbox hanging next to the office door. The lid slipped out of my hand, metal slammed on metal. I hurried out of there. I didn't want to be there when she found the poem.

Mrs Kruse opened the door. She was tall and super thin and had a long neck. Her hair was short and her teeth were very white. She was as elegant as a heron.

Mrs Kruse smiled at me like she'd been waiting for me. At first I thought the secretary had phoned her. Perhaps she'd told her a girl with blue hair would be standing outside her door shortly.

But then Mrs Kruse said: 'Yes?' and I could see in her eyes that she had no idea who I was and what I wanted from her. Then I realized that she was simply friendly. That made me even more nervous. I held my breath. I was afraid to say the wrong thing. I was afraid she'd close her door again.

'Hello, I'm Billie,' I said, and then I didn't know how to continue. I didn't know what to say first. I wanted to do it all at once.

But I didn't need to decide.

Mrs Kruse recognized me without ever having seen me before. 'You're the girl from the sea!' she said, like I had a mermaid's tail instead of legs.

When she said 'Come in,' she'd already taken a step to the side. When she said 'You're just in time for tea,' I stopped worrying. Mrs Kruse took my coat and hung it in the wardrobe in the corridor. Then I followed her into the kitchen.

The kitchen was large and cosy. Almost everything was made of wood. The floorboards were dark, rough wood, and the furniture was walnut brown. The sun was shining above the sink through a large window. The wallpaper had a flowery pattern, and there were a lot of photographs on one of the walls: smiling people on the beach, in front of a Christmas tree and here, in this kitchen. A blonde girl appeared again and again. Sometimes she wore a hat on her baby head, then she was sitting on a rocking horse, then on a real horse, then she was standing outside a primary school on what must have been her first day there.

There was a massive bulky table in the middle of the room with six chairs. I almost expected more visitors to come through the door.

'Take a seat,' Mrs Kruse said. She filled a large metal kettle with water and switched on the stove. Then she put tiny teacups with a rose pattern, a small jug of cream, a small bowl of sugar lumps and a plate of biscuits on the table. The sugar was almost transparent, and the biscuits were made with real butter, not margarine. I could see that straight away.

'First a piece of rock sugar,' Mrs Kruse said. She put a lump into my cup with a small pair of tongs. The lump was quite big compared to the tiny cup. When the water on the stove was bubbling, she poured it into a small china teapot that had the same pattern as the cups. When she poured the tea into my cup, it crackled. Finally she poured in some cream. 'Don't stir it,' she explained. 'First you'll taste the cream, then the tea, then the sweetness.'

I'd never met anyone who made such an effort with tea. Where I came from, you simply put a teabag into the cup and poured hot water on it. That was it.

Mrs Kruse sat down opposite me. 'Right then, now tell me why you're here.'

'I'm looking for my father,' I said. Mrs Kruse stayed silent and looked at me expectantly. 'My mum and dad must have lived somewhere nearby. I want to find out where exactly. At the adult education centre they said you might have taught my mum.'

Mrs Kruse asked for Mum's name, and I told her. But her face didn't move.

'I have a photograph,' I said. I pulled the photo out of my backpack and put it on the table. Mrs Kruse looked at it, and then she smiled. 'I remember. It was a small class.' Mrs Kruse put the photograph back on the table. 'I can't remember names, but your mother was quick and clever. I'd probably have remembered her either way.'

'What do you know about her?' I asked.

'Not much, I fear. Your mother didn't really speak about her private life. But I know she lived on the island.'

'On the island?'

'Here, straight across from the mainland. There's a ferry from the harbour. When the weather is bad, they withdraw the service. I can remember your mother missing class a few times because there was such a storm.'

I took a biscuit and broke it in half.

Mrs Kruse tapped on the photograph. 'Is that you?'

'Yes.'

'Then in some way you're from here.'

'Perhaps,' I said. I said perhaps, but in fact everything had become clear. I thought of how often I'd dreamed about the sea. I thought of how I'd asked my mum if we had ever lived by the sea. And then I heard her laughter. It sounded wrong. I didn't know if it just sounded wrong in my memories. Perhaps it had sounded that way back then, and I simply hadn't heard it.

'Is everything all right?' Mrs Kruse asked.

It was only now that I felt the tension in all my muscles. My entire body was stiff.

I'd been waiting for the anger for quite a while. I wanted to be angry at Mum. I knew the anger would help me because then I'd miss her less. But the anger hadn't come. Until now. Why was I getting angry now, of all times? My body sat in Mrs Kruse's kitchen, but my head was in Marlene's room. I hit at the punchbag until my fists hurt. 'You can't choose your feelings, Billie,' Mum had once said. 'They're just there.'

But now I didn't want to listen to my mum any more. I turned her voice down like the volume on a radio.

'My mum didn't tell me much either,' I said.

Mrs Kruse poured me some more tea. 'And now you're searching not only for your father but also for your mother?'

I nodded. Then my eyes filled with tears. I tried not to blink, but the tears spilled out anyway and ran down my cheeks.

'Do you want to tell me what happened to your mother?' Mrs Kruse said gently.

And then I told her the whole story.

When I was finished, Mrs Kruse said: 'Come with me.'

I didn't ask where she was taking me. I followed her through the house until we came to a bathroom. Mrs Kruse took two white towels from a cupboard and put them on the sink. 'You should wash off the salt,' she said. 'You can use whatever you find here.'

Then she closed the door behind her.

I used Mrs Kruse's shampoo and her shower gel, and when I'd dried myself I used body lotion that smelled of flowers, and I thought about the flowery wallpaper in Mrs Kruse's kitchen and about how they'd smell exactly like this if wallpaper had a smell. I wiped the shower cubicle dry with the second towel. Then I hung both towels over the radiator.

Mrs Kruse was sitting in the living room, quite still. For a second I was worried she'd died. There was a book on her lap. It was open, and several pages seemed to be floating in the air. When I went towards her, the wooden floor creaked and she woke up. 'Oh,' she said.

'I'm sorry, I didn't want to wake you,' I said.

'Rubbish,' Mrs Kruse said. 'It would be better for me to sleep at night anyway.' She got up. 'Where are you sleeping?' It was like this question had been waiting outside the door the entire time.

'With friends,' I said quickly.

Mrs Kruse nodded. I wasn't sure if she believed me, but she didn't say anything.

'I need to go now. Thank you for the information and the shower,' I said.

'No problem,' said Mrs Kruse. 'Call me if there's anything I can do for you.' She wrote something on a piece of paper and handed it to me. Then she accompanied me to the door.

I was standing on the bottom step when I remembered something: 'How did you know it was me who swam in the sea?'

'This place is small. People talk,' Mrs Kruse said. 'Of course, tourists quite often swim out too far and have to be saved.' She paused. 'But normally not at this time of year.' And then she said: 'Good luck with your search, mermaid girl.'

The next ferry left in five hours. It was the last one that day. Mrs Kruse had written her phone number and the departure times on the note. Underneath she'd written: *Careful. The times change each day depending on the tide.*

I went through the various options of what I could do. It would be almost dark by the time I arrived on the island. I was so lost in thought that I didn't realize I was lost until twenty minutes or so had passed. I stopped in the middle of the road and turned around. I must have taken a wrong turn somewhere.

I thought about how often my mum had gone in the wrong direction. Perhaps she'd been too impatient to read maps. But perhaps she just couldn't do it. I had no idea how she'd managed to make her way out of her village to Budapest.

The houses here were all different and yet they were similar too. Some were red brick, some made of timber and painted blue, some were larger, some smaller. But they all looked respectable and expensive. I thought of Luna and how she'd give anything for that kind of house. Perhaps she'd even give her right arm for it if her dream man was waiting in the bedroom for her.

I needed to get back to the beach. That was where the Nissan was. The problem was: there was beach everywhere on a coast.

I decided to go towards the sea, because that was easiest. I couldn't see it, but I knew the wind always came from the sea. I walked back a bit in the direction I'd come from.

A park appeared behind the next crossing. It was only when I came closer that I realized it was a graveyard. I hadn't been to one since Mum's funeral.

I went through the gate and followed the gravel path. The graveyard wasn't big and was surrounded by a forest. I walked among the graves. Most people who were buried here had been ancient, twice as old as my mum.

Then I passed a grave that had a smaller headstone than the rest. The grave looked like a miniature flower meadow, chaotic and beautiful. There were toy horses in between the flowers.

And then I saw the photo. It was embedded in the headstone. Before the image entered my brain, my eyes wandered to the inscription.

Anna Kruse. And underneath: *The sea gives, the sea takes, it took our heart forever.*

I sat down on the ground.

The girl from Mrs Kruse's kitchen. She was six when she died. I closed my eyes and pictured a blonde girl in the waves, I saw Mrs Kruse running into the water, I saw her clasping the child to her chest.

Had Mrs Kruse been on the beach yesterday? Had she called the lifeboat? I tried to remember the people who'd been standing near the ambulance, but I couldn't recall. I couldn't remember if Mrs Kruse had been among them.

Nonetheless, I knew she wouldn't have hesitated to offer me a soft bed. She wouldn't have hesitated to sit down on the edge of the bed and stroke my head until I fell asleep.

For a moment I regretted leaving her.

But then I didn't look back any more. Everyone knows you can't move on if you keep looking back. It's like something freezes inside you.

35

I was standing on deck and waving when the ferry set off. The other passengers were waving too. They waved to their mothers and fathers, their children, their grandparents or their friends. I waved to the Nissan. I'd parked it in the harbour car park. In a few minutes it would just be a silver dot on the horizon.

'Is the car included?' I asked the old man at the counter as I held up the ticket.

'Nope,' he said without looking at me.

'Get used to everything always costing extra,' I heard my mum say. 'Not long now and they'll be charging extra for the gherkins on the hamburger.'

The old man fiddled with his cap. It was too big for his head. Or perhaps his head was too small.

'What does it cost to take the car?' I asked.

'The car has to stay on the mainland,' he said. His eyes were light blue and watery and red at the edges.

'Why?' I asked.

'The island is car-free,' he said. Then he pushed an information leaflet under the Perspex window.

'What?' I stared at the leaflet, but the man had already waved over the next person in the queue.

I smoked the last cigarette as I leaned against the Nissan. My gaze shifted from the sea to the leaflet and back.

The island wasn't far. It was only six kilometres from the mainland. From above, it looked like a prawn. The only town was on the west side of the island. It was tiny. There was a beach in the north, salt marshes in the south and some bird breeding areas in between. I had no idea what a salt marsh was. I read in the leaflet that the island was ideal for those seeking complete peace and quiet and relaxation.

I knew what that meant. It meant: there was absolutely nothing going on there. There was nothing but wind, water, sand, waves and other nature. That's probably what the salt marshes were.

The ferry left in an hour, and I wasn't prepared. I wasn't prepared to be without the Nissan. It felt like I was losing my home for the second time. And these feelings were accompanied by the images and there was nothing I could do about it. I pictured my mum falling. I saw her lying on the floor, not moving.

I stood on deck for almost the entire crossing. I watched the other passengers. They were perfectly equipped. They wore colourful coats and headbands and ponytails. They held their faces in the wind until their cheeks grew red.

But I only had a denim jacket and I was cold. It was lined, but the lining didn't really help against the wind. I was also wearing my mum's cowboy boots. They were a bit too small for me, but all right with thin socks. I'd put my trainers into my backpack. You could spot I was a stranger from ten kilometres away.

I leaned over the railing and looked into the waves. The sea and the sky were so grey that I couldn't see where one started and the other stopped. And then I also started to feel quite grey.

I looked at the horizon. Why was the island still so far away? I tried to make out its outline, but it was already too late.

I puked on the deck right in front of my feet.

A man and a woman had been standing next to me. They jumped to one side and then handed me a packet of tissues. 'First time on the ferry?' the woman asked, and her yellow raincoat shone so brightly that I had to close my eyes. I could only nod. 'It'll pass as soon as you have firm ground beneath your feet,' she said.

The seagulls screeched above me, and all around me was the noise of the ferry.

I suddenly remembered what I'd once read: some seagulls had pecked a dog to death. I closed my eyes again and held on to the railing.

36

Finding the town was easy. There was only one road from the harbour, so I simply followed the crowd from the ferry. My first stop was the tourist information office in the town centre.

The office consisted of a single room, its walls lined with shelves crammed full of brochures, travel guides and timetables. I couldn't believe how much information there was about such a small island. According to the leaflet I'd been given at the ticket desk, only about five hundred people lived here.

Luckily, I'd already decided what I needed: a free map of the island showing every path, no matter how small. The woman behind the desk didn't take long to find it. Within five minutes, I was outside again.

I spread out the map on a nearby wall, determined to be methodical. I had no idea where I would sleep that night, and only a few hours of daylight left.

It was clear that most of the houses were clustered in the town. I worked out how long it would take from one side of the town to the other. I worked out how long it would take me to go from east to west and from north to south. To be on the safe side, I doubled the time, thinking that I'd be zigzagging and stopping frequently. If I hurried, I could check every house in the town before nightfall. However, there were a few pink-coloured squares on the map outside of the town too.

I refolded the map and slipped it into my coat pocket. I stuffed my cowboy boots into my sports bag and put on my trainers instead.

Then I set off.

I'd looked at the photograph of my mother so many times that I didn't even need to get it out of my backpack. It was like the image of the garden with the garden shed had been burned into my memory.

My heart was beating like crazy in the first street. Two-thirds of the first twenty houses were holiday rentals. I wasn't sure if that was good or bad. I hadn't considered the possibility that my father might own a house he rented out to tourists. Maybe the garden belonged to a house that my father didn't even live in. But that didn't really matter. It just meant he lived somewhere else. Everyone lived somewhere. And I would find the house.

By the second street, I'd already accepted that it was going to take longer than I'd hoped. I had accepted that my father wasn't going to be sitting in his living room behind the next hedge.

I crossed out the first two streets on the map and marked the houses whose gardens I couldn't see from the front. I hoped the problem would resolve itself and I'd recognize the house when I saw it. What was I supposed to tell the person who opened the door to me? 'Hello, can I see your garden?' I could already hear the door slamming in my face.

In the third street, I noticed that all the houses had names. I wondered why I'd only just noticed that. I almost considered going back to the beginning, wondering what else I might have missed.

In the fourth street there were only four houses, and none of them was the right one.

In the fifth street, an elderly lady was sitting at the window of the third house on the right. As I walked past, she quickly pulled the net curtain closed. I wondered if she didn't have a telly.

My father's house wasn't in the sixth street either. And so it went on. I just couldn't find the house. But at least I had an idea of where I could spend the night. The sign said READING PAVILION. Once it got dark, I just needed to follow the signs. They were everywhere.

I'd imagined the reading pavilion would be like a library – a place where I could lock myself in and get comfy, surrounded by bookshelves, chairs and reading lamps, with perhaps even an armchair and wooden floors. But it was nothing like that. The reading pavilion didn't even have a door. Just a square opening where the door should have been. The little building sat in the middle of the dunes, hexagonal and made of white planks. It had a couple of windows, and inside there were some wooden chairs and a table, and that was it.

My legs ached and I was cold. I pulled my notebook out of my backpack and, in the last bit of daylight, scribbled: *I've ended up in the crappiest place on earth.*

Outside, I turned in a circle. There were only two options: go back to town or head towards the sea, where I saw some lights shining in the distance.

I found four large houses around a sort of courtyard, with a smaller house to one side. A sign on one of the buildings read PROTESTANT YOUTH SHELTER.

I thought of all the stories where Jesus helped people. I wasn't a Protestant, but I was a youth. And I was in need. Surely no one working for a Protestant youth shelter would turn away a girl in need.

I rang the bell.

A man answered the door. He was middle-aged and wearing a blue polo neck and slippers. He looked as if I had interrupted something – maybe he'd been reading or sleeping.

I tried to sound as polite as possible. 'Good evening,' I said. 'I'm looking for somewhere to sleep. Could you please help me?'

And so I spent the night in a bunk bed – the last free bed in the entire youth shelter. Five other kids on a school trip snored and farted around me, but that didn't bother me. The room was warm, the sheets were clean, and I slept like a queen. Best of all, I didn't have to pay.

'I'm a good writer,' I'd told him. 'I could pay you in poems or in letters or whatever you might need right now.'

The man had laughed.

Just in case, I added: 'I'm also really good at washing up. I'm better than my mum, and she's really thorough.'

Of course, the last part was a lie. I felt bad lying to him, but I had no other choice. He'd asked me dozens of questions: my name, what I was doing here, where my parents were, and why I didn't know where I was sleeping. But I'm good at making up stories. Finally he'd said: 'All right,' and showed me to my bed.

Next morning, I slipped out before the sun was up. I walked east along the beach. There was no one else around, not even the sea. The water had retreated, leaving behind grey-brown mud.

Biro marks almost completely covered the map of the island, with just a few houses in the east left to check. Whoever lived there had no close neighbours. The nearest house was at least half an hour away, no matter which direction you took. I couldn't imagine what it would be like to live without any neighbours. It must be as quiet as a tomb. And who would you ask if you ran out of sugar on a Sunday when you really wanted to bake a cake?

The longer I walked, the more I felt like I was on a different planet. It didn't matter where I stood – there was only wind, mud, grass, water and sand all around me. Clouds raced across the sky, white and grey and lilac, and when I tilted my head back to watch them, I felt a bit dizzy.

After half an hour, I came across a sort of wooden terrace. There were three steps leading up to it and two wide wooden sunloungers, large enough for two people each. Behind the railings was an information board that read WELCOME TO OUR STAR ISLAND. I learned that the island was one of the darkest places in Germany.

I lay down on one of the loungers, imagining how wonderful it would be to lie there with someone who warmed you, someone who loved you so much it took your breath away. But I didn't stay long. The wind made sure I kept moving.

The further I walked, the more restless I became. I knew I'd either find my father very soon, or I'd never find him at all.

It was possible that he'd moved away long ago.

It was possible that he'd died years ago.

But neither of these things was true.

37

I didn't see the garden straight away. It was almost hidden. But as soon as I saw the house, I knew. My body immediately sensed that it had arrived.

The past crashed into the here and now, and somewhere inside me it shuddered and banged. The sky became much lighter, the wind colder and the air saltier.

The house, stables and a barn.

It was a farm.

The farm kept getting closer and I kept getting slower.

I'd imagined this moment so many times. How I'd ring my father's doorbell and we'd stand opposite each other. We would be speechless with joy, of course.

But life is not a film.

What if I didn't like him?

What if he had a new family?

In my thoughts, I took my hand off the doorbell.

I crept around the farm like a burglar. From the telly I knew that American farmers were allowed to shoot anyone who appeared on their property. This obviously wasn't America, but it didn't feel like the Germany I knew either. Where I came from, houses like this didn't exist.

My father's house awakened all my hopes and destroyed them

at the same time. Living alone in a house like this was a complete waste.

The house was huge. I saw how huge when I stood right in front of it. It had a thatched roof that shimmered green in some places. Almost the whole front of the house was covered in ivy. The red stones showed through in a couple of places. There were lots of windows, and each one had a white frame. Every window was divided up into small rectangles which also had white frames, just narrower. I kept looking up at them. My gaze wandered across the windows, from left to right, from top to bottom and back again. Suddenly I thought I saw something. A movement, a shadow? I wasn't sure. If you stare at something for long enough, you start imagining strange things. I sat down on the ground near the house. Then I pulled my notebook from my coat.

I wrote: *The houses wear velvet bonnets here.*

The garden was big, beautiful and wild. On the left side of the house there was a barn bordering it. But the biggest part of the garden was behind the house.

That was where I discovered the shed.

It was bigger than it looked on the photo, and the sun had bleached the colour of the wood. But it was still the same shed. It was still under the same tree. It was a walnut tree. There were nuts all over the ground, and you could just pick them up. I stepped on a shell until it cracked. Then I put the nut in my mouth and thought about my grandma's bejglis. The nuts really did taste better than those from the supermarket.

The garden was overgrown. When I closed my eyes, I felt the hot sun on my face. I could smell the rose bushes and the lilac.

I tasted the redcurrants and the apples. I felt my mum's arms holding me, and her hair that tickled my cheek.

I'm not sure if I actually remembered the moment the photograph was taken. It's possible that it was only because of the photo and the fact that I desperately wanted to remember. But either way, it didn't matter.

The shed wasn't locked. I looked around once again, and then I went in. The room immediately welcomed me. It was like it had been waiting for me.

First I saw the mattress. It was leaning against the left wall. There were shelves on the far side with boxes on them. Only two shelves were empty. On the right-hand side was a window. The curtain was closed. There was a folding chair in one corner and a broom in the other, but it didn't look like anyone had used the place recently. Although it was tidy, there was dust everywhere. On the empty shelves, the dust lay as complete and untouched as a blanket of snow in the early morning. I took a closer look at the boxes. There were signs on the front: PAINT, BRUSHES, FERTILIZER, SEEDS, etc. This was where my father seemed to keep all the things he needed for the house and the garden.

I turned the mattress over. It was dusty but clean. I couldn't see any stains, at least. Perhaps it was even cleaner than the mattress in my bedroom. I lay down on it and crossed my arms behind my head. I looked at the wooden beams on the ceiling and began to count them. I didn't count them for fun, of course. I was questioning the future. I did that often. I counted steps and trees and street lamps and such things. When the number was even, then all was well, but if it was odd, then not really. If the number was even, then my father was a great guy, and if not, he was a loser. I got to twenty-one. I decided to stop counting. After all, I wasn't a child.

If I pushed the curtain in front of the window a little bit to one side, I could see the house and the barn. I put the folding chair in front of the window and sat down. Then I waited.

I waited an eternity. The notebook lay on my lap, but I didn't dare spend any time writing. I knew my father would appear as soon as I lowered my head. At some point I couldn't stand it any more. I pushed the curtain back across the window, put the mattress back against the wall, and hid my things in an empty trunk that stood near the door.

Then I ran over to the stables. I smelled the horses even before I went in. It smelled like pony rides at the funfair. But this was different. Here there were so many horses that I couldn't immediately say how many there were. I walked down the corridor between the boxes and counted. Who owned thirty-five horses? Was my father some sort of cowboy or what? I didn't much like horses. They just stood around in stables or fields. If someone had asked me if I'd rather have a horse or a donkey, I wouldn't have to give it much thought. Donkeys stood around too, but they weren't waiting for someone to come and train them. Donkeys didn't want to please anyone. And donkeys were clever. I'd read somewhere that they recognized you after you'd been away for twenty-five years.

Then I took a closer look at the barn. There was a big table near the entrance with a load of tools on it. Further back was some sort of tractor. And of course there was a lot of hay, probably for the horses.

Now all that was left was the house. I had to wait until my father had gone out. It wasn't enough for him to go into the barn or the stables. I needed time. He needed to go to the village. I couldn't see the front door from the shed. So I climbed one of the trees between the barn and house. I was pretty sure my father wouldn't discover me there.

'Most people aren't like us,' I heard Mum say. 'Most people don't keep looking up in the air, but rather down at the ground under their feet.'

There was a thick branch on one of the trees. I managed to climb up it on my first attempt. It was like the tree knew I'd need it. It was like it had grown the branch especially for me.

38

And then I saw him.

My father left the house without turning around. I saw him from the side first. Then I only saw him from behind. He was tall, or at least I thought so. If you're sitting in a tree, it's hard to estimate someone's height properly. His hair was dark, and he had a beard. When I saw the beard, I immediately thought of stracciatella ice cream but with lots of chocolate. It wasn't a proper beard, it looked more like he hadn't shaved for a few days. He carried a backpack, wore dark green trousers and a red checked shirt with the sleeves rolled up. Over it he wore only a padded gilet.

He was definitely older than my mum. Much older. I could see that even from a distance. I could already picture how Mum had leaned her head against his shoulder. She leaned her head like his shoulder was a pillow.

My father went around the corner, and then he disappeared. I climbed down from the tree.

On the doorbell I looked for the name, but there wasn't one. There was a letterbox in the door, but no name on that either. You probably didn't need one in a place like this. There was probably just one postman, and he knew everyone personally. He probably knew exactly who was in love with who and who was getting divorced. It was he who put the expensive, cream-coloured envelopes through the letterboxes. And it was he who dropped in the cheap brown envelopes that never contained good news.

I rang the doorbell and hoped no one would open the door.

Obviously I'd planned what I'd say. I could hardly claim to have come to the wrong house. But I could pretend I was from the Jehovah's Witnesses. I had no idea if there were Jehovah's Witnesses on the island. If not, then I'd simply be the first. I rang the bell a second and a third time, but no one seemed to be in.

I walked around the house twice before arriving outside the front door again. There were no open windows and no cellar door. I had no idea how to get in the house. But then the problem resolved itself. I leaned against the door, and even before my bum had properly touched the wood, I fell backwards into the hallway.

I lay on the wood floor and didn't move. I listened, but there was nothing to be heard except my own breath. I got up and felt the bottom of my spine. Then I checked the door. For a moment I thought it had broken, but then I discovered the latch. I couldn't believe my father didn't lock his house. Anyone could just walk in.

Once someone had walked into our flat. Sometimes, when the heat had built up in our flat, my mum left the front door open to let the air in. The problem was that we only had windows on one side, on the side that led to the autobahn.

I had woken up in the middle of the night. I heard steps in the hallway, right outside my bedroom. I lay in the dark and held my breath. But whoever had come into our flat changed their mind and disappeared. I ran into the hallway, slammed the front door shut and snuggled up to Mum. The next morning she was surprised to find me lying next to her. I told her someone had been in our flat. I used the word 'burglar' even though I wasn't sure if it was the right word for someone who'd come into our flat through an open front door.

'What's he supposed to steal? Our old sofa?' Mum asked, but after that she didn't leave the front door open at night.

Coming into Mrs Kruse's house had felt like stepping into a hot bubble bath when you're freezing cold. Coming into my father's house felt quite different. Something wasn't right.

At first, I didn't know what it was.

Everything in this house made a noise. Everything creaked. The wooden floor creaked, the stairs creaked, and so did the door handles. It was impossible to open or close a door without making a noise. The heating gurgled and groaned, and I could hear rustling from the attic.

But that wasn't it.

The furnishings were a bit old-fashioned. The wooden doors had coloured glass panels, the floorboards were dark wood. There was wood everywhere, even on the walls. The lower halves of the walls were wood and the top halves wallpapered. There was a huge light-brown leather sofa in the living room. It had so many cracks that an entire household could get lost in it. Or a person. I imagined myself sitting on the sofa and an arm shooting out and grabbing me.

Suddenly I missed our sofa. And I missed the sofa conversations with my mum. She'd often started by asking how things had been at school. Once I'd told her about the E I'd got in art. I hadn't followed the guidelines. 'Did you learn something when you painted the picture?' Mum asked. I'd thought about it and nodded. I'd learned that it can take a while for something to happen between me and the canvas. 'Did you like the result?' I'd been happy. I thought I'd improved in comparison to the picture before. 'Then bugger the grade,' she'd said.

There was a patterned carpet in front of the sofa, white lace curtains hung at the window, and an eight-armed lamp hung from the ceiling. It looked like a shiny spider.

But it wasn't that either that felt strange.

There was a bookshelf in the living room. I quickly skimmed the spines. They weren't novels but reference books. Just like the furniture, they looked like they were at least a hundred years old. I read *Horse Breeding and Feeding*, I read *The Best Tractors Since the 1920s*, and I lost interest in reading further. Next to the books were some old records, mainly classical music.

I walked from one room to the next.

And then I realized what was wrong. There was no stuff. No photographs, no candles, no plants, no things that stood in the corner or on the windowsill and just looked pretty. There was nothing that could have reminded one of something or someone. All I had was a car. But there was more stuff in there than in my father's entire house.

Nothing indicated that anyone else lived here with him. There were no children's or women's shoes in the hallway, there was only one toothbrush in the bathroom, and the double bed in the bedroom was only made on one side. The cover on the duvet didn't match the pillowcase.

There was a fruit basket full of apples in the kitchen. It was full to the brim, and I was hungry. I thought about taking one. No one would notice. And in some way this was my house. There was half a loaf of bread in the bread bin. The crust was floury white and quite soft beneath my fingers. I cut off two thick slices and looked for butter in the fridge. I couldn't find any butter, but I found a piece of ham. I put the apple, the bread and the ham in a bag, and then hurried to get out. I'd been here way too long already.

I sat down on the mattress in the garden shed and had a picnic. I wanted to gobble up the bread in big bites. But I ate slowly so I'd feel full sooner. I'd read that the feeling of fullness kicked in after twenty minutes. And I didn't know when I'd next get something to eat. Anyway, the fridge hadn't been very full.

My next chance was when my father left at the same time as the day before. I slipped into the house. I wanted to look up in the attic, but first I glanced into the kitchen. Everything was the same as the day before, apart from an opened envelope that lay on the kitchen table. My eyes were immediately drawn to the addressee.

Ludger. My father's name was Ludger.

I pulled out the letter. It was from an insurance company.

And then I didn't just have a name, but also a date of birth. My mum, me and my father. That was summer, autumn and winter. My father's birthday was in February. He was fifty-six. He was almost twenty years older than my mum. I put the letter back in the envelope and put it in the same spot it had been before.

PARADISE GARDEN · 249

Then I went up the stairs in the hallway, all the way to the top. Above me was a hatch. That had to be the door to the attic. It seemed to be the only locked door in the entire property. I fetched a chair and took a closer look at the lock. It was a combination lock. I knew most people weren't particularly creative. Lea's bike also had a combination lock, and the code was 1234. I tried that first. Nothing. Then I tried the code backwards. Nothing. Next I tried my father's date of birth. Nothing. Then I put in my mum's date of birth. The lock sprung open. I pulled down the hatch and unfolded the ladder. The whole thing hadn't taken more than four minutes.

I stayed under the black hole for a moment. I thought about the rustling noise I'd heard. Perhaps it wasn't mice but rats. I knew rats could eat people if they were hungry. But I mounted the final rungs anyway. I felt around for a light switch up there. A bulb hung from the ceiling, illuminating the room with a yellow light. The attic was dusty and quite empty. There were a couple of pieces of furniture. Between a wardrobe and four chairs I spotted a cradle. The white wood was spotless. I carefully rocked the cradle and it moved without making a sound.

I pictured Mum standing by the cradle, I heard her saying 'Shush, shush, shush'. I heard her singing a lullaby. I tried to imagine I'd laid in it once.

Next to the cradle was a suitcase, with magazines stacked on top of it. The suitcase looked like a prop for a very old film. I thought it probably contained old clothes or videotapes or something like that. I almost just went past it.

When I opened the suitcase, it didn't contain clothes or videotapes. When I lifted the lid, my mum smiled towards me.

I knew I'd found something that was none of my business. I knew it must be something between my mum and my father. But I couldn't stop myself. There were dozens of sketches, and I looked at every single one.

It was like Mum came alive in my hands. The sketches were very precise, almost like photos, but better. I didn't know exactly why. It was like my mum's spirit had slipped into the paper.

I looked at the little mole on her forehead. It looked like a miniature version of Italy. I held the paper close to my face, leaned my forehead against hers and looked her in the eye. I ran my index finger across her mouth, which had the full lips I'd wanted to inherit.

There were also a few sketches where my mum was naked. I quickly packed them away again. When I left the attic, I set the combination lock back to where it had been. I wasn't stupid. Someone who puts a combination lock on a hatch pays attention to details like that.

I went back into the kitchen. It was only now that I spotted the pot of chilli con carne. I tipped some into a Tupperware box I found in a cupboard and also put a serving spoon in my pocket.

The chilli tasted delicious even though it was cold. After I'd finished eating, I lay on the mattress and played Mau Mau against myself. I'd found the cards in one of the boxes. If Mum had been here, she'd have asked: 'Do you really want to waste your time with that? Can't you think of anything better to do?' If Lea had been here, she'd have shown me how to break open a door with the cards.

After two rounds of Mau Mau I gave up. Playing against myself was definitely the most boring thing I'd ever done.

If I wasn't writing, playing or sleeping, then I listened to the walnut tree. Its leaves rustled in the wind, and its nuts plopped onto the roof.

Sometimes I also spoke to Mum. I said things like: 'You didn't want to tell me anything about him – that's what comes of it.' And of course I thought about my father. I thought about whether I liked him or not. I couldn't decide.

I opened my notebook and made a chart. In one column I wrote *Pros*, and in the other I wrote *Cons*. Lists almost always helped.

On the Pros side I wrote: *He can sketch, he likes animals, he eats healthily (apples, wholemeal bread), he's tidy. He doesn't have a new family.*

On the Cons side I wrote: *He hides my mum in an old suitcase, he likes horses, his fridge is almost empty, he doesn't have any stuff in his house. Perhaps he doesn't have a new family because he's odd.*

This wasn't helping. I closed the notebook.

39

The next morning my father left the house early. I'd only been sitting on the tree for a minute when I saw him go around the corner. Apart from the cellar, I'd seen almost the entire house. But I wasn't sure I wanted to go into the cellar. Cellars were usually scary. Scarier than the attic.

First I needed to eat something. I realized I couldn't survive on one meal a day forever. If I carried on at this rate, I'd be skinny enough to sleep under the mattress at some point.

I saw the note from the hallway. I didn't even need to go into the kitchen to see that it was meant for me. No one props up a note against a vase for no reason.

Either you piss off and don't come back, or you show yourself. Regards, L.

I stared at the words until the paper curled beneath my fingers. I threw myself down on my stomach on the mattress in the shed. Then I opened my notebook. I wrote: *Shit.*

Finally.

Shit.

I was a wimp. That was the truth. But the truth was also that I couldn't simply leave again. Leaving again would mean it would have all been a waste of time. And if there's a feeling I hate, it's the basically-it-was-all-a-waste-of-time feeling.

The next time I was outside the front door, I'd ring the

doorbell. I'd ring like normal people did. I'd just get it over with quickly, like when you rip off a plaster.

I looked down at myself. I hadn't changed my clothes in ages. And my last shower had also been a few days ago. I sniffed my armpits. I stank like a polecat. I definitely couldn't meet my father in this state. I couldn't meet anyone in this state. Then I remembered my mum's perfume. I sprayed it under my armpits. A bit better.

In the next few hours I counted the falling nuts. There were four. Four was a good number. Four seasons, four elements, four phases of the moon. Four meant that nothing would go wrong.

I held out a bunch of flowers to my father. 'For the empty vase in the kitchen,' I said before my father could say anything.

'Ah, the burglar,' he said. And then, as he took the flowers: 'Do these happen to be from my garden?'

I nodded. The flowers weren't proper flowers. Proper flowers had blossoms, not fronds. The fronds looked like squirrels' tails, just lighter. They were very bushy and pretty.

'Come in,' my father said. 'You know your way around already.'

In the hallway I considered taking my shoes off, but I left them on. I hadn't thought to put perfume on my feet.

We sat down opposite each other in the kitchen.

For the first time, I was able to take a proper look at my father. I examined him like he was a painting in a museum. He looked older than he was. I wondered if he'd fibbed about his date of birth. But usually it's only women who do that.

I looked for similarities, for an anchor, something that seemed familiar. His eyes were blue, bluer than any eyes I'd ever seen. His nose wasn't big or small, but my nose was smaller rather than larger. Perhaps the mouth, I thought. We have the same lips.

Everything about my father looked rugged. It was like the island had become part of his body. My father looked like he'd inhaled the storm, drunk the sea and rubbed sand in his eyes.

My gaze wandered to his hands. He had his arms folded across his body, so I could only see his right hand. That was okay, I knew you wore your wedding band on your right ring finger in Germany. There was no ring.

My father examined me too. Then he asked: 'What do you want here? Why did you just come into my house?' He had no idea who I was. And he didn't seem to want to waste any time.

'I've run away from home,' I said. That wasn't a lie. I didn't want to lie. I was determined not to lie to my father.

'And what's that got to do with me?' My father lit himself a cigarette. Then he tucked the packet back in the breast pocket of his shirt.

'Can I have one too?' I had to smoke a cigarette before he found out I was his daughter. My father hesitated, but then he pushed the packet across the table.

'How old are you anyway?' he wanted to know.

'Fifteen,' I said.

'And why have you appeared in my house, of all places?'

'The door was unlocked,' I said, like that was an explanation. 'So I'm not really a proper burglar.'

'Aha,' he said, but he smiled for the first time. 'What is your name?' he asked.

'Elisabeth,' I said.

'And your last name?'

Shit. 'That's a secret.'

My father sighed. 'Elisabeth, I know that you're sleeping in the shed. What's going to happen now? Your parents need to know where you are. I want you to call them.'

I thought maybe he was the perfect father after all. He had said what all parents would say and what no child in the world wants to hear.

'Okay,' I said. 'I'll call them.'

Obviously I wasn't planning on calling anyone.

My father stood up.

'Right now?' I asked.

'Yes, right now.'

I followed him into the living room.

'Sit down,' said my father and brought me the phone.

It rang twice at the other end, then Mrs Kruse picked up. I'd repeated her number over and over like a prayer before I went to sleep each evening.

'Hello, it's me,' I said.

'Who's speaking?' Mrs Kruse asked.

'The mermaid girl,' I said. 'I just wanted to say that I'm doing well and that I'll be coming home soon.' Mrs Kruse wanted to reply, but I quickly hung up.

My father raised his eyebrows.

'It's all right,' I said. 'They're used to it.'

'Is that supposed to mean that you've done this before? Are you often in trouble —'

But I couldn't say any more. I'd stood up too quickly, and a billion stars danced before my eyes. I sank into the darkness. My final thought was that no one nowadays says 'run away'. My very final thought was that I should at least have eaten a few walnuts.

When I came round, I was lying on the sofa. My father held a glass of water in his hand and was staring at me. He was really pale.

'I'm fine,' I said. 'I just haven't eaten anything yet today.'

My father raised the glass to his lips and drank. He drank until the glass was empty. When he'd finished the last sip, he put the glass carefully on the coffee table. Then he turned back to me. 'Billie?' he asked. And then again. 'Billie?'

'That was quick,' I said.

It was the perfume.

'I've never smelled it since,' my father said, and then he said almost nothing for the rest of the evening.

He had warmed up some lasagne from lunch, but didn't eat anything himself. Instead he drank red wine. The bottle and the glass wandered back and forth the entire evening. It wandered from the kitchen to the living room and then back again.

I drank apple juice. My father didn't have any Coke. I didn't even have to ask. I already knew that. When I'd finished my plate, my father cleared the table. I got up to help. But his hands were so big that he almost cleared everything away in one go. He took the plate, the two glasses, the bottle and the bread basket. I just carried my napkin.

Then my father sent me to have a shower. And when I'd showered, he sent me to bed.

'But it's only eight!' I protested.

'Yes,' my father said. 'But I need some peace and quiet tonight.'

How could he not want to speak to me now? How could he stand not knowing why I'd sought him out? I didn't know what to say. I just left my father standing there and walked down the hallway.

'What are you doing?' he asked.

'Putting on my shoes,' I said.

'Why?' he asked.

'I'm going to bed.'

'Not in the shed, please. I've made up the guest bed for you,' my father said.

The room was on the first floor and reminded me of my room at home. It was pretty small. A desk with a chair, a cupboard, a bed and a bedside table just about squeezed in.

My father closed the window. 'We'll talk tomorrow,' he said. Then he was gone.

I thought that my father was probably a there's-always-tomorrow type. I didn't know if I liked that or not. My mum and I were more the I-might-be-dead-by-tomorrow types.

I sat on the bed and pulled the cover over my legs. It was so heavy I needed both hands to do so. I'd never laid under such a heavy cover before.

Perhaps it was the covers, perhaps it was the sea. I could see it from my bed. I felt quite calm.

That evening, I only got up twice more.

I brought my things from the shed to my room. And I fetched a glass of water from the kitchen.

I didn't come across my father. He had disappeared somewhere in the huge house.

40

The next morning my father had already laid the table when I came down. He was in the process of frying some eggs.

'Did you sleep well?' he asked.

I nodded. I'd slept deeply and had no dreams. At least I couldn't remember, which was almost the same thing.

'How would you like your fried egg?'

I didn't understand the question.

'Fried on both sides? The yolk runny or firm?'

'What tastes best?' I asked.

'I prefer mine runny.'

'Okay, me too.'

My father took my plate and put two eggs on it. Then he sat down and spread the two halves of his roll with butter and jam.

'Have you ever tried sea buckthorn jam?'

I shook my head. He held out the roll and I took a bite. The jam tasted sweet and sour at the same time.

'Billie?' said my father. 'Why are you here? What's going on with your mother?'

'I wanted to meet you. But first I needed to spy on you. That's why I moved into the garden shed, and that's why I sneaked into the house.'

'Does your mother know you're here?'

I took a deep breath and then I simply came out with it. 'My mum is dead.'

I could see it came as a real bombshell.

My father put the knife down on the plate. His hand shook. The silver met the porcelain, and it clinked.

I told him about my grandma and that there had been an argument. I told him about the fall and the hospital. I left the rest out.

While I told him, something strange happened. It felt like it hurt a little less than the last time in Mrs Kruse's kitchen.

When I was done, my father buried his face in his hands. He just sat there and didn't move. It was only after a long time that he looked up again. His eyes were red, but dry. My mum had once told me that some people cry on the inside.

'I'm so sorry,' my father said without looking at me. 'I loved your mother very much.'

It seemed to me like he was speaking to himself. I thought of the sketches he'd done of my mum, and I knew that it was true. Now I was annoyed I hadn't taken any of the sketches to hang up in my room.

'But why did you leave us then?'

Now my father stared at me. 'Is that what your mother told you?'

'Yes.'

'I didn't leave you. Your mother left me.'

My stomach started churning.

'I proposed to her. Shortly afterwards, she just disappeared. Just like that. That was twelve years ago.'

I wanted to ask why my mum had left him. I wanted to ask why he'd never come to look for me.

But my father laid the cold fried egg on his roll and took a bite. He looked out of the window and with his mouth full said: 'It'll stay dry today.'

I realized I wouldn't get any more out of him today. I saw that my father was locking himself away, but I couldn't crack his code.

After breakfast my father set off, just like the last few days. 'I'll be back in about three hours,' he said. He had a pair of binoculars hanging around his neck, and he wore dark green trousers. They glistened like they were wet.

'Where are you going?' I asked.

'To the birds,' my father said.

'Which birds?'

'Oh, lots of different ones. Perhaps I'll see a hen harrier.'

I had no idea what my father was talking about. But I knew I couldn't sit in the kitchen all day and look out of the window. 'Can I come too?'

My father froze mid-movement. It was like someone was steering him and had pressed the pause button by mistake. I was just about to uninvite myself when he said: 'You'll need some other footwear. Do you have any waterproof shoes?'

I looked down at my feet. My trainers had been white once upon a time. Now they were grey-brown and the seam was coming apart on the left one. 'No,' I said.

'One moment,' my father said.

A couple of minutes later he returned with a pair of wellies and thick socks. They fitted perfectly. I wondered if Mum had worn the boots. But I preferred not to ask.

I'd only been here a few days, but I'd already learned one thing: the wind always blew, the question was just how strongly.

I pulled the hood of my sweatshirt over my head. But we'd barely stepped out of the front door when it was blown back. 'Quite stormy today,' I said.

'No,' said my father. 'That's just a little bit of wind.' Then he looked me up and down. 'You need different clothes. You won't get far with those city clothes.'

I said nothing. I had no idea if my father knew I couldn't afford new clothes. But he could probably tell.

'We'll have to go and see Swantje on the way,' my father said.

'Who's Swantje?'

'Swantje has a shop and sells coats and rain trousers to tourists.'

'Only to tourists?' I asked.

'No, of course not. But the islanders are born in functional clothing.' The left corner of my father's mouth twitched.

'My mum hated functional clothing,' I said. Then I imitated my mum's voice: 'What is the function of it? To make you look ugly?'

My father didn't react. Instead he asked: 'And what about you?'

'I love functional clothing.'

I'd just decided that. And I said it like the love of my life was standing in front of me.

It was pretty simple: if everyone around you is wearing ugly windcheaters and waterproof trousers, then it doesn't matter if you're wearing them too. And I hadn't come across anyone wearing the latest fashions here yet. Here no one wore leather jackets that you left undone because it looked cooler, regardless of whether you were freezing your arse off. No one teetered about on high heels. No one had tiny handbags in the crook of their arm. Here you carried backpacks and wore headbands and hiking boots.

The paved road had now become a sandy path. There was less moss on the dunes, fewer bushes and some different plants whose names I didn't know. There were almost no trees.

It was only now that I realized how many different faces the island had. If you got bored, then you just had to go around one or two corners and everything looked different. The landscape was lighter here. Suddenly I could see all the way to the horizon again.

'Have you been out here before?' my father asked.

I shook my head.

'That's the most beautiful part,' he said. 'Ahead of us is the Leegde. Behind it is the Ostplate. The entire area belongs to the national park. Around twelve million migratory birds rest here per year.'

Twelve million birds. That was a lot. 'That's quite a tight squeeze,' I said.

My father laughed. 'They don't all come at once.'

'How do they know that it's twelve million?'

'They are counted.'

That sounded like a punishment from hell.

'That would take forever!' I said.

'There are tricks. Only the small flocks are counted. The large ones are estimated.'

I hadn't heard my father speak that much in one go before. It felt a bit like being in geography or biology class, but better. But I had only just thought that when he fell silent.

We walked a long way without either of us saying anything. I breathed in time with my steps. I don't know if it was the wind or the view. Either way, the island made everything inside me smaller, but in a good way. I pictured my thoughts as soap bubbles. They rose up and twirled through the air for a moment and then they suddenly burst.

At some point my father stopped.

'What's the matter?' I asked.

'Look over there,' he said and handed me his binoculars.

There was a group of seals sunning themselves on a sandbank. Occasionally one of them slipped into the water and swam around a bit. Then it would heave its body back onto dry land and flop down on the sand.

'Can we get closer?' I wanted to know, but my father shook his head. This was better than a visit to the zoo, and free besides.

'We're going back now.'

'But what about the bird you wanted to see?'

My father shrugged. 'Maybe tomorrow.'

'What sort of bird is it?' I asked.

'The hen harrier?'

I nodded.

'A raptor.'

'Like an eagle?'

'More like a buzzard with an owl's face,' my father said.

'No idea what a buzzard looks like.'

'The males have blue-grey feathers and black-tipped wings. The females are a bit bigger than the males. They have brown top plumage. The underside is light brown with dark streaks, and the tail feathers are banded.'

'What does banded mean?'

'Do you know what a raccoon looks like?'

I nodded.

'His tail is also banded.'

My father tried his best, but I still kept my eyes open the entire way back for an owl with a raccoon tail.

'I'll show you pictures at home,' he said.

We saw lots of other birds on the way home, and my father knew everything about them. He told me a story about each bird. He knew what they ate, where they spent the winter, where their name came from and if they were on the brink of extinction. We spotted red knots and golden plovers, oystercatchers and grey plovers. They strutted across the salt marshes, flew off in large flocks and returned in large flocks. And we saw gulls. I had no idea there were so many different types of gull. I told my father the story of the seagulls and the dog, but he just laughed.

'Rubbish,' he said.

I had never seen so many birds at one time. It was an absolute birds' paradise. But we didn't see a hen harrier.

'Unfortunately you only seldom get to see them,' my father said. 'In summer they sometimes breed on the island, but now only those migrating from the north come. Some of them at least spend the winter here.'

If I was a migratory bird, I wouldn't have to think twice. The island was beautiful all right, but cold. I'd choose a warmer place, of course. Florida, for example. I was picturing a sunny palm-lined beach, but my father was talking again.

'We'll have to see how much longer they even breed on the island. In summer, the tourists arrive with their dogs and trample through the dunes.'

My father looked like he wanted to report each and every one of them.

The hen harrier is a proud, beautiful bird. I couldn't believe it was threatened with extinction.

I sat on the sofa and looked through the bird guide my father had given me. I used to think that birds were boring and birdwatching was just something for old people and nerds. But now I realized there was a difference between looking at pictures of birds and seeing them in real life. It made a difference whether you saw pigeons on a square in the city or plovers on the mudflats.

My father made a late lunch. The smell of fried onions wafted into the living room and tempted me into the kitchen. He was making fillet of plaice and mashed potato.

It was the best thing I'd eaten in a long time.

'Why is the mashed potato so good?' I asked with my mouth full and thought about the mashed potato Mum and I had often eaten. You just had to put a bit of water into the bag and put the whole thing in the microwave. In comparison to this mashed potato, ours tasted like flour paste.

'The secret is the potatoes,' my father said. 'These here are especially aromatic.'

I put another spoonful into my mouth. 'Nutty somehow,' I said.

My father nodded. 'I also use butter and cream.' And then he said: 'It was your mother's favourite.'

I almost choked. I wanted to immediately open my notebook and write it down. But I was just about able to contain myself.

Later, when I was in my room, I wrote only two sentences: *My mum is already here. All I need to do is wait.*

That evening, I couldn't fall asleep.

I wondered why Mum and I had eaten mashed potato from a packet for years. Potatoes weren't even expensive. Mashed potato wasn't even hard to make. And I wondered how long I'd need to wait. How long would it take for my father to talk?

The wind had picked up too. At first it just whined, but now it howled around the house. The roof beams creaked, and the shutters rattled in their frames. The whole house was groaning and sighing. Surely it wouldn't be long until the sheep flew through the air.

At some point I couldn't stand it any more and I got up.

When I came downstairs, I heard music. For a moment I thought I'd been mistaken. I stayed in the hallway and listened. The living room door was slightly open. My father was lying on the sofa. At first I thought he was asleep, but then I saw he was listening with his eyes closed.

'Miles Davis,' I said, and my father flinched. 'What's the name of the piece?' I asked.

'"Billie's Bounce",' my father said and sat up.

'Really?' I asked.

'Yes. You don't know the piece, but you know that Miles Davis is playing it?'

'That was just a guess,' I said. 'I only know one of his albums. But this piece isn't on it.'

'*Kind of Blue?*'

'Yes.' I didn't tell him I'd found the same album in Mum's things. I didn't tell him how Mum had reacted to the music.

'Do you play an instrument?' my father asked.

I'd never asked my mum. I knew that you could borrow instruments, but you still had to pay for the lessons.

'No,' I said. 'But I'm good at pretending that I do.' I closed my eyes and felt the cold metal at my lips and hands. My heart beat in three-four time, and my fingers and legs moved almost by themselves.

My father laughed. 'Very professional.'

I opened my eyes and sat down next to him on the sofa.

'Can't you sleep?' my father asked.

I shook my head.

'The wind?'

'Yes. The house is too loud.'

'You never forget your first storm,' my father said. 'I was five when there was such a bad storm here that half the roof flew off. And now I barely hear the wind any more.'

'Do you think you can get used to everything?'

'Good question,' my father said. 'I think you get used to what you want to get used to.'

My father got up, walked over to the record player and moved the needle. It scratched and then the first sound began. We listened to the album together from the beginning, and when it ended, the storm had passed.

41

My father woke me early the next morning.

'It's the middle of the night,' I complained and pulled the covers over my head.

'It's seven o'clock,' my father said, and as he left the room he said: 'You can help me muck out the stables and feed the horses. I'll see you downstairs.'

'What about breakfast?' I wanted to know, but my father had already closed the door behind him.

Downstairs I called his name, but no one answered. He had probably gone ahead already. I bit into a roll lying in the bread basket in the kitchen. Then I grabbed my coat.

The air was fresh and damp. I could hear the horses neighing from a long way away.

'Come with me,' my father said as I entered the stables. I followed him. He stopped in front of a huge pile of hay. 'This here is the fresh hay. It needs to be distributed to the individual boxes. But first the old hay needs to be taken out.' He pointed towards one of the two pitchforks that hung from a hook on the wall.

'That pitchfork is much smaller than the other one,' I said.

'Be thankful,' my father said. 'It'll be hard enough as it is.'

And he was right. It was hard work, and I hated it. My father was about a thousand times faster than me, although I tried to be quick. My father started in the box opposite, and so we worked our way down, each on our own side. My father worked efficiently and consistently. For the entire time, he whistled a song I didn't recognize. He had rolled up his sleeves, and after four boxes, his forehead gleamed with sweat.

Whenever my father went into a new box, he greeted the horse that lived there. He greeted each horse by name like it was an old friend. The horses were called Poppy and Gregor, Cinnamon and Adonis, Popcorn and Beauty, Aurora and Moby, and I couldn't hear the rest.

His voice was so quiet and so sweet, like he had a sugar lump under his tongue. My father stroked the horses' necks, ran his hand over their backs and flanks, and held fresh hay under their noses. They lowered their heads, sighed quietly and almost closed their eyes.

I didn't like mucking out, but I started to like the horses. They looked nice. Their fur was all different colours, from white to black, and was a bit shaggy. These horses weren't very tall or thin, but small and muscly like me.

And I liked the way my father handled the horses.

It seemed like my father was suddenly a different person.

It seemed like he was connected to the horses.

When my father had finished his row, he continued in my row. We met in the middle.

'I'm sore all over,' I said.

'That's what your mother always said,' said my father. 'Best thing is to take a hot shower. That's good for your muscles. In the meantime, I'll make breakfast.'

When I came into the kitchen, my father was pouring coffee into large cups. I sat down at the laid table. My father put a cup in front of me. Then he said: 'I wondered how all your hair managed to fit under that blue thing.'

I'd left the wig in my room. I didn't need it any more. My hair had fallen out completely and was now growing back. The new hair was still very short, but it was soft and quite thick. When I ran my hand over my head, it felt like stroking the velvet cover of our sofa. My father didn't ask why I had such short hair. He probably thought that's what you did when you lived in the city and were fifteen.

Instead he said: 'You had such thick hair even as a little child.'

'What was I like?'

'You always knew exactly what you wanted and what you didn't.'

'That's good, isn't it?'

'Definitely,' my father said and spread butter thickly on his roll. Then he put a slice of smoked salmon on it. 'Tell me,' he asked, 'what did you do with the shampoo?'

I had no idea what he was talking about. 'What do you mean?'

'The entire bottle was full of water.'

'Oh, that,' I said, putting the peeled boiled egg in my mouth. It was delicious. I'd been dying for a boiled egg for days. 'I stretched the rest.'

'Why?'

'So it lasts longer.'

'Do you always do that?' he wanted to know.

'Sure,' I said. 'That way you can make a bottle of shampoo last for at least a week longer.'

My father asked which other tricks I knew, and I told him everything. I told him about the shelf with the food supplies that had gone past their sell-by date, I told him how you can save water and electricity by only filling the kettle with the actual amount of water you need, I told him how we saved our good clothes for when we went out, and I told him that you can donate plasma much more often than blood.

While I spoke, I watched my father. I didn't want to miss the pride in his eyes. But there was no pride. When I'd finished, he said nothing instead of applauding.

'What's the matter?' I asked.

'It makes me sad,' my father said. 'That you had to live like that.'

My father said it like our entire life had been a bad joke. My face went hot. I wanted to say something, but I didn't know what. I opened my mouth, but only my shaky breath came out. I probably looked like a stupid fish. I closed my mouth again and clenched my teeth. I jumped up.

'Billie!' my father called, but I was almost out of the hallway. I slammed the front door behind me and ran off. First I ran towards the shed, but then I turned off to the stables.

The horses ignored me. They chewed and stamped their feet and looked around, always just past me. At first I ignored them too, but then I stepped up to one of the boxes.

'Hello, Lucky,' I said and stretched out my arm. The horse briefly raised its head, and then continued eating like I wasn't there. 'You're not very polite,' I said. 'I did clean your home, after all. Do you remember?'

'He definitely remembers you,' I heard a voice behind me say. I turned around, and there was my father.

'Why is he acting like I'm not there?'

'He can sense your anger.'

'I'm not angry,' I said.

'Don't stay too long. It's too cold without a coat.'

Then my father turned to leave.

I watched him until he was gone. Then I put a hand on my heart and a hand on my stomach and breathed with my eyes closed. When I opened my eyes, I stared straight into a pair of eyes just a few centimetres away. The horse had come forward to the door. It had the longest eyelashes I'd ever seen. I carefully moved closer to its muzzle, and the horse let it happen. Its muzzle was warm and soft and velvety.

My father was still sitting at the kitchen table reading the newspaper. When he saw me, he got up. 'You only live your own life,' he said as he filled the kettle with water.

'Our life was beautiful,' I said and especially emphasized the word 'beautiful'.

'Yes,' my father said. 'Your mother might not have had money, but she had imagination.'

My father summarized our life in one sentence, and this time it felt right.

In my head, I took an eraser. Then I simply rubbed away the scene from earlier. Individual words disappeared. Then both sentences. And then the sheet of paper was white again.

'Will you call your grandma later?' my father asked as he put down the cup in front of me.

'But I can't stand her,' I said.

'She still has to know where you are and how you are,' he said. 'Despite everything, she's still your grandma.' And then, perhaps because he saw my face: 'She is particular, yes. But everyone has their story.'

'What do you mean?'

'I mean no one behaves in a particular way without a reason.'

'Okay, but does that make it better?'

'Yes,' my father said. 'I think it does.'

I drank especially slowly. Then I helped clear the table. Then I washed up. I washed up in slow motion. But even if you wash up in slow motion, you finish at some point.

And then I held the phone in my hand for the second time. But my grandma didn't pick up. I wanted to hang up after it had rung three times. I didn't fancy the answering machine. But my father shook his head. So I continued waiting.

'My arm is getting heavy,' I complained, and at some point my father said: 'She doesn't appear to be home.'

'Perhaps she's gone back to Hungary.'

'We'll try again later. Now we're going to pay Swantje a visit.'

But later my father didn't remember that I needed to call my grandma, and of course I didn't remind him. It was a long time until he remembered again. And when I did reach my grandma, everything was different.

Swantje looked pretty young, but she had three children. They were quite small and cavorting around in the shop. When we arrived, Swantje was putting out stock onto the shelves. She didn't just sell clothing but also a few books, postcards, soft toys and other things.

'Morning, Ludger,' Swantje said. 'Long time no see.' Then she looked at me. Her eyes were alert, and everything about her was lively. She ran her hand through her hair. 'Who have you brought along today then?'

My father didn't say: 'This is my daughter.' He said: 'This is Billie. She needs some new clothes.'

Swantje brought me a whole pile of clothes to the changing room. 'Are you staying long?' she asked.

'Not sure,' I said.

Swantje didn't ask any more questions. She probably already had her own thoughts about me.

My father had once said: 'People here know things about you before you know them yourself.' Now I realized what that meant: it meant that there was always someone from the village sitting in your living room listening to all your conversations.

In the end we left the shop with two jumpers, a waterproof jacket and three pairs of trousers. I didn't know why I needed three pairs, but my father insisted, and I didn't complain.

42

I'd been on the island for almost two weeks. And if you have a lot of time, two weeks can feel like half a lifetime.

My father and I didn't talk about how things would continue. They just continued. I lived in constant fear that the police or social services would appear outside the door, of course. I'd got used to being here. No one ever called in. My father didn't have any visitors, and he never visited anyone either.

Each day was a bit different from the one before, but not so much that you'd notice. Everything repeated itself, just as the tide ebbed and flowed every day.

My father got up early every day even though he didn't use an alarm clock.

'How do you know when it's time to wake up?' I asked.

'It's time to get up when I wake up.'

He woke up at roughly the same time each day. Then he woke me. We mucked out, fed the horses and had breakfast. Usually my father went to see the birds afterwards. Sometimes he worked in the stables or in the house instead. And sometimes he ran errands in the village.

In the mornings I usually read or wrote in my notebook.

There wasn't much else to do here. I read almost the entire time, and when I got bored, I wrote. And when I got bored of that, I went back to reading. It was like the thing with crisps and gummy bears.

My father had fetched a couple of old crime novels from the cellar. I didn't really like crime novels, but they were better than nothing. In any case they were better than the books about tractors and horses.

I missed my books that were still in the car. I realized I'd have to fetch them onto the island at some point. I still hadn't finished reading *On the Road*.

'Can we fetch the Nissan onto the island too?' I asked my father.

'But you know the island is —'

'Car-free, yes. We could just fetch the Nissan and put it in the garden and make a flower bed out of it.'

My father laughed. 'I'll think about it.'

We always had a hot meal at lunchtime. The food that my father made was pure luxury. Everything was fresh, everything tasted great.

In the afternoon, we rested. Then we had tea together. I told my father stories from our housing block, and my father told me stories about the island. My stories were always about people I knew; my father's stories were always about nature. I talked about Lea, Ahmed and Luna and about Uta and Heinz. My father told me about marine luminescence, hooded beach chairs and about the oldest house on the island. It had a roof you could use as a raft in case of floods.

We hardly ever spoke about Mum.

At least my father didn't speak about what had happened back then. But he did mention her occasionally. He said things like:

'Your mother would like that!' or 'Did your mother allow that?' It was almost like Mum had just gone to do some shopping. And at least it was more than Mum had told me about my father.

I don't know exactly when the change began. I just know that it was raining that day, raining and raining. In any case, my father stopped talking about nature that afternoon. Instead he talked about himself. And I knew that it was just a small step to my mum.

My father told me that he'd inherited the house from his parents and they'd inherited it from their parents and so on. They'd never lived anywhere else than here on the island. When he was sixteen, his parents wanted him to learn something practical. So he decided to become a carpenter. If there was something that needed doing in the house or the stables, then he could usually deal with it himself.

'But I don't think I would choose the job again today,' my father said.

'Why not?' I asked.

'I prefer working with horses.'

'How long have you had the horses?'

'I grew up with them. My father also had cows and German grey heath – that's a breed of sheep. But I got into business proper with the horses.' My father told me that he bred horses, gave riding lessons and arranged hacks. 'Most people fall in love with them immediately,' he said. 'Icelandic horses are very special animals. They're brave, friendly, playful and confident.'

I took a sip of my juice. My father had mixed blackcurrant and sea buckthorn and topped it up with mineral water. The mixture was really yummy.

'Do you want to learn to ride?' my father asked. 'I taught your mother too. You were too small to learn at the time.'

'Yes,' I said. 'I want to learn to ride.'

I didn't say that because I'd suddenly become a pony girl. I said it because my father's eyes were shining. I said it because daughters should learn things from their fathers. And I said it because it would take a good long time until I learned not to fall off a horse.

In the days after our conversation my father barely had any time. 'We need to postpone the riding lessons,' he said. 'Two of the horses are sick.' He spent most of the time in the stables and only appeared to eat and shower. We ate frozen pizza and tinned ravioli. It almost felt like being back home. Every day I saw the vet come up the path. He carried a heavy bag and reminded me of a doctor from an old movie.

After three days, my father smiled when he came back into the house. It was like a dark cloud that had been hanging over the house had dissolved. When it became apparent that both horses would make it, my father cooked a feast. We had fish in white wine sauce with potatoes and samphire. I'd learned that samphire was the island's asparagus.

'There's going to be a shower of shooting stars tonight,' I said. 'They said on the radio earlier.'

I thought my father would be pleased with this news. Everyone knew you could make a wish when you saw a shooting star. The two horses were already on their way to being better, but it couldn't do any harm to wish them good health. I also had lots of other wishes, and the thing with God had somehow sort of taken care of itself.

'Did you know that the island is one of the darkest places in Germany?' my father asked.

'Yes,' I said. 'I read it on a sign in the dunes. Where the sunbeds are.'

'It's going to be a clear night. You should check it out later,' my father said and squeezed lemon on his fish.

'But you'll come too, right?'

My father yawned. 'I'm tired. I'm looking forward to my sofa.'

By now I knew what that meant. Instead of going to bed early, my father would play one record after the other. The later it got, the sadder the music became. And at some point he fell asleep on the sofa. I couldn't understand it. Why would you sleep on a sofa full of cracks when you have a large comfy bed waiting for you?

'But the shooting stars are only going to be happening tonight,' I said.

'There'll be others,' was all he said.

I had an idea. 'But you can wish for a hen harrier.'

My father laughed. 'Do you know that you start almost every sentence with "But"?'

'But that's one of my basic principles,' I said. Obviously I knew a 'but' didn't fit at the beginning of this sentence. I wasn't stupid. But I said it anyway. 'And you start almost every sentence with "Do you know?" or "Did you know?" Do you know that I know a great deal? But I know almost nothing about you and my mum.'

And then my dad said nothing more.

I wanted to head out straight away. When it got dark, I put a torch, my notebook, a jumper and a thermos with tea in my backpack. Then I grabbed my wellies and a blanket and set off.

I was still a bit hurt that my dad didn't want to come. I thought his life could do with a bit of glitter.

It wasn't proper day any more, but not proper night either. The sun had only just disappeared behind the horizon, and the slender, narrow moon stood high in the cloudless sky. The island and the sea spread out in front of me in a bluish light. I lay down on one of the two wooden sunbeds. Then I waited. I took an occasional sip of tea.

'Is this space free?' a voice suddenly asked from behind me.

First I saw the huge white telescope. It glowed in the dark. Then my father appeared behind it. 'Sure,' I said and moved over a bit.

My father sat down next to me.

The shower of shooting stars hadn't even begun, but the sky was already the most beautiful chaos I'd ever seen. Billions of stars glowed in the darkness. A white veil was stretched across the sky, like the sky was wearing a wedding dress.

'Can I look through the telescope?' I asked.

My father handed it to me. Then he showed me where to twist it to sharpen the image. 'You can see not only the Milky Way, but also our neighbouring galaxy, the Andromeda Galaxy,' he said.

'Do you think there's some sort of second Earth there?'

'Yes. And if not there, then somewhere else.'

'Imagine if there was a parallel universe somewhere, where we live a second life,' I said.

'Would you like to visit yourself?' my father asked.

'I think so.'

'Perhaps that would be a journey into the past.'

'I'd visit us. Mum and me. I'd tell her that she mustn't open the door to my grandma.'

My father thought for a moment. Perhaps he thought about whether he'd visit himself or not. But perhaps he was thinking about what he'd say to my mum if she was still alive.

'It's starting!' my father said.

I counted three shooting stars, then I closed my eyes and made a wish. I only made one. Three shooting stars were a lot for a single wish. I was sure that increased the probability of my wish coming true.

I'd never tell anyone what I wished for, of course. Everyone knows that shooting star wishes don't come true if you tell someone.

'Let's play a game,' I said.

'What sort of game?' my father asked.

'I just made it up. With each shooting star, we remember something to do with my mum.'

In the darkness, I could see my father tense up.

'I don't know if I —'

'One: she collected perfume samples, and that's why she sometimes smelled of roses and sometimes of lemons.'

'Billie, I —'

'Two: the way she looked at me when I did the washing-up with the water running. Come on. We're meant to take turns.'

And then my father caved in. 'Three,' he said. 'Her grin when she won a board game.'

Yes, I knew that grin. My mum was a terrible loser.

'Four: when she read me a story, she kept falling asleep. It annoyed me so much that I taught myself to read when I was five.'

'Five: she had a beautiful voice. She sang to you when you couldn't sleep.'

Automatically, I thought of the white cradle in the attic.

'Six: we could watch a film a thousand times and she'd still laugh like it was the first time.'

'Seven: how she kept everything even if it was broken.'

We played until the real fireworks in the sky began. There were so many shooting stars at the same time that it became impossible to count them. We drank tea and just watched.

I thought Mum might be up there too. I thought if she saw us sitting down here, then she definitely wouldn't be cross with me. She'd understand that I'd needed to find my father. I needed someone to talk about her with. And she couldn't blame me for that.

43

The next morning my father woke me with the words: 'You're learning to ride today!'

I was still tired. But I jumped out of bed nonetheless and headed straight for the shower.

We only had a slice of bread for breakfast. Then my father said what he said every morning: 'We'll meet outside.' And off he went.

In the hallway, I slipped into my trainers, but then I had an idea. I ran to my room and fetched the cowboy boots from the sports bag.

'Howdy,' I said when I looked at myself in the mirror. I'd seen on the telly that cowboys greet each other like that.

My father had already selected a horse for me and was placing a blanket on its back. It was Lucky.

'Do you think I look like a real cowgirl?' I asked. I twirled around and raised my right foot so he could see the boots close-up.

'You look more like a Las Vegas showgirl,' my father said. He was right. The shoes were better suited to a stage than a horse's back.

'Mum didn't want them to get dirty. That's why she never wore them,' I said. 'You should have given her a display case as well as the boots.' I briefly considered putting on my trainers again, but decided against it. We'd be starting soon, and I didn't want to waste any time.

'A display case, that's good,' my father said and heaved a saddle onto the blanket. 'But it wasn't me who gave her the boots. I found them quite naff at the time. She got them from László.'

It took a moment, but then I understood. It was like a puzzle piece had fallen into place.

And when I understood, I fell.

I fell and fell and fell and couldn't believe it.

I hadn't even asked the question yet but still knew the answer. I knew the answer even before the question left my mouth.

'You were six months old,' Ludger said. He had sat down on an upturned apple crate. His chin rested in his hand. Without looking at me, he asked: 'Didn't your mum tell you that?'

'No!' I screamed. 'No! No! She didn't! Never! Never!'

I tore off one and then the other boot and threw them into the horse's box.

And then I ran. Ludger tried to stop me, but I was quicker. As I ran, I screamed. I just couldn't stop. It's not that easy, screaming when you're running. And at some point you have to stop doing one of the two. I stopped screaming and continued running. I didn't turn around.

I ran all the way to the village. Then I had to stop. My socks were tattered, my feet were cut open, and my lungs were burning. Each breath hurt. I didn't know where I should go, so I went to the church.

The church was empty.

I was too.

The wind had cooled my heart.

I felt in my trouser pocket for money, but of course I didn't find any. I lit two candles without putting any money in the box. I looked at the two burning candles and said: 'Fuck you, God!'

'Fuck you, Mum!'

I said it extra loud. I wanted to make sure they heard me.

And then I got up and limped back.

What else could I have done? An island is an island. There are limits.

I didn't have my notebook with me. That's why I talked to myself. The people who came towards me got out of my way. They probably thought I'd gone mad. But the opposite was true.

I said: 'I'm never running away again.'

I said: 'This here is my story, not yours.'

I said: 'Please forgive me, Mum.'

Ludger met me halfway. He put his coat around my shoulders, and then he picked me up. He carried me like I was a baby.

At home he put me down on the sofa. He fetched a bucket of water, a cloth, iodine, bandages and a pill. Then he pulled the last tatters of my socks from my feet.

'Ouch!' I said.

'I'm so sorry,' said Ludger and handed me the pill.

'I'm so tired,' I said, and Ludger put a blanket over me.

I slept through the entire afternoon.

When I woke up, I heard sounds from the kitchen. I wanted to get up, but then I remembered the thing with my feet.

Ludger appeared in the doorway. 'Feeling better?'

I nodded.

'Don't put any weight on your left foot,' he said and leaned a pair of crutches against the sofa. 'For later. We can eat here for now.'

'Where did you get those from?'

'I broke my leg once. It was years ago.'

Ludger had made spaghetti bolognaise. We rested the plates on our thighs.

Ludger said: 'I genuinely thought you knew who I am.'

'It's not your fault,' I said. 'It's my mum's fault.'

Ludger wiped his mouth. He cleared his throat and said: 'It's your right to know where you come from. Do you want to know?'

I nodded.

And then he told me about my father. He told me everything he knew without me having to ask.

My mum had met my father at the Academy of Dance in Budapest. He was her dance teacher and, as Ludger said, the first man she'd been in love with. I could imagine what that meant. It meant that she couldn't eat during the day and couldn't sleep at night. I imagined her standing at the window in her flat all the time instead, dreaming.

Ludger told me that László had promised to give my mum the stars from the sky. And that my mum had never been so happy before. László had promised to marry her. He promised to buy her a house, no, to build her a house, with his own two hands, just like her father had done for her mother. He promised her that he'd always be there for her. And my mum had believed it all. Even later, when she was several months pregnant.

I pictured a handsome guy placing his hands on my mum's stomach. They'd probably discussed what to call me. My mum had surely imagined what it would be like to have a family.

'But at some point,' Ludger said, 'your mother couldn't dance any more. Her belly was too big.' And while my mum sewed baby clothes in her flat, László just carried on with his life. The less she came to the Academy, the less he called her. And at some point, he just stopped coming. He just didn't reply to her calls any more.

My mum must have known he would leave her. My mum had a sixth sense for that kind of thing.

'What happened then?' I asked.

'Your mother was angry. Very angry.'

She'd stomped over to the Academy to confront László. But he wasn't there. She was told he'd got a contract at the theatre in Sofia. 'What does the bastard want in Bulgaria?' my mother is said to have screamed. In any case, one of the dancers told her that he'd been seen with another woman, a Bulgarian woman.

My mum got so worked up about it that she started having contractions that same day. She didn't know who to turn to for help, so she called her mother.

'The two of them didn't get on very well,' Ludger said. 'Your grandma didn't even know that your mother was pregnant.'

The journey from my mum's home town to Budapest was long. When my grandma arrived at my mum's the next morning, I was already born. Mum had delivered me all by herself.

When Ludger told me that, I pictured myself lying on Mum's stomach. I saw my tiny hands and feet and the long, white umbilical cord.

'Your grandma cried when she saw your mum. And your grandma's tears haunted your mum.'

Mum had at least two interpretations of why my grandma cried. Firstly: because my mum had had to go through it all alone. Secondly: because it was a scandal to have a child when you weren't married.

From then on, my grandma used every opportunity to tell my mum how irresponsible she'd been. And there were a lot of opportunities. My mum had a tiny baby and no idea what to do next, which is why she went back home with my grandma.

'She never saw your father again,' Ludger said. 'I'm sorry, but he must have been a real shit.'

So that's what it was, I thought. The secret around my father fitted on two pages.

'It would have been your mother's job to tell you.'

'And why didn't she?' I wanted to know.

'Perhaps it was too painful for her. Perhaps it was still too painful after all these years.'

'Do you think that's why she never told me about you either?'

'Possibly.'

'Is that why you didn't tell me anything about my mum the whole time too?'

'Possibly.' Ludger looked slightly past me.

'And my mum never tried to contact you again?'

'Never again,' he said.

We stayed silent.

And then Ludger said: 'It was as if you were my daughter. I didn't just lose Marika, but you too.'

'But I'm here now.'

'Yes,' Ludger said. 'You're here now.'

'Can I ask you something else?'

'Of course,' Ludger said.

'Was my father a Romani?'

Ludger looked at me in surprise. 'No,' he said. 'Not that I know of.'

After dinner I limped to my room and sat down on the bed. Then I pulled my notebook out from under my pillow. I wrote: *As of today, I have a story.*

44

All at once, the thought of calling my grandma wasn't that bad any more. I was just about to reach for the receiver when something rang. For a moment I thought it was the phone. But it was the doorbell. Ludger was in the kitchen clearing away the lunch things. We'd had fish soup.

I heard his footsteps in the hallway.

I couldn't see who he asked to come in, but the voice sounded familiar. I limped over to the living room door. I was managing quite well now without the crutches. My feet were almost healed.

It was Mrs Kruse.

I wanted to run over to her, but stayed in the doorway. 'Hello, Mrs Kruse,' I said instead and waved with a tissue I was holding in my hand.

'Hello, mermaid girl,' said Mrs Kruse. Her gaze asked questions.

Ludger's gaze also asked questions.

'It's been a long time,' Mrs Kruse said, turning to Ludger. 'You gave my daughter riding lessons.'

As Mrs Kruse spoke, her voice changed. It grew soft, like she was afraid of breaking something.

'Yes, of course. Edda. Do come in,' said Ludger. He reached out to take Mrs Kruse's coat. Mrs Kruse turned to the side at the same time, and the coat slipped off her shoulders. Ludger caught it. It looked like a little dance.

We sat down in the kitchen. Ludger warmed up some fish soup for Mrs Kruse. 'How do you two know each other?' he asked.

'Billie, do you want to tell him?' Mrs Kruse said and dipped her spoon into the soup. She'd hung her handbag over the back of the chair.

I told him about my mum's certificates among her things, about the woman at the adult education centre and about my visit to Mrs Kruse. The only thing I didn't tell him was my discovery at the graveyard. I didn't know if Ludger knew about it. And I didn't want to put Mrs Kruse in an awkward situation.

'I was worried after your call,' Mrs Kruse said and looked at me. 'I didn't know what you meant by saying that you'd be home soon. First your swim in the sea, then your call…'

'What swim in the sea? What call?' Ludger said.

Ludger opened a bottle of wine and filled our glasses. Perhaps he'd forgotten it was only early afternoon. Perhaps he didn't think about the fact that I was too young to drink alcohol. But perhaps he simply didn't care at that moment.

'I called Mrs Kruse when you wanted me to phone my parents.'

'And when did you go swimming in the sea?'

'That was before. But it doesn't really matter now.'

Ludger nodded.

Mrs Kruse dabbed her mouth with the napkin and took a sip of wine. 'Ludger, I didn't know that you have a daughter too.'

Mrs Kruse said *too*. She spoke about her daughter like she was still alive. Perhaps Mrs Kruse spoke to her daughter like I spoke to my mum. Perhaps it would be like that forever now.

Ludger looked at me. Then he said: 'Marika brought Billie with her at the time. She isn't my biological daughter.'

'Ah,' said Mrs Kruse. 'And your father…'

'Is a loser,' I said and shrugged.

'How did you know that Billie had found me?' Ludger asked.

Mrs Kruse smiled. 'My sister saw you – with a girl. It wasn't hard to find out that it was Billie.'

'Did you think I'd kidnapped Billie?'

Mrs Kruse almost choked on her wine. 'No, obviously not! And if that had been the case, you wouldn't have got far.'

'But you still wanted to make sure everything was all right?'

'Of course.'

'Because I'm an old codger who barely has any contact with the outside world?'

Oh, Ludger, I thought, and had to smile. Suddenly he seemed like someone who I could actually be related to. Perhaps Mum had rubbed off on him. I'd once read that couples even start looking like each other. But that only happens after fifty years or so. So no chance of a man running around out there who looked like my mum.

Mrs Kruse stayed completely calm. She rested her slender hand with the long fingers on the table. She wasn't wearing a wedding ring, but wore a large silver ring on her middle finger. Then she leaned forward and said: 'I like your sense of humour. I simply wanted to know how Billie's story continued. And I wanted to make sure that she was doing all right.'

'And?' Ludger asked in my direction.

I was still smiling, and I couldn't do anything about it. 'I'm doing well,' I said.

And that was true.

Mrs Kruse and Ludger carried on talking. The longer they chatted, the less they seemed to notice that I was still sitting at the table too, like I was invisible. But they were only speaking about people I didn't know anyway, and about island politics that didn't interest me.

I dozed with my eyes open until Ludger took my wine glass away from me. 'Hey,' I said.

'You've had enough now,' he said, and I didn't protest. My tongue lay in my mouth like a heavy dead fish. The next thing I remember is lying on the sofa. Ludger handed me a cup.

'Yuk,' I said, as I took a sip.

'Drink up,' said Ludger.

'Where's Mrs Kruse?' I asked and started to feel a bit better.

'She's gone.'

'Why?'

'It's past six. Mrs Kruse has her own home. Did you forget? You were there.'

Of course I hadn't forgotten.

But I had forgotten that a day on the island is almost over by five.

'Shall we go outside for a bit?' I asked.

'Good idea,' said Ludger. 'Meet you outside.'

The moon had just risen, and the sand crunched beneath our shoes.

'I loved your mother very much. She was clever and beautiful,' Ludger said.

Finally, I thought. And I wasn't surprised. The moon softens the heart, and a soft heart makes you chatty. I knew that from my mum.

'She wasn't clever enough. Otherwise she wouldn't have left you.'

'Clever people can be afraid too,' Ludger said.

'What do you mean?'

I couldn't remember Mum ever being afraid of anything. Mum could stroke spiders like they were cats. She was never scared in the dark, and she jumped from the ten-metre platform. And I was sure that if it had been a fifteen-metre platform, she'd have jumped from there too.

'Your mother always sought adventure. I think she was afraid of leading a conventional life.'

'What's a conventional life?'

'No idea,' said Ludger. 'Living in a house. Marriage. Having children. Things like that.'

God liked it when people got married and had children. At least that's what the Bible said.

'Do you think Mum died because God wanted to punish her?'

Ludger looked horrified. 'No, of course not!' Then he said quietly: 'It's so sad that she died just when she wanted to tidy up after herself.'

Obviously I knew what he meant. But I wasn't sure if Ludger was right. After all, she'd opened the door to my grandma on one condition: no talking about the past.

'My mum hated tidying up.'

Ludger nodded. 'I know.'

'How lonely were you, from one to ten, when my mum left?' I asked.

'Twelve,' Ludger said. 'But probably still not as lonely as you.'

'Did your hair fall out too?'

'No,' said Ludger. 'But a tooth did.'

'A tooth?'

'Look,' he said and showed me his teeth. One of his back teeth was missing. 'But I don't think that has anything to do with your mother. It was a coincidence. Everyone in my family had bad teeth. Be thankful that I'm not your biological father.'

Something shimmered in the sand in front of us. I bent down. It was a shell. It was beautiful. It looked like it came directly from paradise. I held it out to Ludger. 'What sort of shell is that?'

'I don't know,' he said. 'Perhaps a stray. I've never seen one like that.'

I wanted to put the shell in my trouser pocket, but it was too big. So I kept it in my hand.

'Best thing is probably if you put it back,' Ludger said.

'Why?'

'There's bound to be a reason why it's here, don't you think?'

I put the shell back on the sand. Then I asked: 'Can we go back to the beginning? Can you tell me how you met my mum?'

He had met my mum in Hungary at a horse show. She'd been working there as a hostess. Ludger had seen my mum – and bang, he had fallen for her. 'We went out a few times and then I was allowed to meet you both.'

'Us both?'

'You and your grandma. Your mother was living back at home. Your grandma invited me over for coffee and cake. And I can tell you one thing: that was the only sweet thing about that day.'

I laughed. 'And then? What happened next?'

'Then your mother came to Germany with me. In the beginning it was all new and exciting, but then normal life resumed.'

I thought this summary was pretty short, but I didn't want to complain. Instead I said: 'That was after the photograph, right?'

'What photograph?' Ludger asked.

The photo was in my notebook, and I always had my notebook with me. I pulled it out and held it right under Ludger's nose. 'That's your arm, isn't it?'

'Yes, that's my arm,' he said.

And I said: 'Mum looks happy.'

And he said: 'Yes, that was at the beginning.'

I tried to imagine Mum on the island. I sat her down on the ugly sofa, I put a pitchfork in her hand and put her in the stables, I had her walk on the beach, I laid her beneath the heavy covers. Something about it didn't work. It was like the image was fuzzy.

'And the end?' I asked.

'That was still unexpected,' Ludger said. 'I asked myself for a long time what part of it was my fault.'

'And do you know now?'

Ludger put his hands in his coat. It had got cold. 'No. Perhaps I should have talked more to your mother.'

'You can just copy me if you want to practise. I'm pretty good at talking.'

'You're also pretty good at running away,' Ludger said.
'That was before.'
'Then we can go home now.'
And that's what we did.

45

I discovered the ring three days later. It lay on the sink in the guest toilet, right next to the soap. From the telly I knew that women leave things lying around on purpose when they like someone. I put the ring in my trouser pocket.

Mrs Kruse was probably sitting with a cup of tea, looking out to sea and thinking about Ludger. I'd ask Ludger to invite her for dinner. I'd think of a reason.

I imagined how it would be if Mrs Kruse moved in with us. I imagined Mrs Kruse and Ludger walking hand in hand. I imaged how it would be to be a proper family.

I thought of my grandma and looked at the clock. It was 8 p.m. If she didn't answer now, she'd either gone back to Hungary or she was dead.

My grandma picked up after the first ring.

'Hello, Nagymama,' I said. 'You're there after all!'

'Where else would I be?' she said. 'Where are you?'

'I thought you'd gone back to Hungary.'

'Rubbish! I can't go back to Hungary when my granddaughter has been missing for weeks.'

'Did you report it to the police?' I asked.

'Of course. What do you think? But they were completely useless. Where are you?'

'I'm with Ludger,' I said.

'With whom?'

'With Ludger. In North Germany.'

The line went quiet for a moment. 'Oh goodness,' she then said. 'What do you want up there?'

'To stay,' I said.

'Are you going to school at least?'

'Probably,' I said.

And then something strange happened.

My grandma said in German: 'How are you, Billie?' I was so surprised that I didn't know what to say. 'I German learn,' said my grandma and then switched back to Hungarian. 'I have to do something. I can't just sit in this flat and wait for you to get in touch. I almost went mad with worry. You could have been dead!' My grandma's voice quivered.

'I'm sorry,' I said quietly.

My grandma blew her nose. Then she said: 'It was Ahmed's idea. He took me along to a cultural centre. I am taking part in a beginner's class.'

'That was kind of him.'

'Yes, your neighbours are very kind. Ahmed does my shopping for me sometimes. And Luna sometimes brings me a piece of cake. By the way, she's got a contract with some sort of film company.'

'What?' I couldn't believe it. I pictured Luna's name in the credits of a film. I saw her wearing an evening gown on the red carpet.

'She got lucky,' my grandma said.

I don't know why I remembered the *Swan Lake* thing then. Suddenly Luna turned into my mum, her evening gown turned into a tutu, the red carpet became a stage. Had Mum been a prima ballerina or not? It didn't really matter anyway. I knew she had wanted it. She could have been the prima ballerina. She'd dreamed about it. And perhaps that's exactly what mattered.

'Billie?' my grandma asked.

'Yes?'

'Will you give me your phone number?'

'Do you have a pen?' I asked back.

Then I gave her the number. I'd known it off by heart for a while now.

Following the conversation with my grandma, I said goodnight to Ludger and went to my room. I sat on my bed and thought about what Ludger had said: everyone has a story.

My grandma had a story, my mum had one, and I did too. I was in the middle of it.

I pulled the notebook out from under my pillow.

Then I wrote on an empty page: *My mum died that summer.*

Transforming a manuscript into the book you hold in your hands is a group project.

Elena would like to thank everyone who helped to publish *Paradise Garden*.

THE INDIGO PRESS TEAM
Susie Nicklin
Phoebe Barker
Phoebe Evans

JACKET DESIGN
Sarah Schulte

PUBLICITY
Sophie Portas

EDITORIAL PRODUCTION
Tetragon

COPY-EDITOR
Sarah Terry

PROOFREADER
Ian Howe

I
THE
INDIGO
PRESS

The Indigo Press is an independent publisher of contemporary fiction and non-fiction, based in London. Guided by a spirit of internationalism, feminism and social justice, we publish books to make readers see the world afresh, question their behaviour and beliefs, and imagine a better future.

Browse our books and sign up to our newsletter for special offers and discounts:

theindigopress.com

Follow *The Indigo Press* on social media for the latest news, events and more:

- @PressIndigoThe
- @TheIndigoPress
- @TheIndigoPress
- The Indigo Press
- @theindigopress